MW01385755

COYOTE

COYOTE

An Indian Casino Blues

BY RICHARD MILLER

> We live in a world of lies.
> ----Jacques Cousteau

Published by
Synergy International of the Americas, Ltd.,
4684 NW 69th Avenue,
Miami, FL 33166,
In conjunction with
DFI Books, Dada Foundation Imprints, LLC,
Box 621,
Monterey, CA 93942

ISBN 0-9658423-3-9

Library of Congress Control Number: 00-092681.

Primary Distributor: Lightning Source/ Ingram, Inc.
of LaVergne, TN.

Rights: Joan Fulton
Harold Matson Co., Inc.
276 Fifth Avenue
New York, NY 10001.

Set in Goudy Old Style.

The title page image of a Mayan embodiment of
Coyote was photographed by
Heidi Elizabeth McGurrin.
Here, Coyote waits for a minion to serve him a
succulent human heart.
The images of other Mayan Gods are or derive from
photographs by Heidi Elizabeth McGurran.
The original terra cotta figures may be seen at
Peppers Mexicali Café,
170 Forest Avenue, Pacific Grove, CA.
The cover design derives in part from
"Medicine Man's Headpiece,"
an assemblage by Marcus Amerman.
The Mayan ceramic pictured on the back cover
is in the National Museum of the American Indian,
Smithsonian Institute, Washington, DC.

To all you readers in the post-literate generation.

PART ONE

Do you ever think about
What you're thinking about?

--The Beer Fairy aka Beffle
aka Theodora Eliot Braun,
Westlake, Ohio, 2003 a.d.

ONE

WALKING IN THE WOODS by the creek I turn that flat gray rock and feel moisture and moss and smell maybe death, maybe change, and from among all the wriggling fear and idiotic indifference abruptly exposed to daylight and to all my omnis, present and potent, I select the most alien, no, revolting specimens, and, one after another, imagine being *it*, that sticky slug, that black claw-mouthed beetle, that cigar-colored armor-plated worm gorging ants, and one after another I am they, each one, and live its life for a while. You try it. What do they see? Do they feel cold and wet? This can't be envy. How's it smell down there? My dream of dreams? Can a slug hear? Fun with fetishes? No. So, not long ago driving across Rocky River gorge into the village, I spy a ragged hitchhiker thumbing on the corner by my favorite deli, and I stop. The rearview frames him limping toward me, and I flash away, but curiosity about what's under that slab draws me back and I let him in. This guy smells. He stinks. It's not science, or art, but grease that makes his cotton jacket look like leather; his hair is grizzle-blond matte. But it's not a he. It's a *her*. Too late to flop that rock back and cap her *her* world. Alice has decayed for homeless years on my side of the looking-glass. Alice sits snarling in the shotgun seat. "I'm the Beer Fairy," says Alice in an alto radio voice. "I'm on the road to my thirtieth high-school reunion."

I ask her where.

"Down the road a piece, Westlake. Holiday Inn."

"I'll drop you off."

She'd have to be forty-eight. I'm more than that, but I can pass for less. My beetle, my slug, my worm, my new me, squats next to me, peering over the wiper past the yellow of smashed-bug spots at the road, at where wildlife goes to flatten and feed. She smiles at me and I see I, this new me, have nice clean even teeth. She shrugs her pack off her back.

"Could you stop at a gas station so I can wash up?"

Sure, why not.

As she walks toward the ladies' room by a flower bed dense with pansy faces, she favors her left leg. High-school reunion! Me, I didn't even go to my graduation. Re*union*. Re-*onion*. Not me, no way. Gas rushes and money meters spin. A swirl of tenths, as cents turn and dollars pop. She'd stained my seat! Leave her here! I pay, and she clambers back in, this Beer Fairy.

"Dada," says she, "ist für Ruhe und Orden."

"What?"

"Dada is for tranquillity and medals."

I shift into drive; she slides into silence. If I'm her, am I still me? Am I any cleaner? I don't look that way. She pays me no mind. I tell her I missed my graduation. No comment. "What are you thinking about?" I ask.

"Die Frau in Gelb ist gegangen."

"What?"

"The woman in yellow is gone."

Why did she-- I-- say that? What would I, no, *will* I do at the Holiday Inn? Panhandle my school mates? Abuse them? Can they really be homesick for 1973? For dope and Nixon? For zits and bulimia and rebellion? For booze and foreplay on some back seat? An odor steeps and cloys: dead fish and vomit. Beer Fairy? In-fucking-deed! Under this rock it should smell like beer.

"Did you go to your graduation?"

"Yes, and the prom too."

So in a few minutes, remembering the graduation and prom, there I'd be, in the Holiday Inn, in my grease jacket and ragged jeans, reeking of dead fish and vomit, my chest embellished by a nametag proclaiming: BEER FAIRY. Whoahhhh. Will I really?

"Are you homesick for 1973?

"Home is where you pay your bills."

The Holiday Inn looms ahead.

"Are you *really* going in there?"

She nods green-eyed scorn.

"With no money?"

"In a money economy, mister, if you don't have an anarchy garden with plenty of cabbage, a cabin, woods, water, tools, a fishing hole, and a swimming hole too, why, then, much as you may detest it, hateful as it is, you've got to suck up to Washington, Lincoln, U.S. Grant, Alexander, Ben, and Jack. Dig it! You have to keep your mind on the buck, and hold a few. Otherwise, when the mule train comes back from the seashore, it won't bring no salt for you."

"In there, when they see you, won't they give you the bum's rush?"

"They may get a bit uncomfortable."

"They might call the cops."

"Not if I control their perceptions."

"And your homesick classmates?"

"My classmates! Sure. They'll come to show off success, or pretend to it. Or curiosity will lure them. Or boredom. And some will miss it, from shame, from indifference, from disgust. And some are going to miss it because they're dead, some of them long-time dead, in the war." She shifted her pack from the floor to her lap. "In high school, most of them seemed dead. Do they still? Thirty years in zombieville. So, what the hell. Maybe I can vivify them. I'll be the same old alarm clock, with new tricks. I'm the paint that won't dry, the cement that won't set, the wound that won't heal."

At the grand entrance, I stop behind a taxi.

The Beer Fairy says thanks, and steps out.

I set the rock back in place.

TWO

SHE, THE BEER FAIRY, watched the car drive off, and smiled, spit, and limped through the portal of the Holiday Inn into the lobby. She'd been on the road for days and despite her ablutions still smelled like it. A banner, blue and gold, spread above the reception desk, declared WELCOME LAKEWOOD HIGH THIRTIETH REUNION. A TV greenly announced in-house events: for the reunion a no-host-bar Welcome Party starting at six; a bus trip to Downtown Cleveland and Lakewood High in the morning; and, for the evening, The Silver Reunion Dinner Dance, casual dress acceptable. Are they ready for the ultimate lesson in informal grooming? Defying an intense outgoing current of glare, she strode upstream to the desk, where, haughtily, with master-class confidence, she told the clerk:

You have a room for Theodora Eliot Braun, III. *Prepaid.*

"Madame, we always ask for identification."

She drew a passport from her pack, opened it to a page rubber-stamped IF YOU'RE TOO DRUNK TO WALK, *DRIVE*, and smiled as the clerk turned to the document pages, and looked from the photo to her, and back at the photo, and back at her, and back and back, and gave her the keycard to room 5221.

And now, she thought, as she limped to the elevators, he should call the fumigation service.

A lone man in the elevator began inspecting the safety certificate as she pressed the button for 5.

He turned and stared at her.

"Beffle!" he said.

"You remember my nickname?"

"How could I forget?"

She studied his smiling face, trying to recover it, the who of it, the where and why of it. Nametags would come with registration. The floor gauge flashed 5. "See you at suppertime." She followed the arrows, slid in the card, limped into 5221. The baggage she'd sent ahead from the casino now stood neatly stacked just inside the door. She peered into the full-length mirror by the honor bar and wondered how he could have recognized her. She stripped and showered. Be the Frau in Gelb. She put on her yellow dress, the one she'd packed along with her masks, her theatrical makeup, wigs, and a history of piracy in the Caribbean, published in Paris in 1852, a book some Canadian friends had given her. They said it would afford her a fresh perspective on her current profession. She poured a drink and sat by the window. The inside rooms had been built around a skylit atrium. Imagining herself a hovering hawk, she looked down on people walking about and socializing at café tables and splashing in the pool and herding children. Lakewood High! Its odors drifted back. Locker room. Cafeteria. Wet summer grass; wet winter wool. Somebody, some group, was trying to kill the casino. But who? Am I being watched? Lakewood High had been on occasion a sanctuary in an adolescent then as she hoped it would be in today's now, this Holiday silver anniversary retreat, her momentary refuge. Sanctuary? Refuge? Often

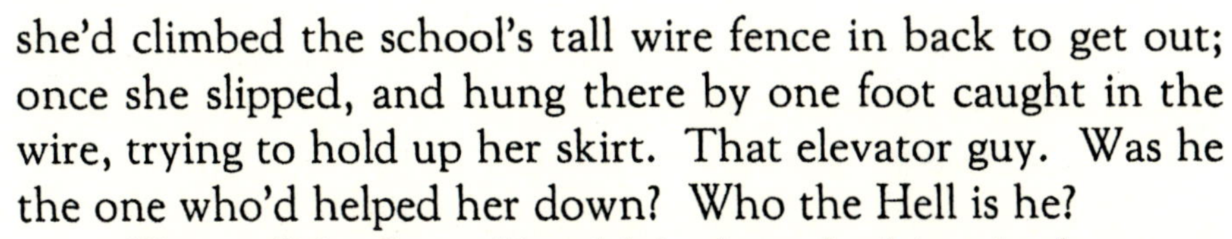

she'd climbed the school's tall wire fence in back to get out; once she slipped, and hung there by one foot caught in the wire, trying to hold up her skirt. That elevator guy. Was he the one who'd helped her down? Who the Hell is he?

This will be fun. Trouble? A snakeskin, shed out on the Coast, wrapped for a while around Two Bears, her boss.

She rubbed cream into her face, the same features, but devoid of the rough hobo complexion she'd been wearing on the road. She finished dressing, and preening, and went downstairs to register. They gave her a customized Hello-My-Name-Is tag bearing her yearbook picture and inscribed Theodora Eliot, her maiden name, only even then she wasn't. On the way across the atrium to the bar she saw more tags, everyone two-faced, on both sides of their prime, looking zitty and puerile, battered and weary. Can we strip *those* masks? At the end of the bar the elevator rider sat. He turned toward her, beaming.

"Beffle."

Memory racing, she smiled back. There were his old face and name under his new face. Those stick-out ears! Exposed now by a Nazi haircut, concealed then by cascades of brownish black hippie hair. And back then he'd paraded a nice butt. Her prime opponent in debate club. Eddy Jones. "What a treat!" said Eddy. "What's happening with you these days?"

Can't tell him about the Indians and the casino, the truth, as always, much too complicated. "I live out in California, on the coast, near Carmel."

"What do you do."

"You won't believe this, but *try*. Good. You're ready. I have a rat farm. You know, pets, science, that sort of thing. Big bucks in rats."

"No kidding." His old ironic smile beamed at her. "I'm in law enforcement, myself."

"Which is to say you keep order in *our* rat farm."

"Where you find ants, there you'll find ant-eaters."

"As in the parable of the prez and the parrot."

He'd put muscle onto his pigeon chest. He displayed it in an expensive, stylish, green, made-in-Indonesia-by-female-slave-labor jogging shirt. "Oh?" said he.

"The prez and the parrot were in the Oval Office, arguing about the effect of animals on the vote. At length, exasperated by still yet another contradiction, the prez said: 'I'm the President, and you're just a lowlife parrot.'"

Eddy interrupted in a mirthful voice. "And the parrot replied: 'I can talk, can you fly?'"

"All of which goes to show, Edward, in any species, males are superfluous. They're only good for procreating and causing trouble."

"Meaning me?"

"Starting with you."

"That makes me think of Terry Thompson. You remember, he was quarterback and student president. He quit college and married Melissa Green."

"That redhead?"

"Yes, Beffle. That redhead. Just after we graduated. Terry dumped his jock scholarship to Ohio State and married her. About a year later she was killed in a car wreck. Terry went to Nam. Nowadays he clerks in a shoe store at the Lakeview Mall. Ten gets you one we don't see him here." He embraced Beffle. "Do you still believe in fun?"

She took him by the ears. "What do you think?"

They spent the rest of the evening eating and drinking and reminiscing and joking and dancing and teasing long lost classmates, most of whom had divorced Miss Fun, if, indeed, they'd ever been married, or even acquainted. Giddy and tired, and by herself, Beffle went back to 5221 and turned on TV. Indians in the wildwood, in living color, abruptly occupied the screen, ghosts, perhaps, of people who'd lived here, not in the rooms, but on this spot, for ten thousand years before George Holiday planted his five-story-building seed and it gestated and grew to maturity.

The Mohecans gave way to a beer commercial. Smiling at thoughts of her recent role as Beer Fairy, and of how that would play pushing beer on TV, Beffle stripped and slid into bed. She rose early for breakfast, surprisingly refreshed, and went down to the coffee shop and ate her usual grits with maple syrup and orange juice as she read the Cleveland *Plain Dealer*.

Now for Melissa.

Melissa! *Yes.* Yes!

Time for the resurrection.

Beffle rushed by the swimming pool to the elevators and along the hall into her room. Beffle drew her laptop computer from its nest of rubbery masks, jacked it into the phone line, set it on the writing table by the window whence she could watch the atrium action. At the casino one of her duties was running the eye-in-the-sky crew and so, she said to herself, I'm used to looking down on people. Adolescents and two hairy fatties frolicked in the pool, their wet skins glistening in the sunlight. She turned on, no-- not turned on, *opened* the computer, for this briefcase-sized screen and key board, when active, connected to the casino's system, and through it admitted to the mind of the whole world, to a vast filament of web, strewn with flyspeck chips, pulsing with minute currents, where almost everything ever recorded, every survivor that is to say, had found place and connection. "So," she muttered, sliding her fingers over the magic keys, clicking icons and typing codes, "Madame Overlord, spirit of this ouija board, Clairvoyant Queen of Tarot, Mistress of Tea Leaves and Tin Trumpets, Goddess of the Crystal Ball and the Internet, I, Beffle, thine loyal minion, doth implore thee, O! mighty monarch of the World Mind, to bring Melissa Green back from the dead, to join in our reunion."

And then, lo and behold, . . . on the screen, tiling and merging, Melissa's bio, sucked from a multitude of sources, . . . and, save for the contents of a mummy box in Lawn View Cemetery, the screen scrolled through the artifacts and databits her dull crushed life had left behind.

And, so . . . .

There they are, piled up, her desolate vitae, some of which she herself did not know, enough and more to cover me in my act, and to asphyxiate me with boredom.

Beffle took it in, the history of her latest multiple personality.

But the net had not snared all.

Melissa, jealous Melissa, in the shower room, streaming water and tears, pert tits and curly red triangle, undone by faltering in the tryouts for the gymnastics team; Melissa, sweet Melissa, soul-bruised by losing to Ed the assignment to write the *High Times* humor column; pissed-off Melissa, bad acid-trip Melissa, attacking, trying to kill, who knows whom? And now for the chores.

Beffle unpacked her bags and trunk, hanging clothes, stuffing others into drawers, stocking the bathroom cabinet. She poured a drink and opened the *1973 Cinema*-- their yearbook-- and thumbed her way to the graduating class portraits. Here it's sweetface Melissa. Ready for the printer? She fetched the printer from the trunk and connected it,

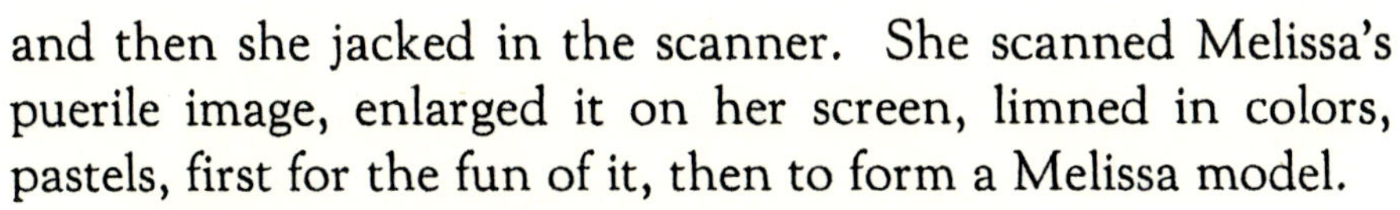

and then she jacked in the scanner. She scanned Melissa's puerile image, enlarged it on her screen, limned in colors, pastels, first for the fun of it, then to form a Melissa model.

Beffle printed a life-sized enlargement.

Beffle went to the mirror.

She compared the likeness of Melissa with her own.

We're both roundheads.

How should I look in my Melissa manifestation?

Hideous? I was in an auto wreck, crushed. When I emerged from the hospital a year later, I looked so awful, I never came out, but stayed at home, studying investment, and built my insurance settlement up to a fortune.

Rich and ugly? Is that my part? Poor and pretty? Friendly and fanatic? That would be fun. Ribald and romantic? Well, let it work itself out. Hair first. Redhead is what they'll remember. She took her redhead wig and worked gray into it, and dulled it. Yes. And now, the mask. She set the mask matrix on the dresser before the mirror, the picture beside it, got the materials, and formed Melissa's features. And now for a big ugly scar. She worked rapidly, skillfully, and, eventually, thinking of Pygmalion, and Mary Shelley and Frankenstein's monster, she stood before the closet door, gazing into the full-length mirror, at the resurrected Melissa Green.

She poured a drink, raised and clicked a toast.

"To your second coming!"

She made Melissa make a face.

"Together, we're going to live a short story. 'The Second Coming of Melissa Green.' Not a bad title. Now to go find the story."

Would Melissa Green wear green?

No.

Now to get Melissa's reunion badge.

Masked and wigged and dressed in green, Beffle went down to the atrium and on to the registration table by the door to the ballroom. Shirley Renovic's two faces looked up at her and the big, wrinkled one asked if she were here to register. "Oh yes, Shirley. I wouldn't miss this for the world!"

"I'm, uh, sorry-- it's awful embarrassing, but, well, it's been so long, and I don't recognize everybody."

"Melissa Green."

"Melissa Green?" said Shirley, then, in an arctic tone. "*Melissa Green*." She looked through her papers. "You're not here."

"Look at me. Am I here?"

"Well, you're not."

"But I must be! I wrote in for a reservation!" Beffle reached for *Cinema/1973*, opened to the pictures. "Here I am. You should have a badge for me, with my picture!"

"I don't have anything for you, until you pay."

Beffle paid. Shirley typed a badge, slid it into a transparent holder, presented it, along with the reunion booklet, the menu for the dinner-- she was asked to chose between roast beef and orange roughy-- and the program of events.

"The picture! I've paid my money, now I want a badge picture."

"We're getting awfully feisty, aren't we, Miss Mouse?"

"How come you hate me so much?"

"You should know."

"The picture."

"No picture. Even if I liked you, there's no way to get a picture now."

"I'll make one."

"How."

"Magic, Raggedy Anne, magic." On hearing her hated old high-school-behind-her-back name, Shirley flinched. Yes! And it suited her still. "Catch you later, Raggedy. I might bite, too. As you see, I ain't no mouse no more."

Back in 5221, Beffle invoked an electronic Fairy who retrieved the *Cinema/73* portrait of Melissa. Beffle imprinted it on a clone of the faceless nametag fed to her by Scanner, King of Counterfeiters, then slid the tag back into its holder and pinned it onto her dress. Now comes the bus tour of downtown Cleveland and the visit to Lakewood High. In memory of Cleveland's purged streetcars they called their tour Lolly the Trolley. Beffle went down to the atrium and out to the main driveway. The ankle seemed much better today. Thank you Ms Green. Faces showed at most of the windows; more people were getting on and a few were scouting the windows of the three buses looking for favorites or enemies. Every single one of them was forty-eight, give or take a year. How many of them know Melissa the Mouse is dead. Does anyone miss her? Beffle strode slowly by the rank of windows, letting everyone have a look at her. My red head should attract attention. *Redheads.* No more than one in a hundred people. Do any of these folks know Washington, Hamilton, Jefferson, and Churchill were redheads? And, as the pirate book revealed, Henry Morgan? How could Melissa be such a pussy. Time to change that. An old man's voice sounded behind . . . . Who?

"How nice to see you, Melissa. Do you remember me? Don't be embarrassed. I taught you mathematics, and you were really special. Remember how you used to come for individual assignments after class."

"That was so long ago."

"Surely you remember. I'm Mr. Jellenich."

Now what?

Flee.

She embraced Mr Jellenich, bussed his cheek, and strode onto a bus.

Forty-eight-year-old-plus-or-minus-one faces smiled as she walked toward the back, seeking . . . .

Yes!

Ed!

Ed sat peering out a window on the street side near the back. He thinks I'm *dead.* She slid in next to him. Curiosity turned Ed's head to look at her. He blanched. The bus drew out into traffic. The high-school fight song rang and echoed from the speakers. His sight seemed fixed on the nametag. "Melissa! What a nice surprise."

Now to fake a voice.

"Why, Edward Jones! I declare!" She embraced him. She asked him what he'd been up to for the last thirty years, a question which seemed to pull his plug, because he babbled out an endless answer, draining the subject into her ear, pouring it in while, probably, behind the flow, he wondered how to calmly share the ride with this resurrected corpse, burned face and scar, and at the same time here I sit wondering can I disguise my voice well enough to keep him fooled. Why not? So far, I am who I want to be. I'm gifted. I can fake voices and play-act parts. Two Bears still thinks I'm half Huron. Something else I can do that he doesn't know about, something that makes me virtually unique. I can puke at will. Barf when I want to. Retch and vomit any time, anywhere. Now there's a talent! You may not envy it, but think it over. It sure can come in handy. And does. Two Bears! Two Bears is so well gulled he calls me Little Sister, and speaks of me so intensely, with such empathy, that they've all taken to calling me One Bear.

The buses entered the expressway and hurtled along.

Ed Jones' monologue ran out of gas. How much of it had he invented? "Rats! I've been talking too long. Guess you've got lots to say about your thirty years."

"Huh Unh."

School songs gave way to Dylan, to if *Ever-body'd jus git stoned!*

Ed smiled. "Musical nostalgia. Re-*Jew*-vin-a-tion. Get it?"

"Nope."

The bus rolled across a long concrete span over Rocky River Gorge and through some Rolling Stones and the Led Zeppelin and onto the shoreway along Lake Erie. Beffle glanced at her crew-cut companion. "Edward, how can it be? I'm already used to you being forty-eight."

This evoked babble about the pains of aging, and Beffle looked out the window at a gigantic electric sign depicting an immense can of paint pouring a rainbow of colors out over the earth until it dripped off the bottom. She closed her eyes, Ed's voice a background buzz mixing in with Beatles as she mulled over the morality of treating him this way. Her eyes, open again, fixed on the lonely spike of Terminal Tower rearing over the downtown skyline. Ed's voice sounded a softer tone.

"Back in the old days, I was always keen on you."

"Yes. But you had a crush on Beffle."

"That bitch?"

"It's all right, Ed. You can tell me."

"I don't think she knew it, but she used to drive me fucking *wild*."

"You have better taste now, I hope."

"She's here, you know."

"Really?"

They were rolling up Ninth Street toward Euclid.

"I think I could still go for her."

Beffle saw the dead empty skull-face of the Kit Kat Klub, where in the dear sweet days beyond recall, beginning when she was seventeen, they used to sell her booze to go.

"No offense meant, Melissa, but Beffle's still sexy as hell." She made no response, and, as they listened silently to The Doors light a fire, the bus carried them back up onto the expressway and on toward Lakewood, and, with Janis Joplin screaming *down on me*, off on to suburban streets, where, with the help of the Grateful Dead, they rolled along to Franklin Boulevard, and stopped before Lakewood High. The tour monitor took the microphone and announced, "After thirty years, dear old school, we're back!"

"I knew that already," said Eddy.

"And now, brothers and sisters of Lakewood nineteen-seventy-three, we will all join in the Alma Mater song." Band music burst out; a group of curious students gathered beside the bus. Beffle smiled at the tired, proud 1909 pseudo-Roman building as she sang along, a contralto counterpoint to the tenor beside her, surprised that after so long they both remembered the words, wondering why she'd bothered learning them in the first place.

Lakewood High,
We're proud of thee,
All allied in Loy-al-ty,
May thy counsels
Ever be
With-in our mem-o-ry!

She felt Eddy's hand clasping hers.

Honor then
To Lakewood High,
Thy dear name up-hold,
We shall ne'er for-get

The purple *and the gold!*

She rose, dragging Eddy with her. "Come on, let's go buy a *High Times*."

"You mean you don't care any more?"

"Hell, no. You're funnier than I am." They walked off the bus and joined the other Lolly the Trolley excursionists on the lawn. "Eddy, do you see Beffle?"

They both looked around. He let go her hand. "I don't see her anywhere."

"You'd think she'd come to this."

The principal made a short speech, then led them up the walk into the main building. The hall was thick with students, mostly wearing the absurd adolescent-fashion-clothes of the early Twenty First Century. Absurd, well, yes . . . but not nearly as much so as 1973's muumuus and bell-bottoms and love beads. "Why are people avoiding me, Eddy? Because I'm supposed to be dead?" Last week, when Two Bears told her the truth about their business troubles, that onset of fiscal diabetes affecting the robust life of the casino, he'd said somebody wanted to kill him and maybe her. "I thought you *were* dead," said Eddy.

"I am."

"You don't smell like it."

The principal explained that due to the new system of staggered classes, one adopted for more efficient use of the buildings shortly after the mailing of the reunion programs, most of the older students now took Saturday classes. This, he said, might not be necessary next year, after the music, gymnasium, and extra-curricular programs finished phasing out. Unfortunately, however, this year he'd been forced to cancel the alumni tour. Thanking them for coming, reminding them of the school's great need for contributions, grants, and bequests, he led them out to the buses.

Jimi Hendrix played them back into the traffic of Franklin Boulevard.

To ease escape, Beffle had pushed Eddy into the window seat. "When you croaked," he asked, "did you leave your fortune to dear old L.H.S."

"You mean my insurance settlement?" She kneaded her knuckles, producing a loud crack. "Remember how loud it sounds in class?" This opened a back and forth of trivial reminiscence under which Beffle felt a surge of anxiety urging her to stay linked to Eddy for the evening's events. Too bad Beffle, Melissa will have all the fun. After all, it's not every day you can come back from the dead. Not even Houdini managed it. What happens to you when you die? Whatever you expect. Rain hissed and pounded on the roof of the bus, a strong rhythm section behind Elvis doing the Jailhouse Rock. They stepped out into sunlight sparkling on the Holiday grass, steeped in a wet links fragrance. "Mel, I shot eleven birdies last week."

"What'd you do with them?"

"That was in only two games!" In the lobby, some grayheads came rushing over, and embraced her. "Melissa! Remember us? We were in your homeroom!" Oh sure, yes, easy to say so, with their names showing. "We heard about your accident, and, oh, well . . . what we heard . . . oh, I mean it's just wonderful to see you're all right!"

She motioned at Eddy. "Recognize him? Long hair? Love beads? Used to chase balls at Westlake? I haven't seen him since. Until today. What a change! I'm sure you noticed. From golf caddie to golf Nazi in thirty event-filled years." Oh, Melissa, sweetheart, the old girls said in reply, Do you remember the time we all went to that football game in Berea, and we ate all that luscious acid heart candy marked Be My Baby and Beffle made you and Shirley take off your clothes and poured cooking oil all over you and pushed you into that room with all those boys?

Eddy took her arm and led her into the ballroom to the no-host bar. Waiters were swarming among the tables, setting them for dinner, and a band called Ziplock played electric sixties memory music from a bandstand by a podium embellished with the Lakewood High seal. They traded more hellos. Someone called her Carrot Top. Rather than scandal, or awe, her resurrection seemed to have run aground on indifference. "So she didn't get killed in that auto wreck," said someone in range of eavesdrop. "So what? Look how ugly she is! Those *burns*. Skin like a baseball mitt! Brrrrrrrrrr."

Eddy looked at her wide-eyed. "I heard that too." He hugged her. "I think you're swell." The hostess bade everyone to find seats. They went to the E-through-G roughy-table. "Catch you after, babe, as near to the bar as possible," he said, as he set off in search of the J roast-beef table. Beffle found her Melissa place card, scrawled with a marker, crowded in among the printed reservations. Soon, E-F-G fish-eaters, none of whom she recognized, surrounded her. Probably from the January class. The principal mounted to the podium and tapped the mike for order, preparatory to what the program announced as the Welcoming Address.

He looked out over the hungry crowd, smiled, and said: "The great poet, Robert Frost, whom many of you first encountered in the rooms at Lakewood High, tells us, and I quote: . . . a poem begins as a lump in the throat, a sense of wrong, a homesickness, a lovesickness. It finds the thought, and the thought finds the words. . . . Well, mine is to find, to mirror your thought in welcoming you to the Silver Anniversary Banquet, and to do so in words commensurate and expressive. For us, our presence here is a poem, a right and a rite, a homesickness, and, yes, a lovesickness, a return, a renewal of becoming, of hope, of an endless future, of a solidarity, each with the other, a rightsickness, a lovesickness, a homesickness for an almost tribal time when idealism was pure, the future bright, and the heart, warm. O! Tribe, O! Class of 1973, O! cohorts of January and June, I welcome your return to your beginnings. From a heart warm with affection, I salute you. Welcome to the reunion! Bon appétit!"

Beffle cracked her knuckles, a sound alone in the silent instant before applause begins.

Twaddle! Drivel!

Hands clapped around the room.

Beffle imagined the old boy boozing in his suite, where he'd consulted his banquet speakers' book of quotations, found Frost, and practiced before the mirror. Drinking more, his past and future collapsing into a glorious *now*, he'd imagined himself as he'd appear to the audience, then became the audience, and projected its warmth into the words.

Applause swelled.

Got to be for brevity, not content.

The E-*through*-G roughy crowd clapped loudly.

January fools!

She saw death in their eyes.

Reflected?

Waiters served plates of orange-roughy, with baked potatoes and peas, salad, tea, coffee, but-- because dinner was prepaid, no wine. Beffle went to the bar and bought three bottles. Imagining the anonymous casino customer who'd inadvertently paid for them, she brought them back. Some E-*through*-G's stared disapproval. The waiter brought glasses. A fat woman in pearls looked at her oddly, thanked her, remarked what a miracle it was that the food and the music, like the class, had come from everywhere to be here, the fish all the way from New Zealand, spuds from Idaho, lettuce from California, peas from Mexico, wine from Chile. Feeling uncomfortable, sensing the woman somehow familiar, Beffle smiled, but did not reply. Ziplock played some Motown, then Peter, Paul & Mary. Eddy came over, took Beffle onto the dance floor, told her his roast beef had tasted like roadkill. "It's amazing, Mel," he said into her ear, during a tight and dreamy dance, "most of these people have not left Cleveland. Ever. So all those do-you-remember-whens, such a big deal to them, bring back trifles life has wiped right out of my head. Makes me wonder how the Hell they can be so homesick when they've never left home."

Ziplock played Nowhere Man and as she let Eddy swirl her around in tight embrace, hearing about nowhere plans, she drifted off into an affable temper, wondering how Eddy spent his nowhere days, and lived his nowhere dreams. Could that be truly law enforcement? And now, cheek to cheek, a whisper saying, "Mel, you make me feel twenty years younger," and the music stopped, and they dipped, and went to the no-host bar in the corner.

The fat roughyphage came and embraced Beffle while saying, "Melissa, honey, Melissa, it really *is* you! You *ain't* dead like they say! Don't think I'm a buttinski, but I'm not no cheapskate, neither, and I want to buy you a drink, and thank you for getting that wine, and saving me from them temperance freaks." She wouldn't take no for an answer and soon their glasses were raised and consecrated with Here's-looking-at-you. And after the click and the smiles, she touched her necklaces, and said, "I don't need a name tag, I'm Pearl. Remember? I used to hang around with Beffle."

"Sure, Pearl, it's coming back . . . ."

And she's put on weight and she's exaggerating and I always called her Sis.

"You and your pal, Beffle, in the drama club, in the chess club." Pearl took Beffle by the shoulders and squeezed. "And them slumber parties, sweetie; remember, we even let you come sometimes."

Beffle turned Pearl toward Eddy. "You know who *this is* don't you?"

"Eddy! Oh, you bet!" She bussed his cheek. "Eddy," she said in her squeaky voice, "how could I ever forget how nice and groovy you looked in those bell-bottoms with the big buttons on the front, and all that hair? Where the Hell'd it go? China?"

"Beffle's here some place. Have you seen her around?"

"No." Pearl called for another drink. "Say, honey," she said to Beffle, "Beffle's house, remember when me and you swiped her brother's Johnson-Smith catalog?"

So they were the ones who'd done it!

"And he blamed *her* and beat *her* up for it." She leaned toward Eddy. "He wouldn't let us look at it cause that's where he bought all his trick stuff. So we sent for a whoopee cushion, and some itching powder, and got him with that, too, and he beat her up again, and she got so sore, so hot under the collar, she set his car on fire."

"She wouldn't do that."

"Not now, maybe"

"Not then, either."

"Eddy, the things a child will do!"

"True! She was pretty wild, and she did mean things, but she'd never do anything like that."

"How the Hell do you know, smartypants?"

"I just know."

"You hardly even went with her."

He shrugged. "Enough to know."

"She did worse than just raise Cain."

"Seen from these days, Beffle was cool. And fun. With her around, I was never bored."

"She was nasty."

"No way."

"A pervert!"

"Come on!"

"All right, Eddy, I never told anybody before, but lots of time's gone by, so now I can let the cat out of the bag. Melissa, this is really rich!" She paused, rattled the ice in her glass, doubtless to build suspense. "We were thirteen, and me, I was staying over at her house, in her room. Her mutt-- that cuddly little beagle-- bet it's dead now, her dog was in her room too. Must have been after midnight. We were just learning about the birds and the bees. Well, anyway, we had our clothes off-- it was a hot night, and I didn't know much about boys. Zero. Doodeley squat. That was then. I do now, Eddy, believe it! Sometimes I'm even a go-getter. But then, well-- I was kind of dumb. So Beffle laid that dog on its back, and rubbed its thing, till it got all hard. And, well, you could have knocked me down with a feather! The color! The smell! It looked so funny! Then she gets me to rub it till milk comes out. And it did! So she wipes her finger in it, and licks a little off, and offers me some, and I say no, and she says that's where milk comes from, really. That milk don't have nothing to do with tits, or udders, that cows have big soft hoses that drop out of their bellies and the hicks rub them to make them hard, and then the hoses squirt milk, and adults lie to us kids about that, just like they lie to kids about everything else."

Beffle smiled, remembering, then began to blush, under the Melissa mask.

"And *then*, believe it or not, then she lays back on her bed, spreads her legs, puts a candy bar into her *thing*, and gets the dog to eat it! And she says it's great fun, and wants me to try it, but I won't, Hell no, not then, or now for that matter, not in a month of Sundays!"

"Why not?" said Beffle.

"Well, can't say I haven't thought about it, but I ain't never been that hard up."

Eddy whooped with mirth, slapping the bar.

"For the love of Pete, silly, it ain't *that* funny."

"The Hell if it ain't. I pushed a candy bar up my ass once, and let my pooch lick it out."

Beffle broke into laughter. "Now that, dear friends, is what, around here, they call putting-on-the-*dog*."

Eddy rose from his stool, scanned the far corner of the room. "Pearl, *look*, there she is. *Beffle!* I just saw her, over there, by the wall, in that crowd."

Leaving a trail of warm good-byes, Pearl went away, and Beffle said, "She's not really there, is she?"

"She could be."

"I suppose so."

"It'd be fun to see her."

"Hey, aren't I fun!"

"Oh, sure. But, well, you know . . . most of the time I'm utterly fucking bored, and maybe, when I see her, I can fix it so we can get back together."

"Back?"

"You know what I mean."

"No. What do you mean?"

He smiled. They sat quietly, not speaking. Beffle felt content, at peace. Does he feel that way? Or something else? Boredom? Ennui? How would Melissa stir him up? Action swirled all around them, but no one since Pearl seemed willing to approach the dead. Have the casino's enemies followed me here? Is danger hounding me? Dog eat dog! With a candy bar up his sexy butt! "Eddy, I'll bet you're a cop."

"And why would you be thinking that now?"

"Melissa intuition."

I should tell him the truth, but how?

"Where do you think Beffle is?"

"I have no idea, but I'm watching for her. If she's in the building, she'll come in here. If she does, I'll see her." He slapped the bar. "Melissa, honey, is it really you?" He laughed softly. "That Pearl! Double-damn!" He took Beffle's hand, and examined her palm. "I'm going to read your future."

"You a palm reader?"

"It's my biz, my profession. I can read feet, too. But I can't begin before I know my client's occupation. What do you do all day? What's *your* biz."

"Cleaning. I manage a company of cleaners." True, in a way. Two Bears' in-house term for the casino: The Cleaners. The CIA calling itself The Company had sparked the idea. The Cleaners. When using the term, they both were more inclined to think of vacuum than of fluid, as the victims are more apt to be sucked dry than soaked. Eddy drew a fingertip across her lifeline.

"Where I live now, Mel, we have lots of cleaners. My favorites are the Cypress Cleaners, who really make one wonder how dirty trees can get, and the Owl Cleaners. How the fuck they get enough soiled owls to stay in business beats me. Maybe people bring dirty birds from all over the state. But the one that sets the ultimate enigma is the

Rainbow Cleaners. How the Hell they do it? Why? Do they pick up and deliver?"

"Do they advertise on TV?"

He looked around the no-host bar, a row of moveable sections serviced by three barmaids who were swiftly reaching into racks and coolers, opening bottles, pouring drinks, exchanging dirty glasses snatched from carts brought by busboys for clean ones. "We'll never find out here, in the world's only bar not graced by television." The women shifted into top speed as the drinking intensified. Boozers thronged around the stools, crowding tightly, making Beffle feel constrained.

"Ready for my eugenic dream?" she said. "It's getting squeezed out of me like toothpaste." Eddy nodded assent. "In the old days, when driving around, I used to notice as I glanced into view windows whole families seated before their TV, their boob tube, their cathode ray tube, steeped in its evil green light. In my youthful idealism I had high hopes that television's radiation would sterilize habitual viewers and vastly improve the human race."

A guest, standing at the bar beside them, eavesdropping, broke in angrily, saying: "Melissa, you're probably a child-killer too!"

He wore a nametag, but she did not bother to read it.

"You mean favor abortion?"

"I mean murder children."

"Birth control and abortion aren't nearly enough. Think of it! Mister, the momentum of history, of population, sweeping us along, has to be redirected. Shut up! Don't say anything! That's better. We have to stop growth, hold a balance. We should promote homosexuality. Reward it. Get men to lay off of women and fuck each other. Or, better yet, we could go back to *exposure*. Until age six-months parents can leave infants in the woods. Expose girls. Like the ancient Greeks did. Each girl you let live can add at least ten to the next generation. Expose boys. Those who promise to cause trouble. Like Oedipus. Like Moses. Leave them in the forest. On doorsteps. In the bulrushes on the banks of the Nile. Those God loves, God will care for."

"You're a vicious woman, and you'll be punished."

Eddy stepped over to him, peered into his eyes. "And this is a private conversation, *asshole.*" The man backed away. "Do you really believe that, Mel?"

"Maybe. I don't know."

"One thing for sure, we have to make big changes, and fast."

"Exposure would help."

"You do believe in it."

"I'm not going to crusade for it."

"We have to do something."

"Yes. And soon."

"Like, let's get the Hell out of here."

"You can see me to my door."

They went up in the elevator, and along to her door, which was close by. She became suddenly aware of the poisonous hotel/motel carpet smell. Eddy stood before the brass 5221, waiting. "Open it; let's go in."

"To my door, not *through*. Remember?"

"Invite me in."

"If you promise to grow your hair back."

"I promise."

"And if you promise to give up golf."

"Whoa."

"You can play football instead."

"Football?"

"Football takes brains. A robot can play golf." She slipped the card into the lock. "Promise?"

"Hair and golf? How long?"

"So long." She stroked his cheek. "See you in the morning bright."

He pushed in front of her, blocked her door.

What's my move now?

Push!

She pushed; he stood firm,

Smiling a teasing, taunting, mocking smile.

Abruptly, out of the elevator swarmed a noisy crowd.

From somewhere in it Pearl's voice shrieked, "Hey, everybody, look who's here! Loverboy and Carrot Top!" They crowded around; Flora and Fauna hugged her and kissed her cheek. "Remember us?" She pushed them back a step. Identical twins. "You make it easy." Flora wore a flowered muumuu and Fauna sported leathers, just as they'd done as teenagers standing on the walk in front of Lakewood High, selling the Berkeley *Barb* for one buck a copy. People were touching her, tugging. Flora's always been too skinny for a muumuu. Could those be their real names? Got to get out of here! She pulled Eddy into her room and slammed the door.

"Well, double-damn!"

Carrot Top mixed drinks at the courtesy bar whilst Eddy nosed around. "You bored now, Mr. Jones?" He sat down on her trunk and lifted the tag and glanced at it. "This ain't your room."

"We're in here, aren't we?"

He looked at some of the other tags, tore one off, held it up to read aloud.

"Theodora Eliot Braun."

She held up the door card.

"I've got the key, don't I?"

"Theodora . . . Eliot."

"A very common name."

"This is *Beffle*'s room."

"How would I get the door card to Beffle's room?"

"And this laptop computer!" He was at the table, inspecting it. "Here, see? Right *here*, in gold letters, her name, plus Braun, probably some husband." He glanced out the window, down into the atrium, trying to sight Beffle, perhaps. "What the Hell you doing in Beffle's room?" He was still slender enough to look good in drag.

"You still bored, Mr. Jones?"

"What the fuck is going on?"

"There's lots going on, but you don't know what it is, *do you Mister Jones.*"

Eddy leapt to his feet, looking angry, then relaxed back into his chair, shook his head, and said no, he did not, he hadn't a clue as to what was going on.

"Guess."

"I give up. Tell me."

"If you don't try," she snarled, "I'll flip my wig."

"Don't do that."

She did it.

She ripped off her wig, and stripped off her mask.

Eddy stood, aghast, then howled with mirth.

"Goddamnit, Beffle, you *have* learned something in thirty years!"

"I've learned something else, too. Come here."

He came.

She embraced him, and French kissed. "Loverboy, it's time to show you." Eddy held her tightly, pulling her to him, and kissed her all over her face. She pushed him away.

"No more golf?"

"What do you know about golf?"

"The Scots invented it, but I've yet to reason why."

"You don't know the difference between a birdie and a bogie."

"You don't know the difference between Mel and Beff." She took him by the hands. "So come on, I'll show you." She unbuttoned his shirt. "How'd you get so dog-gone *hairy*?" Over his shoulder she spied the security-fax-line light on her printer, flashing. He unsheathed her from the green dress. She swished over to the printer and plucked out its message. He came up behind, sliding a hand under her waistband on down to her mount of Venus, and tickled, as she bent over for a private read. Signed 2-B. Addressed to TEB, her initials, which is what Two Bears called her when not calling her Dora, or Foul Owl to tease her for not yet having earned her Indian name, or Woman, when driven by aggressive male machismo. Now Eddy's chin rested on her shoulder and she felt a finger touch her *there*. The message:

EAST SUN HAWK.

In their private code, because great evil-- the Anglos, the French, the Spaniards-- had mainly come to Native Americans from the East, East indicated danger. Sun, because of its heat and light and immediacy, signified *hot*, maybe even *extreme*; and, because a hawk can see a mouse from high in the air, hawk would mean *watched*, as in you're under surveillance. Eddy's finger curled and slid in and he whispered into her ear, "East sun hawk?" A kiss. "Meaning . . . ?" Another finger, pressing in. "Sunny Sue *Hawk* is winging from New *Yawk*?" said he. Because he's with me, he's in danger. I should tell him. "The airplane arrives at sunrise." Should I leave right now for home? "True enlighten*ment* is flying here from the Ori*ent*?"

Tomorrow.

I'll tell him then.
After the Gala Farewell Breakfast.
Maybe even stay through the Good-bye Nostalgia Get-together.
Tonight?
But how?
A sudden fear surged through her.
She surrendered to her favorite dominatrix,
To Miss Fun,
To Ms Lizard Mind,
And they had fun,
And cuddled,
And fell asleep.

THREE

EDDY REARED UP in bed, screaming, sobbing. "Another death dream!" Beffle, shocked awake, held him, stroked him, comforted him. He turned on the night-light. "Oh my *God* it's *awful* to *fear* your *dreams.*" Sweating, moaning trembling, sobbing, ---- what can it be? Beffle pushed him back to the pillow and massaged his shoulders, his chest. "Eddy, what is it?" He sat up again. "I have these dreams. About me dying. Each time death comes in a different way. It's all so *real.*" He clasped his hands. "I don't think I ever told anyone about that before." His voice, soft, had risen up into its tenor range. "Just now, I died screaming with pain in an auto wreck, and, yes, I was crushed in tight, and it was night, and warm rain was rushing in on me through the broken windshield, and, my God! I'm still half there now!"

"Eddy, if you train yourself to it, you can control your dreams, you could push your way out of the wreck, you can fall for a mile and land lightly on your feet. In dreams you can *will* what you *want* . . . and *get* it!"

"No, no that can't be possible."

"It *is* possible; it happens all the time."

"Where?"

"In tribes."

"What the Hell you know about tribes?"

"Plenty. I've a master's in anthropology from U.C. Berkeley." She took both his hands in hers. "You can control dreams. Asleep, you can be all powerful, all knowing, omni everything, just like the Big Man Upstairs!"

"It's too good to be true."

"It *is* true."

"Can you do it?"

"Yes, to a degree. Maybe that's because I'm half Indian."

Just because you live that lie, you don't have to tell it.

"*Beffle*! How do you do it."

"Before you fall asleep, you resolve to use your omnis if you need them. So there's nothing to fear. In tribes raised to it, people select their dreams before drifting off into dreamland."

"Well, damn it to Hell, you know, I'm going to have to try that." Eddy swung out of the bed, tugged on his briefs, and mixed drinks at the bar. Hair curled on his legs and tufted his back. Beffle went to the window, closed the blinds, and sat naked at the table next to him. Me, I should resolve to tell him all about it. Would that help him through the night? Tomorrow. I'll warn him tomorrow. "So, now, Eddy, I guess you're going to tell me we are at once everything and nothing, the center of the cosmos and a mote existing for a nanosecond."

"I hadn't planned to." He smiled his old smile. "You're a cynic by choice, and I'm a cynic by nightmare." He gently touched her shoulder. "I have to be a Marine one day a week."

"Yes, okay."

"Beff, I try. I really do."

She pinched him.

He pinched her back. "What do you do on the tenth of November?"

"Mess around. Wait for the eleventh, the holiday."

"Understand, every day, me, being taught and dreaming mass murder of strangers. Then Nam. Intense. They have a ten-foot wall on Parris Island. It's intimidating. They tell us to run up the wall, flip over the top. They know we can do it. We don't. Until we do it. Dare. Believe. The attitude. Intensity. Service. Every day a week, then. Just one day a week, now. Why not? A model? Chesty Puller, no. How about Lou Diamond? That's funny. But I'm too smart. Fucking woman. You don't get what I'm saying. I ain't saying it all that goddamned well, either. No? No. My model is . . . ." He thought who, then wondered why say it at all? The name's enough. "Smedley Butler." He squeezed her shoulder. "So, hey Beff, how many Marine Corps generals can you remember?"

"Eddy, sweetheart, this is not my first bed."

Why didn't I say the truth?

Never was this close to a Marine before.

"Never was this close to a Marine before."

He sprang to his feet, as in some kind of poetic power move. He spoke softly. "That was a long long time ago." Something from memory, anyway. "I was a platoon leader. I didn't believe I'd live to be twenty-one. But here I fucking am! No, don't make faces at me, the median life of a platoon leader in combat-- believe me, it's been studied, is *two minutes.*" He stood there, motionless, naked, trembling with energy, and began singing, "If you want to have some fun, jine the ca-val-ree . . . ." He gave his leg a stinging slap. "That's Jeb Stuart's song from the Civil War. It's what you tell the romantic boy. So, how's that for nightmare cynicism in the mega-dimension?"

She put an arm around his waist. "Come on, back to bed."

"Not yet."

"You called me a fucking woman."

"Meaning what?"

"Meaning you called me a fucking woman."

"Do you ever say what you're thinking about?"

"Do you ever *think about* what you're thinking about?"

He held her at arm's length and scrutinized her, her pale bare body, and, smiling a loving smile exploded into laughter. "Occasionally, I do," he said to her. "And I follow Linus Pauling's advice. Question the question." She sat him down at the table, and opened her pirate book before him, the French book her Canadian friends had given her, and indicated a marked passage.

Standing behind him, holding his bare shoulders, translating, she read it aloud.

"Between the tributary de la Magdelaine and the Orinoco River, extends a long series of coasts, which occupy an immense space. They were discovered in 1499 by Ojeda, Juan de la Cosas and Amerigo Vespucci, who with four ships came up to a place that they named *Venezuela,* because of the resemblance they found in it to Venice. The settlements that these innovators and their imitators tried to plant on the continent did not form with anywhere near the facility of those in the islands. The natives, mutually accustomed to making war, offered resistance, and, sometimes even, defended themselves with advantage. But, eventually, these small isolated nations, which, by character or as a result of their perpetual state of war, rarely had a fixed abode, sank into the earth, or submitted. . . . Open to this, Eddy, it's going to help me explain myself."

Eddy grasped one of her hands.

"They built then a large number of little villages, of which the best known are: Cumana, Caracas, Veregna, Coro, Maracaibo, and Santa Marta. The territory of some of them offered gold mines which were from the very first exploited. Their product was large enough in early times; but this success did not last long; it was soon necessary to abandon them. In the settlements that lacked mines, the Spanish, alternating between gold and blood, went into the interior of the country to massacre the Indians or snatch from them what they had collected of this precious sand from the riverbeds to make into various ornaments. The last recourse of these madmen was to enslave these Indians, in order to transport them to far-away islands which their barbarity had already depopulated."

She sat down next to Eddy and cuddled against him.

"In 1528, Charles V, King of Spain, pledged the territory of Venezuela to a company of wholesale merchants from Augsburg who undertook its colonization. These merchants sent four hundred and eighty Germans there, whose avarice and ferocity surpassed anything yet seen in the New World. History accuses them of having massacred, or caused to die in slavery, one million Indians. Their tyranny ended in a horrible catastrophe; and, far from thinking of replacing them, one is reduced to regarding as good fortune that this country, which they had devastated, had returned to Spanish domination. Unfortunately, the atrocious scenes which the Germans had set as an example were renewed by Caravajal, who was charged with the government of this unfortunate country. This monster, it is true, carried his head to the scaffold, but this punishment did not enable his victims to leave the tombs into which he had thrust them. The depopulation had become so complete, that they transported from Africa, in 1550, a great number of Negroes, upon whom they built hope for an unlimited prosperity. But the habit of tyranny made them treat these slaves with such hardness that they revolted. Their rebellion authorized the cutting of the throats of all the males, and the colony again became a wilderness mingled with the cinders of Blacks, Spaniards, Indians, and Germans."

She stood, went to the bar, fetched two drinks, and sat down across from him.

Looking at Eddy, who sat silently puzzling his way into the book, she saw Two Bears, scraggly beard, massive in his office chair, and heard his deep voice contradicting what she had just said about Indians and white supremacy. "Don't say *whites* when you talk about our enemy. Woman, you have one Hell of a lot to learn. You call yourself half *white*.

You may be fair (a momentary sense of fare-- as in prey-- flashed through her thoughts), but that could be your Indian side showing through. We true Americans are fairer than most Anglos with their hairy faces, and bodies. White! Compared to us, are Italians *white*? How about Spaniards? Persians? Jews?" To get along with Two Bears, she thought, you have to come back at him, hard. "Boss," she replied, "You're climbing up the wrong tree. Nobody's *white*. Tan. Swart. Pink. Red-faced. Sure. The only *red*men I have ever seen-- and believe me, even though some of these guys, thanks to genes, sun, and booze are bright red, they all think of themselves as *white*. It makes a dramatic contrast when they dress up in their white KKK sheets and pointy hoods. True white supremacy would have to be rule by ghosts." And there sits Eddy, furry Eddy, with his five-o'clock shadow. Doubtless he regards himself as *white*.

Eddy looked up at her. "Why'd you show me this?"

"I'm working up to telling you something."

"Telling me what? About the Halls of Montezuma, and his priests, tearing open the chests of gorgeous people, and throwing their hearts down the church stairs for the crowd to eat, and then, flaying their bodies, and dressing in their skins, and *dancing*? He closed the book. "Excuse me, I'm upset. What it says here is still happening."

"That's why I studied anthropology and history. We have to do something about it. About bringing justice to Native Americans, to us." She remembered her play act. "In me, they live side-by-side, at peace. I concentrated on learning about it. But that's not enough. Learning. *Doing* is what counts."

"Are you doing something?"

"Yes. I'll tell you all about it in the morning."

"Tell me now."

"No. It's too complicated."

"All right. In the morning."

They fell silent. He looked sad and lonely. She led him to bed, and, obsessed by the urgency and intensity of Two Bears' warning flaring in her heart, she stroked Eddy into peaceful sleep.

At ten a.m. they awoke in high spirits, feeling fit.

They sprang from bed, and to imaginary music, Beff gave Eddy a big happy, swirling, dancing kiss.

"Let's trade skins, and dance again."

"And jine the cav-al-reeeeee!"

She nuzzled him.

"You want to have some fun?"

"Yeahhhh," he said. "Yeahhhhh."

"Over, Rover, Over. To this mirror."

"So, now what?"

"I'm Jeb Stuart, telling you what to do."

"So, okay babe, stars and bars."

An evil grin twisting his face, he went to the honor bar and, into two glasses, poured straight tequila.

"For the stars."

"And see these two beauties in the mirror?" She pulled him back. "Who'll try to skin them for the good-bye dance?"

"Could be anybody our size. As you're trying to show me, for some mad reason, our bodies resemble."

"Yes. And with that, we'll stoke the class pyre." She put a Beffle wig on his head. "Now pull your prick back under your crotch, and know you are now Beffle."

Laughing, he did it.

"Ratchet your tenor up to alto. Think of yourself as half Indian, as Foul Owl."

She stuffed her bra with two wash cloths and strapped it onto him.

"You have some demented Beffle reason?"

"Ignite the fires of gossip."

She sheathed him in her favorite dress.

"Now you're the squaw in gelb."

She put a Beffle mask on him. "Humans are the only animals whose faces change with age." She adjusted things, rubbed in makeup. "Now you're me." She slipped into her Melissa drag. "Time to break fast."

"And let people see us both in the same place."

Hysterically mirthful, they slapped a loud high-five.

"And be lovers!"

Hoping to encounter Pearl and her pals, who, after all, had clamped them together, they stepped out into the hall.

Empty.

They did a big sloppy kiss anyway.

And held hands in the elevator.

And walked by the tables, whence came a few hellos, then to the pool, and looked into it, at fat fish swish.

Their eyes flashed: Why Not?

Papa Tequila said, do it.

Upstage now, they embraced passionately and shared an immense wet kiss.

And then, holding hands, they leaned back, dancing.

"For the skins."

We did it! The skin trade!

"Hey Beff, did we really truly miss the Good-Bye Lakewood High Breakfast?"

The no-host already made its tempting promise. "So, hey Beff, let's go for the stars and bar."

They went to star at the bar.

More tequila.

And Eddy began singing *The Raggedy Ass Marines Are on Parade.*

And Beffle lured him into tenor/contralto harmony.

Come landlord fill the flowing bowl,
Until it doth run o-ver,
Come landlord fill the flowing bowl,
Until it doth run o-ver;
For tonight we'll merry merry be
For tonight we'll merry merry *be*
For tonight we'll merry merry be,
Tomorrow we'll be ***sober***

An arm, another, around their backs.

Pearl! Necklaces from the bottom of the sea or from some factory in Delaware: Pearl.

Once three jolly post boys
Were seated in a tav-ern,
Once three jolly post boys,
Were seated in a tav-ern;
Then they decided it;
Then they decided it;
Then they de-ci-ded **it;**
Let's have an-other flagon!

"Birds of a feather! Raising Cain!"

They embraced her, and broke loose, and escaped into the restaurant for morning food.

Smiling an open smile, Eddy said, "You ready to tell me?"

"No."

Must! It's the right thing to do.

"Oh, *there* you are!" Pearl! "Mind if I sit down?" She snagged a chair from the next table, and sagged into it. "Oh Beffle, Beffle. You're a sight for sore eyes! Melissa here and Eddy told me you came. Those two lovebirds get along one

Hell of a lot better then they used to." She ran a finger down Eddy's cheek. "Beffle, honey, you sure cake on the makeup!"

"I have a skin condition."

"And something wrong with your voice."

"It's an Indian Summer cold. Colds always make me hoarse."

"Out there by the pool, you two were sure getting mushy, not that I mind. With me, anything goes."

"We're in love," said Melissa, taking Eddy's hand.

"Can you keep a secret, Pearl?"

"Try me."

"Promise?"

"Won't tell a soul."

No matter what, you won't tell anybody at all?"

"Honest Injun."

"Melissa and I went to San Francisco last week, and got married."

"*Married?*"

"Yes. Married."

"For the love of Pete!"

"And this starts our honeymoon."

"What can I say?" She squeezed their hands. "Congratulations."

And now Melissa, carrot top, somewhat grayed out, saw her husband, Terry Thompson, come out of the elevator, and walk toward the pool.

He sat at a table by himself.

No *Plain Dealer*, no coffee.

By himself.

Beffle glanced at Eddy. He'd seen Terry too. Fortunately, no one had taken their order. Melissa stood, and hugged Pearl. "Beffle and I have to go." They walked to the elevators. When the gossip seeds germinated, and that would be soon, this joke would devastate Terry, and there was no way to reverse it. "Melissa has to vanish instantly into the empyrean."

"We'll say space aliens got her."

"I'll go to Melissa's room and change back into me. Melissa in, Beffle out, that should feed the bonfire." She stopped the elevator at four. Standing in the doorway, she said, "Ed, here's the card to my room. Go up there and metamorphose into your genuine lovely self, and wait for me. I'll knock."

The elevator closed and rose. She walked toward Melissa's room. Gossip will blaze. The conflagration I started will flare out of control, utterly beyond my power to quench.

A door flung open, and out came the twins.

On seeing her, Flora and Fauna shrieked welcome, seized her by the hands, and drew her into their room.

They pressed her down into an easy chair.

No muumuu this time. Both, bare from the waist up, sported costly leathers, and long hair, dyed silver. And they still had those weird baby tits. At least they'd never have a sag problem.

"It's goddamned good to see you, Carrot Top."

"Which are you?"

"Fauna."

Beffle took a green marker off their writing desk and stroked a line down the center of Fauna's chest.

"One of you should wear a nose ring or a tattoo."

"You sure have changed," said Flora, in their soprano voice. "If you didn't have that red hair, I wouldn't have known you."

"The auto wreck-- I guess you heard about it . . . ." They nodded. "It messed up my face."

"Yes, but there's more to it than that."

"Flora means you used to be a weak sister, and now you're almost as kick-ass as Beffle."

"You guys look like you do a little kick-ass yourselves."

"We're really living now. Last June, we rode our Harleys to San Francisco."

"And rode at the front of the Gay Pride Parade with Dykes on Bikes."

"And went to that big Indian gambling casino up north and won a *thousand* bucks!"

"Melissa, we've always dug girls, but we just came out this year."

"You came out to me at that motel party at Cedar Point. Remember? Nineteen hundred and seventy . . . one! A'swillin' and a'smokin' and a'eatin out."

"Southern Comfort and hash and beaver burgers."

"More like Southern Cunt-fort, Flora. Cunt-fort."

"And when I got completely out of my mind, Beffle pushed me into bed with you two."

"You had one Hell of a tasty pretty pussy."

"All framed in red." Fauna slid a hand up Beffle's thigh, toward her crotch. "Did you ever wonder," asked Beffle, "what it would be like if people remembered each other, not by their faces-- because faces change, but by their *genitals*? Imagine the family album, the driver's license, the class year book." Beffle sprang to her feet. "Sorry, sweetie. Saving that for Mr. Right." Whooping with mirth, she stepped back into the hall and followed the numbers and arrows to Melissa's room. Now, to call the big Bear from a neutral phone.

But not yet.

She stripped and showered, and wishing time would stop for an hour or two, slumped into a chair. I haven't told Eddy yet. So go do it. But, first, check in with the double Bear. Her father called her Wild Child, and she'd loved it, because he *liked* her being wild. He was wild himself. Almost goofy. "All right, Wild Child, get wild!" She'd called him Feral Frank. "Up! Up!" She rose and sat on the bed by the phone. Once, when her diction slid well over onto the wild side, her mother had actually washed out her mouth with soap. Feral Frank steamed around the Great Lakes as first mate on Cleveland Cliffs ore ships and when the lakes froze, he took the family to winter in hot places. Once, in Australia, near Adelaide, when their dog had been impounded and officials confronted them with a long long scroll of must-do-before-Fido's-free paper work, Feral Frank, late one night, led her to the pound, where he cut the lock off the gate to the exercise yard, dragged it open, unlocked the big cage, and some smaller ones inside, and ran all the animals out. This created a gorgeous chaos affording plenty of cover for Poopy Puppy's escape to home.

The attendants got most of the animals back

Two Bears is still loose.

He'll be in . . . Santa Cruz. At his office in the *Mercury-News* Building, where he usually stays on Saturday night.

California is minus three hours from Cleveland, making it about nine a.m. out there.

Ignoring the bad music they produced, she touched the phone numbers.

Tomorrow, the big Bear would be in their San Francisco office, covering political expediencies, and, Tuesday, he'd be handling affairs in Monterey. Bear's phone rang. She pictured him stumbling from his couch to his solid walnut executive desk, him all smooth and fleshy in his boxers and Ohlone Valley Casino T-shirt. O.V.C.'s three branch offices struggled against rivals trying to infiltrate the territory she and Two Bears had persuaded Clio, which is what Bear called history, to award to the Ohlone Tribe. Clio discreetly questioned whether any real Ohlone existed at all. Big Bear would now be sitting at his desk there in the *Mercury-News* Building, groping for cold coffee. The floor above had been leased to a contemptible weekly, which began as an alternative paper, and now snuggled in the shelter of a Murdoch umbrella, seemingly entrusted with the sole mission of harassing its downstairs neighbors: Ohlone Gaming Enterprises and the San Jose *Mercury-News*.

"Hello," said the phone in an angry voice. "James Two Bears Jones speaking."

"Hello Mr. Jones." Yes, he recognized my voice. "My name is Clio and I represent The Seaside Investment Corporation. I'm calling to invite you to subscribe to our future's plan."

"Futures! My motto about futures is be wary, be careful, and be open to help from Owl."

Sometimes I wish he didn't think I'm part Indian, and wasn't obsessed with the idea that Owl is my protector. That's one bird I'd like to send to Eddy's Owl Cleaners!

"Futures, young woman, at the best look extremely dangerous."

What a year! Security! Talking in innuendo and code! Paranoia? No, that's when you think more guys are out to get you than really are. "I would like, Mr. Jones, to bring you a copy of our futures plan as soon as possible."

"Very well, young woman. I want to see if you're serious. Bring it to me tomorrow."

"It will have to be Tuesday, Mr. Jones."

"Very well, Tuesday." He hung up.

Her adrenaline raced.

She *still* hadn't warned Eddy.

She rang her room, five, ten, fifteen rings.

No answer.

Did they think he's me and kidnap him?

Maybe even kill him?

She dressed and hastily gathered her things, rushed out, down the hall, up the stairs, and, wondering what to do about having no card to the lock, came to her door.

It stood ajar.

And, inside, . . . no Eddy.

She shouted for him.

No answer.

She looked in the bathroom, under the bed.

No Eddy.

Maybe, in the closet, waiting to spring out and shout *Boooooo!*

Plenty of clothes inside, but no Eddy.

Her door still gaped open.

In a flare of panic, she slammed it, secured all the locks and bolts, jammed a chair under the doorknob, leaned against the wall, heart racing, intensely aerobic, waiting quietly for calm.

He'd left by himself, or he'd been abducted.

Someone had taken the computer.

And the Beffle mask, and the yellow dress, and the rest of the Beffle paraphernalia he'd been wearing.

Anything else missing?

She looked down at the busy pool café and the swimmers sporting about, and then began to inventory her possessions.

Kidnapped.

But if so, why had they deliberately left the door open?

Too nervous to sit, she flopped onto the bed, and sprawled on her back, and closed her eyes, and saw nothing save the marbled matte red-orange of her eyelids. And now, Wild Child, don't do anything until you reason out a sense of what's happening. Eddy. My laptop computer. My yellow dress and Beffle disguise. They're gone. The printer and all else are still here. What more do I know? The Bear and I thought coming here I'd be out of danger, but now he makes an effort to warn me my situation is perilous. So I have to go straight back as fast I can. Bear will be in Monterey, but I'll cab directly from Monterey airport to Carmel Valley and the Casino. That would be safest. No. Not really. I'll wing from here to Boston, and then to L.A., and up to San Luis Obispo, and taxi back. But how do I get from here to Cleveland airport?

She bounced out of bed and began packing. Work always seemed to produce poise and tranquillity. First, I have to build a hypothesis about what's happening. Another certainty: more and more things seem to be going wrong for Bear and me and the business. It's a pattern. It must be by plan. But who wants to wreck us.

Everybody.

Bear and I have made it too successful.

She though of the beginnings. Of the bare-fist politics which had driven Congressional recognition of the Ensen, Salinan, Rumsen, Mutsen, and Salson septs of the Ohlone group, and of continuing attempts of other self-defined groups to be accepted. Clint Eastwood, for one dollar, had sold his Carmel Valley land to the Rumsens so they could establish his part of their ancient home as a legal reservation. Secretly hoping to develop a casino, the elders had engaged Two Bears-- a full-blooded Cherokee and a lawyer specialized in land titles-- to organize the enterprise. Land titles in most of California, he told them, trace back to Spanish grants which, in turn, trace back to soldiers and other royal agents who claimed Indian lands in the name of their King. So with the help of Eastwood's lawyers and further research at the Bancroft Library, Two Bears requested and received a writ dissolving the Spanish grants, thusly returning both title and sovereignty to the Rumsens.

Packing some of her Indian jewelry, she remembered her first days as Two Bears' administrative assistant when he'd confided in her that Clio had alerted him to the contradiction of the Spanish grants presented by the absence of any treaty between Spain and the Ohlone confirming Spanish sovereignty or land titles.

"And then, deep into that dialectic, Clio clued me to the fact that most likely no pure-bred Ohlone exist at all."

And then, after they'd opened the Ohlone Valley Casino, the Salson Ohlone, organized a multi-tribal casino near San Juan Bautista.

And the two had been fighting for territory ever since.

So, our troubles may trace back to that, or to other Ohlone, or to jealousy, or to the Mafia, or the Triads, or to multi-national finance . . . or . . . or to all of them.

Criminal synergy.

She folded some dresses, put them in her carrying case, zipped it, and stacked it on the others.

Now for the theatrical paraphernalia.

Decide now.

Disguise, or not?

Be the Beer Fairy? Melissa?

Being Eddy would take too long.

Be me?

If I knew what was going on, deductive logic, my dear Watson, would serve to disclose the best bet. But . . . ?

Ah! She took her book off the table. *Histoire des Marins Pirates et Corsaires de l'Océanie et de la Méditerranée Comprenant la Conquête de l'Algérie* par P. Christian, PARIS, P.-H. Krabbe, Libraire-Editeur, 12, rue de Savoi. 1852. *Of course . . . !* Consult an oracle!

Clio is surely embodied in this tome.

Open it at random.

"O! Mighty Clio, she who knoweth all and see-eth all, I invoke thy presence in these pages to reveal what I, thy humble and loyal servant, should do now."

She hefted her pirate history.

The leather back fell off.

Revealing reused printed paper.

From a medical book!

Il est préférable de prendre cette tisane avant les repas et avant de se coucher.

So, uh, yes, Clio has disclosed: It is preferable to take this tisane before meals and before going to bed.

So, what in Hell is a tisane?

Herb tea.

And in street slang: *correction*, as in Department of Corrections, punishment, *imprisonment.*

"Now is the optimum time for the tisane, Clio, but I scorn both herb tea and punishment."

She stuffed her theatrical gear into the suitcase, and snapped it shut.

So, Wild Child, I'm told to be me.

Done. I'm me. What's my next move?

From the clothing she'd left unpacked till deciding who to be, she selected charcoal gray slacks and a black blouse, dressed, and packed the rest. She took some hundreds from her money belt, zipped it, cinched it on. She dumped out her big shoulder-strap purse, packed in her collapsible umbrella and some toiletries and her address book and her wallet. A light jacket? No. If I need one, I'll buy one. After all, most problems are soluble in money.

And now for further guidance, and as Clio's alternative to all those moron magazines airlines provide, the pirate book. She slipped a rubber band around *Histoire des Marins*, and thrust it in.

She slung her bag and stepped to the mirror.

Not bad!

Grunge in; vogue out.

She gazed at her neatly piled baggage as the next series of moves took shape in her head. Call the desk; say I'm staying through Tuesday, but won't need maid service. Walk out a side door and around to the front. Catch a cab. Or the airport shuttle? No. Then, Tuesday, phone them from home to check out, and have them forward my baggage to the casino. What did I forget? Whatever I don't remember. So much for the tactics. Strategy? Don't be seen; leave no clues. Minimize their opportunities to intercept.

Ready and confident, concerned about Eddy, she stepped into the hall and, favoring her left leg somewhat, went down the stairs and into the parking basement, thence out a side door to the main entrance.

A cab stood at the curb.

So far so good!

Wrong!

"Beffle, sweetie. You're as pretty as a picture!"

Pearl.

"How'd you change so fast?"

"Change?"

"Why yes, your yellow dress."

"What are you talking about?"

"I just saw you in the lobby, in your yellow dress, walking with that man."

"Eddy?"

"No, silly, not Eddy."

"Who?"

"You know."

"Goddamnit Pearl! Who?"

"Hold your horses."

"With whom did you see me?"

"Cool your jets."

Oracle, you double-crossed me! I should be the Beer Fairy.

"Beffle, honey, don't look at me like that."

"Which man, Pearl?"

"I won't tell you, smarty pants, because I know you know, and you're being a tease."

"Just tell me."

"Only if you'll tell me something I've always wanted to know. Why'd we all call you Beffle?"

A plan!

She motioned the taxi over, opened the door, pushed Pearl in, slammed the door. "Downtown Elyria, driver, and then bring my friend back."

"What the Hell you doing . . . ?"

"I've an appointment, Pearl. This way we can have a visit and I won't be late. But if you don't want to chat, I'll tell him to turn around and take you back."

"Why, dear, ain't that just like you. Sounds like more fun than a pile of monkeys."

"Settle back, and I'll answer your question."

"I don't mean to be a nosy Parker, but I always did wonder about your nickname."

"Tell me about the man, and I'll tell you the story."

"The man who was carrying that big dispatch case?"

"Yes. There's got to be more."

"Oh, there's more all right, but first tell me the story."

"Gladly. If you promise to tell me everything you saw."

"Swear to die!"

The cab sped by trees through dappled sunlight.

"Pearl you remember, in our junior year, the second half, they made me editor of the *Lakewood High Times*?" Pearl nodded, yes. "Well, I sort of felt then what I know now. As my boss puts it, when you're chief of something, you want everyone to feel they're part of the enterprise. He says, from the national level to the family level, *that* is the secret of successful and orderly government. Back then, we handset all the headlines, then proofed them, and pasted them onto the layout sheet. We had lots of different kinds of loose type that had accumulated in the printshop for anyway fifty years. All the lower case was stored somewhere, but, for heads and subheads, we kept all the capital letters twenty point or larger easily available. Believe me, in those days, I was your archetypical ink-stained wretch."

Beffle studied her companion, slouching there on the seat beside her, toying with the strings of fake pearls decorating her massive décolletage, waiting cowlike for more story. O! Wild Child, rejoice! Imagine, instead of being born from the cream of the gene pool and being me, being born from the dregs and for all of my life having to be *her*. How can she *stand* it? One Pearly blessing is that nobody can imagine being smarter than they are.

"Remember old Fart Face?" Do you also remember when I stuck a Kick-Me sign on your back? "Fart Face, the janitor?"

"I'll say! Used to tell us he'd been gassed in World War I, but we didn't think he could be *that* old."

"His car displayed a BACK UP OUR BOYS bumper sticker, and he always tried to make us think he favored the Vietnam war, but he got me to sneak him copies of the *Berkeley Barb* I bought from the twins."

"How 'bout the time he crossed the picket line in front of the school, you know, when Nixon attacked Cambodia, and Eddy got real sore at him and yelled, 'You can kiss my *ass*,' and he looked Eddy up and down and said, 'Well, all right, son, but I think I'd rather kiss your *horse*.'"

They burst into laughter, and outside the window the flat Ohio farmscape flowed by.

"Well, yes, that was a killer, but, anyway, even though I did slip him those papers, he was pretty sloppy about cleaning up the printshop, so, trying to get him into the enterprise, I asked him to pick the headline type for the April Fool issue. And he picked **BEFFLE**. Why? Because, said he, in all the years he'd worked there, he'd never seen it used. On anything. It truly is a stupid looking type-face, wild and silly, so I wrote a long article about the beauties of beffle, and from then on in his humor column, Eddy kept calling me Beffle, and finding in beffle qualities like wild, foolish, stupid, moronic, absurd, always criticizing the type face, but everybody knew he meant me, and that sure was a *gas*."

"Oh, silly, I remember all that. I'm just checking up."

Pearl cranked down her window, and the dry hot breath of the countryside came in, touched with manure. "Okay. So then you remember that April Fool issue. An immense banner all in beffle announced **JANITOR FINDS BODIES**. And right under it I ran a photo of ten boys in gym shorts, all piled up. **CUSTODIAN FINDS TEN CORPSES**, and under the picture: **COUNT 'EM**."

"Oh, I loved that. You razzed the Hell out of the big papers for running body counts every day. But you was just as bad in class. Remember? In chem lab? You hitched the gas line for the Bunsen burners to the water, and one after another the burners turned into geysers and smashed up all those funny glass jars they was supposed to be heating."

"And in that issue-- remember--? one story announced the abolition of football so the field could be plowed up for a Victory Garden. And another proposed auctioning off grades to raise money to pay for the war. And, yes, the *Times* proposed teachers be drafted into the K-9 Corps."

"Sure, I read that paper, and Eddy's columns, but I didn't really catch the type stuff."

"So Pearl, me, I'm an Indian, I must be, because people keep giving me new names. And only one-- Braun, is for being married. Imagine, my son, he's twenty-eight-- is named Charley *Braun*." The cab was now rolling through elm shaded streets in the outskirts of Elyria. "Your turn, Pearl. Who was that man?"

"Well, if you insist." How could this big lump of meat have such a squeaky voice? "When I was drinking at the bar with Eddy and Melissa, this fellow butts into our conversation and goes ballistic about birth control and abortion. That's the guy you was with, and you know who he is as well as I do. He looks like a real stuffed shirt to me!"

"True." Later it proved far from being so.

The cab turned into a main street-- Main Street? Beffle spied a neon sign blinking Teeney Weeney Lucky Spot.

"That bar there, cabby. That's where I'm going." They drew up in front and she paid him double-the-meter plus twenty dollars. "Well, here's where I get off." She stepped out and Pearl slid over and they embraced. "Pearl, I enjoyed all that, going back to Lakewood High and seeing old friends. Strange, but I sort of miss the place."

"Me too."

"Maybe it's just that I'd like some of those in-between years back."

"You can say that again."

"Even so, I still find plenty of excitement."

"Honey, about all I do any more that's fun is fly out to Las Vegas and sink right into it. So what if it costs a few bucks? I really dig them marble tubs they have in the rooms at Caesar's Palace."

"Well, so long."

"Toodle--oo."

The cab drew away, leaving her standing before the Teeney Weeney Lucky Spot. She went to a street phone on the corner and called Greyhound. She could go to Toledo in fifty-five minutes. Once there, she'd cab to the airport; buy a ticket to San Luis Obispo, via L.A. In Chicago, doubtless, there'd be a layover at O'Hare. She walked three blocks to the bus station, bought a ticket, and then went across the street to the Okay Lounge, and sat at the bar. A smiling young barkeep came up to her. "What'll it be, Lady." She ordered a draft beer. Lady! *Another* name. Lady would do as a transition, now that Beffle was suddenly out of style. An image radiated of Eddy in Beffle drag and the mystery man carrying her desktop stepping out of the elevator. She studied it, worried it, doggedly chewing and shaking it, but nothing resolved; it produced naught but a sharp feeling of concern for Eddy. Bet he's sorry he went to the re-onion and met me. Charley slipped into her thoughts. She forced her attention back to Eddy, the golf Nazi. Wild Child, think about what you're thinking about! Charley slid back in. Homesick? What for-- jerking off? She asked for more beer. At twenty, Charley had been converted by a Mormon missionary. Nothing she said could crack this folly. A high crime among Mormon males is masturbation. Virtually the supreme sin. "For Christ sake, Charley, stop reading that *Book of Moron* and go upstairs and jack off!" She'd named him for a guitar player, hoping he'd make a serious try at music, but no. As a boy, in hopes of making him follow imagination, and be a bit crazy, she called *him* Wild Child. She couldn't even make him silly. And then in adolescence, even though he had all the gifts, he did everything he was told to do. "Feral Frank, was like me, Charley. He didn't like to give orders, and he didn't like to take them. Your grandfather is a great model. Try to emulate him." Hopeless. Jack off, you little twit! No. Instead, he went to Brigham Young University. Because there's safety in numbers, money too, Brigham Young, a world-class scoundrel, shaped every institution of the Latter Day Saints toward maximizing births in order to increase his following. Have six wives, Charley; don't ever ever beat your meat. And you'll be fulfilling God's plan as preached by that old charlatan they named your college for. My God! Charlatan alliterates with Charley. Charley! Leaving his major, archaeology, and studying there for an Ed.D.! A degree as phony as the school that awards it.

"Hey Lady."

"Yes . . . ?"

"You have a phone call."

PART TWO

When we know why people get old, we can fix it. Save for disease or a railroad wreck, eternal youth can be yours. Fat? We can fix that too. Longer legs? Sure. Bigger tits? Even if you're male, okay. We can do it. A tail? Why not. Three arms are in style? Pay the price; you've got them.

--Theodora Eliot Braun
Las Vegas, Nevada, 2003

FOUR

TWO BEARS WATCHED **Dora** across the glass-topped table as she ate her usual of grits and maple syrup and orange juice. Despite her age, in her dark-green shorts and blouse, white socks and running shoes, she seemed almost sexy. He bit into a grease-dripping sausage he'd had sent up along with a Denver omelet, and studied Dora as she wolfed into her breakfast. As ever, she's thoroughly feminine, yet even so, she carries herself, expresses herself, with boyish insolence. He opened a window to fresh, sweet air, and said, "All right, now, Woman, this Eddy you were telling me about? An ex-Marine, probably in law enforcement. You cross-dressed him, masked him to impersonate you, then sent him alone to your room. Returning, you found the door ajar. He'd vanished. Later someone told you he came out of the elevator, still dressed as you, and crossed the lobby with a man carrying what probably is your laptop. So this Eddy is now kidnapped, or dead, or laughing his butt off for having fooled you so thoroughly and at this very moment is working with *them* to learn as much about us as they can from your computer."

"That's it. Why don't you wipe that sausage goo off your face before they start calling you Bear Grease?"

He shook his head and laughed.

"Did you report it, Dora?"

"Report what?"

"*That.*"

"No. What was there to report, except the theft of my laptop? And had I done so, I'd have attracted one Hell of a lot of superfluous attention." She poured some syrup. "I love this stuff." She took a piece of Bear's toast and wiped her plate. "What shook me, I think, more than anything else, was when that barman in Elyria said I had a phone call. I'd thought myself safe. I had fantasies of being tracked by killers. Death squads. But I was sure nobody could find me. Imagine! The call turned out to be a *mistake.* Someone was looking around town for his wife." She ate one of Bear's sausages. "Why did you send me that warning, telling me to come back. What do you think is going to happen?"

"I'll reply to that after while."

"Now!"

"I don't want to ruin your breakfast."

She wiped another slice of toast around her plate, and pushed the plate aside. Why, she wondered, after working a year with him, does this guy still manage to make me feel like a child. "Bear, I'm the best paid girl Friday in Monterey County."

He drew a sheet of paper from a file, and, handing it to her, he said, "This came to me from a public fax machine in Santa Cruz. Anonymously. That's why I sent you the message."

It was printed in computer script:

> *As a warning to clean up your*
> *act we're going to hit your lady*
> *in Westlake.*

"Doesn't say much, Bear, except . . . well, start sweating."

"That's all I know about it. I don't even have a theory."

"It could be from any one of those groups we think are trying to knock us over. Or from one we don't even know about."

"I'm going to hire more security types. I want you to stay here, in the casino compound, until I can get a sharp fix on what's going on." His servant-- an Anglo-- came in and cleared the dishes. "I have to go to Monterey. I'll be back in the morning, for breakfast, and I'll stay for a while, and we'll plan our next move."

"Bear, before you go." He stopped in the doorway, turned to face her. "At the reunion, they were calling me by my old high-school nickname. Beffle."

"Beffle? What's that?"

"A funny fancy type face. I never liked being called Dora. You know, who wants to be opened, or closed, or *slammed*?"

"So?"

"So, forget Dora. Call me Beffle."

"You've got too many names now."

"We Indians are supposed to have lots of names."

"You're no Indian, you're a half-breed, half Huron, and half . . . Irish."

"So what? Most Americans are half-breeds, at best. We're a nation of *mongrels*."

He smiled.

"So, come on, call me Beffle. It's the only name I ever earned, so it must be my Indian name."

"What kind of medicine can you make out of lead type? You going to carry it around? When you're in trouble, is it-- is Beffle, going to drop from the sky or rush out of the woods and help you?" He made a face. "Okay. Beffle it is."

She waved good-bye, then walked to Bear's desk, and sat, and hefted the lucky rock he'd found in Greece, at Lambi Beach near Patmos, where Saint John wrote *Revelations.* Sea-worn marble, with blue-gray veins. She rubbed it gently along her forearm. Now what. Call the garage and tell them to get a car ready? Come back after noon and sort out the mail and take care of whatever it brings? Heave the rock through the big window? Close the casino and give everyone the day off? Call 911 and scream for help? She contemplated her plight. Danger might be anywhere, everywhere. She should be frightened. "I *am* frightened." But only feel a softly buzzing background anxiety. Maybe some things are too scary to be scared of. "Wild Child, like everyone else, you live in a cocoon of denial." Eddy had told her he could sometimes be reached at 1-800-MURDER 1. *Busy.* Try again. Still busy.

She called the garage. The Morgan convertible would be ready in half-an-hour. That car is as old as I am! Power corrupts? No, for cars and men alike, middle age corrupts. Why do old ladies paint their faces? Busy! Hell with it.

Favoring her left leg, distressed that her arthritis had come back, she went out by the front desk and, with a wave to the receptionist, entered the office elevator, rode it down to the main gaming floor, and stepped out into a blasting energy-flush steeped in bright noise, marinating in musical motion-flash, action *action* **aktion**. Limping slightly, she strode between rows of busy slots and their sucklings, suckers these mechanized money cows had lured here in midmorning by hope and greed and excitement, bait the casino's ads trolled in nearby waters. She stopped behind a distinguished seeming gentleman in frenzied colloquy with a one-dollar money eater and thought of Two Bears pacing through these rooms, stern, inscrutable, jubilant, rejoicing at the sight of all these fools feeding casino bank accounts and investment portfolios that someday would help finance creation of a confederacy of the tribes. Euro-Christian lust for property exploited by the casinos, Two Bears often said, would revive and solidify the tribes and produce unity and prosperity for all Native Americans. "Money is Anglo blood. Bleed the occupying nation to build our union! Solidarity! Their own folly will destroy them!"

Outside, on the lawn, it was the warm sweet-smelling peace of the Carmel Valley.

She stood there, alone, on cropped grass, calmed by the serenity of the sunny green ridge rising behind the casino and its family of smaller buildings. Taken together, these formed an ensemble resembling Ventana at Big Sur or one of the rustic campuses of the University of California at Santa Cruz. An electric golf-cart approached on a path from the hotel. Blind Badger, an antique Klamath, the grounds manager, stepped out. His T-shirt proclaimed: **I'M NOT 83; I'M A FAILED EXPERIMENT.** "Boss, we got big trouble." She was boss to him because, like all the other department heads, he had to report to her, the chief of staff, and she dealt with the problem, or passed it on to Bear.

"And what, pray tell, might that be?"

"Them goddamned pigs are back to rooting up the gardens."

In the early 1900's some tycoon with delusions of nobility had released European wild boars and sows into the Big Sur wilderness where they'd thrived and multiplied.

"So, my friend, what do you propose to do about it?"

"We've tried everything."

She motioned him back into the cart, slid in beside him.

"Poison?"

"Huh-uh."

"Show me; then take me to the garage."

"Boss, lot's of things we can't fix. Columbus, Portola, Serra-- they broke the cycle of life, and we been in a twister ever since."

"Making all of us a failed experiment?"

"Uh-huh."

The beer garden behind the hotel looked like it had been plowed overnight. The feral hogs had even upset a concrete Cupid. Maybe *swine* are our secret enemies! She began to laugh. "Get High Hawk out here with a rifle and a sniper scope. Yes! Yes! A midnight ambush-- free pork at happy hour."

Looking perplexed, Blind Badger let her out by the garage.

Slowly, feeling the shame of living in hypocrisy as acutely as do the devout when living in sin, she walked around the building to an obscure fire door, and, for a moment, stood before it. "*Every* job, Wild Child, is to a degree show biz; *every* job has its act."

She thrust her master key into the lock and silently opened the door.

All the department chiefs, no matter what they do, should always feel the presence of my presence.

My act is to be omnipresent. Ubiquitous. *Every*where at once.

She stepped inside.

As always on coming here, she noted the place seemed clean as a hospital. Here is an active garage which doesn't even *smell*. Still yet more remarkable than that, it always gave her a holy feeling. She looked around at the auto god, Brahma-like in its many manifestations, each of which David Running Deer, the master mechanic, and his helpers, kept in perfect condition. The auto god's usual embodiments, cars, trucks, limos, mini-buses, stood ranked against the far wall presenting their shining radiators. The clean blue legs of Running Deer extended from beneath a Jeep Cherokee drawn from its place to front-and-center. Away from work, Running Deer, handsome as a movie star, normally braided his long black hair into a pony tail secured by a silver clip, and wore a tan trench coat, and radiated intense fey power through the passive shell of perfect grooming.

Here is the yin to the Bear-slob yang.

In front, alone, in places of honor, were Bear's two favorite toys, a Rolls-Royce limousine with tan fenders and a mottled marbled golden-colored body which had been built in 1933 especially for the Sultan of Morocco, a car Bear occasionally dispatched to Monterey and Carmel Valley Airports to fetch high rollers---- and that marvelous Morgan, a flat open car with wire wheels and a leather strap securing the hood, spinach green, with the rich baked enamel of the best cars from the legendary long ago.

She limped over to it and slid into the seat.

Bear allowed no one to drive it save her and David Running Deer.

Sensing her presence, Running Deer rolled himself out from under the Jeep, sprang from the caster-board to his feet, and, a gentleman as always, came over, greeted her, and wished her a pleasant day. She threw him a kiss and drove out. As she went by the hotel, and the casino, and the cabins for the sporting girls, she stroked the car's wooden dash, with its round gauges resembling those the Bloody Red Baron must have consulted in flight over the Western Front. "Well, Morgan, here goes." While she sped-- while *they* sped by the guardhouse and the fences, she sang a phrase from an Ohlone song she'd read somewhere, "Now we're *dancing on the brink of the world.*" Morgan, you're as wild as I am. The sound of His antique engine evoked Bear's voice saying I want you to stay here, in the casino compound. Until I get a sharp fix on what's going on. That would be never. Morgan ran her swiftly downhill toward the Carmel Valley Road. All right, Morgan, I *am* defying Bear, but Defiance is my middle name! Feral Frank used to say I should have been born in Defiance or Independence Ohio instead of Lakewood. They turned west on the main road. But even Feral Frank had been pissed off when she defied him and married Arthur Braun, a Catholic, an engineer. One 'l' Eliots never married Catholics, or, for that matter, engineers. Frank didn't mind her breaking those rules. What exasperated him was Braun himself. Arthur was a smoothie, very much like David Running Deer, but unlike David, no energy shined through his surface. Frank had proved to be right. What more evidence could be required than that embodied in Charley. Our son. No. *Arthur*'s son. Morgan, I want a son like *you.* One one steers from the *right.* One who *masturbates.*

Risky?

So what?

Defiance exhilarates.

They blasted through ranches and over cattle guards into Carmel Valley Village and slid to a stop before the Running Iron.

Beffle swung out, patted Morgan on his hot hood.

"I wish I could take you in with me."

She remembered the time she'd brought her own stool into a club, a Harley she'd ridden in from the street up to the bar.

She limped inside.

She drank a classic Coke.

Booze could only be a downer.

She limped back out and squirmed into the seat.

"Home James."

A surging roar came in reply as they backed out and then sped westward toward Carmel-by-the-Sea.

James, doubtless, is Morgan's first name. Here's one powerful male I dominate. He's strong and able and can do what I can't do. What? Yes, of course I rule him! I hold dominion! They zip by a line of cars. He's not very smart. Not like the star of *Histoire des Marins, Pirates et Corsaires*, Sir Henry Morgan, nor the most successful pirate of all, the one who named his yacht *Corsair*, J.P. Morgan, a.k.a. John Pierpont Morgan. The road follows along the Carmel River, which is always there but seldom seen. Beffle spies a metal bridge crossing over to a farm. "Pier-*pont*, James, in broken French, means *stone* bridge." She strokes the dashboard. "I christen thee James Steelbridge Morgan-- J.S. Morgan." James honks for joy and squeals the curve. "Screaming Eagle, my friend, that's your Indian name."

They sped by the Mid-Valley Shopping Center, stopped at Highway One. James turned left, rushed by the Barnyard, slid right into Rio Road, raced by the Mission and River School, went left into Mission Fields, and drew into the driveway of her house, or, as she usually put it, her studio.

Any mail?

She found a wad of it in the box and carried it inside where she spread it on the sideboard of the sink. Nothing but flack detritus, mainly seeking contributions, and *Native Peoples* magazine, which always brought information useful for her Native American impersonation act. *Native Peoples* went to Two Bears as well and he always used it to tease her about being a half-Huron who'd never learn what it really means to be an Indian.

He has *that* right!

Then she walked around her ceramic sculptures, completed and in progress, and they comforted, drew her in, into giving life to clay.

And she glanced at her costumes and masks, and at her sleeping couch, and her futon pile, and her computer ensemble, and her tool shelves and work tables and sewing machine. Who should I be today? The Beer Fairy? That would be fun, the Beer Fairy driving Jimmy-the-Morgan, but the BF's skin was still in Ohio. She could drive Jimmy around wearing her ape suit had she not given her ape suit away before moving down from San Francisco. The memory of driving around Frisco in her ape suit made her smile. Back to work. Soon. To wrestle the mail, and, like a living ghost invoked by their guilty consciences, appear to the supervisors and croupiers and dealers. Nothing in her house had changed while she'd been gone. The trip to Westlake seemed an illusion, a delusion.

No Beer Fairy or driving ape. Not today.

She slid into Jimmy-the-Morgan, and cranked the starter, and J.S. sat there, purring, waiting for her to decide what to do. "I can't call you Jimmy! You're almost seventy years old!" She backed out and drove a few blocks to the beach at the mouth of the river, parked J.S, and walked over a dune to the sea. The lagoon, the sand, the rocky cliffs, the sensual brown hills, Point Lobos, together, formed a silent awesome verity.

Opening to it all, the ensemble, the prospect, the aroma, and the quiet natural music composed of sounds from land and sea, breathing warm sweet air, open, part of it now, she felt intense joy and wonder.

"The truth that can be said is not the truth."

Sure! She burst into merry laughter, because, after all, her statement of the greatest truth, by its own definition, could not itself be *true*.

And now on the beach extending along the lagoon over the dunes to the sea, she saw the round huts of Ohlone camps, men, women, and children from inland digging for shellfish, out in the water stripping abalone from the rocks, opening shells, laying them out face up in the sun to dry the meat, a food dance on the brink of the world.

As she trudged back through loose sand toward the parking lot, she peered at Jimmy-the-M, who, although a mere machine, seemed truly gorgeous. She stroked his hood. "You're so patient!" She slipped in and he began his purrrrrr. "And now, J.S., off to the mountains." They went back by Carmel Mission via River School and Mission Ranch and across the highway, through the rich kitsch of the Barnyard Shopping Center, eastward on the Carmel Valley Road to the village, by the Running Iron, then over the river on Rosie's Newbridge, "Pontneuf, James, Pontneuf de Rosie," a concrete replacement for Rosie's Bridge finished just in time to be underwater in the Great Flood of '95.

They parked at Rosie's Cracker Barrel.

"J.S., you'd have loved that flood. The Highway One bridge washed out, making an island of all the country on this side."

She walked through the store into the bar.

Some cowboys at the other end were rolling liars' dice from a leather cup.

Beffle drank a Coke, and went back to Jimmy-the-M. "Sorry, pal. They don't carry ten-forty oil."

They went along Cachagua Road, turned off for another Coke at Prince's Camp, quondam terminus of the wagon road where in the old days goods were reloaded onto donkeys and mules, then they drove to Tassahara Road, southward, upward, out of civilization into the greenwood.

The way became rugged, steep, and narrow, often reduced to a curving single lane.

This led to another Coke, but no oil, in the hamlet of Jamesburg.

"Your town, Jimmy, but we cannot linger. Onward noble self-propelling quadricycle! Into Los Padres National Forest! *En avant!*"

The road became rougher and narrower as it ascended Chews Ridge. Beffle basked in leafy sunshine and sensational vistas and the pleasure of meeting no traffic whatsoever since beginning their climb. Bouncing on stiff springs, sliding sometimes, humming in loud contentment, Jimmy rolled ever upward, until Beffle steered him into the parking space of a small campground. She blew him a kiss and walked away into the wildwood, limping through the underbrush among rocks and pines until she felt herself alone. Somewhere ahead, in the national forest, the road ascended to Tassajara Hot Springs and the Zen monastery, and then climbed yet higher in the Santa Lucia range to end in the realm of wild boar and mountain hippie and vigilant dope farmer, a rugged and impulsive world of marginals and fugitives and outlaws who seldom if ever go back to civilization, one encompassing places where no human, Latino, Anglo, or even over thousands of years, Ohlone, has ever set foot. *Hic sunt Leones*, here are lions, as medieval cartographers wrote on unexplored areas. Likewise, hic sunt gigantic elk and wolves and grizzly bear, and saber-toothed tigers, and Sasquatch, and eagles and condors and dinosaurs. Birds are the last of the breed. Science now accepts that truth. Imagination clothes plesiosaurus with bright feathers and makes the woods ring and tremble to the cheep cheep of dino-birdsong.

She lay on her back under a dead redwood on a soft pad of needles and looked skyward at branches radiating out from the trunk in silhouette against blue sky. The aggravated cough-cough-cough gargling of a helicopter sounded somewhere up there. She closed her eyes and saw bright orange and imagined, when she rose, it would be into these woods as they existed in the days when animals and humans were of the same family and still talked with one another. And then she found herself in the stone-age Ohlone community of before the Euro-Americans, when men went naked and wore plumes and women, skirted with tule reeds, tattooed their cheeks and chins, and she'd painted her face with the sacred hunting designs, and put on a deer-head mask, and now she was in the valley running close to deer, hoping to get near enough to spear one.

She stood, and walked over pine needles toward J.S. Morgan.

Back then, women did not hunt.

She resolved to make herself a deer-head mask, and test her skill at deception.

And she, like they, would bring home the meat, but not eat any. "I had it wrong, Jimmy. The men seldom wore plumes. They pierced their noses and ears." She clambered in, and J.S. began his purrrrr. "And they wore shards of abalone. And, occasionally, short rabbit-fur capes." She turned off the engine. Attending the voice of the forest, they coasted silently, and, due to her snubbing the brakes, slowly, down the steep grade.

Ahead, on a sharp curve, at the center of the road in a bright spot, sunning itself . . . freshly emerged from dino days . . . a tarantula! Big as my hand!

She slowed to a stop and set the brake.

Cautiously she slid out of J.S., and sank to her knees, mindful her shadow did not block the sun.

Truly a noble living sculpture.

Three rows of eyes.

Four small ones ranked in front; two larger ones next, and behind them, two more, somewhat farther apart.

My two eyes see a small brown body at the center of six long furry legs.

What do those eight eyes see looking at *me*?

I see *you* in Renaissance perspective.

And, because you seem so big, in psychological perspective as well. You are designed to seek prey and detect danger.

What is your eight-eye perspective?

How do I look to you?

You don't attack, or run, so I'm neither prey nor danger.

Am I, then, scenery, or . . . *art*?

For what am I designed?

She drew back and looked up.

!!!!!!!!!!!!!!!!!!!!!!!!!!!!!!!!!!

There, standing about ten yards away, a caped figure, broad-brimmed hat, motionless, all in black. Joaquin Murietta? Black Bart? The Lone Ranger? Batman? Rambo? Zorro!

No.

He's wearing a black domino over a crude *Nixon* mask.

She stood.

"Your life or your money."

"Highway robbery's out of style."

"Guns aren't."

From inside his cape he drew a 9mm Glock.

Arthritis said, Don't run.

So did Clio.

Suddenly Beffle became sharply aware of the **whuk** *cooo cooo cooo* of the rain dove.

"Bend over the hood with your hands behind your back."

"Eat shit and choke to death."

A shocking sharp explosion.

He'd shot a round into Jimmy-the-Morgan's radiator.

Green blood flowed and pooled.

Surging against control, like nausea-driven vomit, fear, terror.

Stay cool.

Another explosion and Jimmy's windshield shattered.

"Do it."

She bent over the hood, her hands behind her back.

He bound her wrists with plastic-strip cuffs.

He jerked her away from Jimmy . . . .

"On your knees."

He reached into Jimmy, popped him out of gear, released his handbrake.

Jimmy began moving toward the curve.

Beffle chanted Jimmy's death song, Dancing on the brink of the world, over and over, as he rolled toward the cliff.

And then he vanished over the edge, and produced his own death song, composed of muted thumping and tearing sounds, then silence.

"Get up and walk ahead of me."

She walked around the curve to where a black pick-up truck stood parked in the road.

"Get in."

A familiar voice?

Awkwardly, helped by a shove on the butt, she clambered in.

He belted her to the seat, bound her ankles.

Regarding the sunny scene as they followed the road downward, Beffle thought that though nothing seemed to have changed, everything had changed.

Where'd I hear that voice before?

Her captor stripped off the domino, then the crude Nixon mask.

And revealed, beneath it, a very well executed face mask of . . . *Eddy*.

Talk about dancing in his skin!

Will he be dancing in *my* skin?

In Jamesburg, the cabins, the store, a dog asleep in the sun, all abruptly as remote as Antarctica.

"Hey, Batman, go get me a Coke."

They kept on rolling downward.

"One eight-hundred murder one. Your phone, Batman, is always busy."

"Yes."

"Why have it, then?"

"Because we're always busy."

Who the Hell is this?

The voice? Might be Eddy's, and might not.

"Who in fucking Hell are you?"

"Your conscience."

"I don't have one."

"Your Nemesis."

Beffle shuddered.

Electric windows; he controls them.

When we get down with people, I can't open mine and yell for help.

They turned left onto Cachagua Road.

Beffle resolved when he blindfolded her, as he surely would, to memorize turns, and count the intervening seconds.

They came to the main road, and went left.

He's *not* going to blindfold me.

Meaning, he won't let me live to tell the tale.

This is *real*, said the observer within. Stop treating it like a melodrama.

He turned right into Vista Verde, then right again, took them down a long driveway, stopped before a faux-adobe house, and, then, he taped her mouth shut.

He opened her door, picked her up, lifted her out, and said: "Theodora, your ordeal is almost over."

Keep cool!

He's made no effort to conceal where he's taken me.

She'd even read the street number on the mailbox.

"Give me a nice, sweet smile."

He bore her through sunshine by the house to the garage; he opened the side door, carried her over the threshold, his blushing bride, and stood her before the workbench.

He came close to her, his eyes bright behind the rubberized Eddy-face.

"Now the fun begins."

Who *else* is here?

He stripped off the tape.

"Scream all you like. Nobody can hear you."

All right Wild Child, play your ace of trumps.

Can I still do it?

His eyes are dilating!

"You don't like this," he said. "Do you?"

Did you ever meet anybody before, Mr. Hubris, who can vomit at will?

She opened her mouth, as if to reply.

Out of it erupted a jet of projectile vomit.

It soiled the mask.

It blinded her captor.

She dropped to her knees; sprang toward him and rammed her head into his groin.

He howled and clutched his nuts.

She dropped onto her back and kicked his hands full force.

He shrieked and she kicked his shins.

He dropped, howling and writhing, and his hat came off, and she kicked his head until he went limp.

Who else is here?

Awkwardly, she struggled to her feet, backed up to the bench, took a chisel, and, close to panic, she hopped to the door, backed up to it, turned the knob, and hopped along the drive to some thick bushes. And she flopped into them and squirmed back and back some more until fully concealed. She, Wild Child, sat up. Grateful to the DNA gods who had made her slim, she slid her hands under her butt, drew her legs up tightly against herself, brought her hands up over her feet, and knees---- and then her hands lay on her lap.

No sounds but birds and a car in the street.

She braced the chisel between her feet, vertically, and cut the plastic strip binding her hands. She cut the bonds away from her ankles and wrists, and burst out of the bushes and ran to the street.

She walked to the road.

Traffic ran steadily; the village loomed in sight.

Sunny and hot!

They can't get me now!

She'd be safe at the Running Iron.

Inside, the usual mix of blue-haired women, bikers, business types, and cowboys. A stuffed mountain lion as tawny as Charley reclined on the brick facade of the barbecue pit, its features expressing boredom? indigestion? in a look akin to her son's customary mien.

Lady Luck had put coins into the pockets of her shorts.

Keep the sheriffs out of it. At least for now.

She fed a quarter to the phone and dialed Two Bear's private number at the Monterey office. He answered Hello.

"*Bear.*"

"Beff. What's new in Foul Owl City?"

Keep it cryptic on my side.

"I'm at the Running Iron."

He'll understand the subtleties.

"So?"

"I'll stay till you come for me."

"Something bad happen?"

"To understate it, yes."

"I'll call the casino now and send the Running Iron two new customers."

"Good plan."

"How about a Hawk and a Turtle?"

"I hear that!"

"You stay there."

"For sure. Wouldn't want to miss happy hour."

"I'll leave now, so I'll be there shortly."

"See you then."

She sat at a table near the bar and ordered a large iced tea, sans lemon. Ten-to-four. This would be a very happy hour, indeed. Downright joyful! When Bear gets here, what to say? Tell him my new Cherokee joke. Jubilation time! It would be as merry as once when in a Union Street yuppie gourmet wine-doctor fern bar in Frisco, to shake up her husband, she'd taken the beer bottles for their party off the waiter's tray and opened them all with her teeth. She glanced toward the doorway. As if by magic, materialized there, walking toward the end of the bar, were High Hawk and Blood Turtle, whom everyone called Ace. They ordered pints of Irish lager. No human being could be as muscular as Ace, a pure-bred Navajo, who according to legend had once smashed open a sandwich machine and eaten *all* the sandwiches. The taste for blood, and the hard turtle shell, symbolized his qualities as a fighter. As if that weren't enough to give a girl confidence, High Hawk-- a champion marksman who was said to be as sharp-eyed as a hawk flying at great altitude, or even a satellite, one which could see a mouse on the ground-- always went armed. She suddenly felt as safe as she had as a child when escorted by Feral Frank.

They began rolling dice on the bar.

She sat basking in warm contentment, rejoicing in her lifelong good luck, smiling at the lion and even at the thought of Charley who at this very moment might be reading *The Book of Moron.*

Better, their holy owners' manual, The Book of *Morgan.*

Along with and through that thought guilt feelings slithered.

In came Two Bears.

He didn't even glance at Ace and Hawk.

He came right to the table and sat.

Another very formidable looking guy.

"So, Foul Owl, what's new?"

"Did you hear what happened to the Cherokee who's in the paper today-- the one who tried to blow up that bus?"

"Haven't read the paper yet."

"So you don't know what happened?"

"No. What?"

"He burned his lips."

Bear made a snarling smile-- a snile.

"Why," he asked, "don't they let halfbreeds swim in the reservoir?"

"Beats me."

"They leave rings."

Bear ordered a rum-and-coke, and when it came, they argued about the latest movies.

He looked at his watch.

"It's getting late. Let's hit the road."

They walked outside where Bear's cream colored Mercedes waited. "Why didn't you bring the Morgan?" asked Beffle. "Nice day like this, perfect for an open car."

After backing out, Bear turned to her and said: "Where the Hell *is* the Morgan?"

"You guessed it. Judging from our Morgan's many counts of accessory before, during, and after the felonious fact, Hell's the only place it could be."

"Meaning what?"

"Meaning Jimmy-the-Morgan was murdered."

He parked in front of a store. "Hawk and Turtle are going to follow us." He put his pager in the coffee-cup bracket. Beffle began sobbing, weeping away some of the stress. Bear put an arm around her shoulder. High Hawk and Blood Turtle, in a blue van, parked nearby. "Beffle, I don't really care about the Morgan. When you're ready, tell me the story." He gave her his handkerchief and she dried her eyes.

"They were going to kill me, but I got away."

"Who?"

"I don't know." She shook a smile onto her face. "I was terrified. I was so scared, that . . . that I thought I'd have to be toilet trained all over again."

"But, at the time, you were your usual cool, observant self. Otherwise, you never would have got away."

"If I'd have listened to you, your Morgan would still be in the garage."

"I don't *care* about the Morgan; I care about *you.*"

She burst into tears again, then drew in a deep breath, held it for a moment, and said, "What do I have to worry about? I don't know about you other guys, but I am immortal."

"Except that you'll get old and die."

"Not me. Aging results from insufficient will power. Will power, Bear, *will power*, that's the secret of eternal youth."

"Now the story. Begin at the beginning."

She began at the beginning, and the story flowed easily, and Bear listened intently without interrupting. When she'd finished, he said: "Who do you think he was? Eddy?"

"I should have stripped his mask. But I panicked, and bolted."

"Let's find out now." He called Ace on the pager. "We're going to reconnoiter a house and garage, then break in." He gave them the address. "Find out who's there, then call back." They all drove east, and parked on the street near the house. Hawk and Ace got out and vanished into the bushes. Beffle snapped a Zydeco cassette into the player. Presently, Ace's voice spoke from the pager. "Come on down. Ain't nobody there."

Beffle and Bear met them in front of the garage. The side door was unlocked, so they walked in. Everything seemed exactly the same. It's as if nothing happened here! Like I'd never been here! An old oil smell cloyed. That would annoy Running Deer. Odd, that I didn't notice it before. And there, on the bench. *The chisel*! It must be the same chisel. Why would they have a twin? Bear looked around, until satisfied. "Let's try the house."

High Hawk picked the lock on the back door. They searched through all the rooms. A gigantic color TV ruled. The place seemed the very embodiment of bourgeois banality. Except there was no computer. And no documents, none at all, no notes, mail, bills, books, letters, or even magazines. In that respect, the place was as paper-free as ancient Rome. "Now, we'll go look for the Morgan."

They crossed Rosie's Newbridge, drove to Cachagua Road, Ace and Bear following behind. "Beff, we'll find out about that house. My guess is summer house-sitters are living there now, and they went out of town, making it possible for our adversaries, whomever they might be, to use it for this caper." He smacked her on the leg. "I guess you gave old Funny Face a big surprise. Right at this moment he must be somewhere weeping and rubbing his balls."

They turned into Tassahara Road, and soon were climbing Chews Ridge. "You know, Beff, if it weren't for all these troubles, we'd be on Easy Street. I'd give anything to have things running smoothly so I could give all my energy to unifying the tribes around our coordinated money-sucking casinos. And you know what I want to do? I don't remember if I told you before, but I want to use most of our profits like the Pequots in Connecticut do. They use Anglo money flowing in from their casino to buy back the lands the Anglos stole from them in the first place. Before long, they'll own the whole state! All the tribes should do that. Continuously expand their reservations." He flashed her an affectionate snile. "But can I focus on that? No. Just think of the fires we've had, the fraud we've uncovered, the missing mail, the death threats, the ugly rumors, the mysterious law suits, the power failures, and all the rest of it!" He spit out the window. "Tell me, whom can we trust? Our operation must be infested with spies and agents provocateurs."

And now, Jamesburg again. Quite utterly the same as the last time going through, bound hand and foot. The dog's still there, sleeping in the sun. While all that was happening to me---- here, in Jamesburg, absolutely nothing took place. Yes. Well, now, pay attention. She studied the road reeling under them from ahead. "Stop, just around that curve. Right there's where the Morgan went off."

They stopped. "Ace will stay with you. I'll take Hawk, and we'll go down and look."

Ace leaned against her side of the car by her open window and watched them vanish over the edge. He turned and spoke.

"Wanta arm wrestle?"

"Hadn't thought of it."

He snickered a strange squeaky snort.

"One thing for sure, Ace, I'm glad they went down instead of me."

"Me too," quoth a smiling Ace. "They gave us a chance to grab this Mercedes and cut out for Miami."

Can he be serious? Music time. She clicked on the Zydeco tape and the car filled with the loud French singing of Queen Ida. Through the pulsing music mist, Beffle saw Hawk, then Bear, clamber back up over the brink. Bear radiated joy. He beckoned. "Hey Beff, come on over and have a look at *this*."

She rushed over and looked down. The slope was not nearly as steep as it seemed from the road. The Morgan had come to rest against a tree about ten feet below. Except for the windshield, it still looked pristine. She gave Bear a big, strong hug.

"It's dented on the other side," he said. "But there's nothing wrong with it Running Deer can't fix easily." He hugged her back. "We'll lift it out with a helicopter and take it home."

They got back in their car and steeping in the accordion sounds of Zydeco they started down toward town.

In Jamesburg, something had happened.

The dog had crossed the street.

Feeling sunny warm and content through and through, Beffle looked over at Bear, driving, but not breaking into her thoughts, and marveled at how solicitous he was being about the whole thing. He's really and truly been nice to me! Considerate! But, yes, he always is when something serious is happening. Soon it was civilization again, the flatland, and Rosy's Newbridge. Bear, a powerful presence, sat silently in the sunshine and music, guiding his Mercedes. A feeling of guilt began to overwhelm her. He's truly good to me; he never asserts his boss power by making passes, and yet every day, deceitful bitch that I am, I live the lie, and reinforce it. Bear, I'm no more of an Indian than Jimmy-the-Morgan is. Nor am I Irish. I'm pure New England aristocrat.

She thought it, but didn't say it.

She kept on studying Bear. He's truly an enigma. I don't know anything about his private life. Nada. Nunca. Zilch. What's he do after work when he stays in Monterey, or Santa Cruz, or San Francisco? She'd seen him once in Carmel, at night, in Jimmy-the-Morgan, a classy young woman at his side. On the job, he always seems relaxed, and content. His private life, whatever it is, seems more interesting than mine. And now, it's almost as if I'm in jail! They drove up toward the casino, and passed by the guardhouse into the fenced compound.

Safe at last!

Oh . . . sure.

Under house arrest.

They stopped before the hotel, where she and Bear each had a suite.

Bear came around and opened her door. They exchanged greetings with the doorman, crossed the lobby to their private elevator, and went up to her place. She mixed drinks, and they sat at her table, where one could enjoy a gorgeous panoramic view of the compound and the ridge behind it. She looked at his serene face. What in Hell is happening to us? Is he keeping something from me?

"Bear. Level with me. I've got to know what's going on."

"I understand that."

"Is there something you're *not* telling me?"

"Beff. Believe me. *I* don't know what's going on either. I don't know who or what's behind it. I have detectives studying it, but no luck there, so far, anyway. It was bad before. But now! After what's happened to you! We have to do something, something aggressive, something drastic. But what? You tell me. I don't have a clue."

FIVE

BEFFLE POURED HER SYRUP and glanced across the glass table at the gross sight of Two Bears eating Polish sausage, and then out the big window at deer rambling on the lawn near to a slim Apache riding a mower. Blind Badger's sense of irony had placed this young descendent of generations of warmen on a steel saddle whence he could slice down armies of grass blades. Bear wiped his mouth with the back of his hand. "What's on your mind, Owl?" He picked at his teeth. "Bad dreams?"

"Dammit, Bear, I feel like a rat in a cage! I can't live like this!" She stabbed her waffle. "I've got to have my liberty; I've got to keep making sculpture, art."

"We can move all your stuff out here."

"I can't work here."

"Take one of the cabins for a studio."

"No, no. This place embodies everything art hates. Right now, at nine a--fucking-em, *already*, morons are swarming, feeding machines, watching cards fall and roulettes spin, frenzied, asking God's help in catching Keno numbers, sucking up to Lady Luck, stupefied by the get-rich-quick power dream." She clenched her fists. "They're spellbound livestock, gorging on our feedlot!"

"We're hunters; they're prey."

"Right, Grease Face, right! But art won't run with prey."

"We're *hunters.*"

"I'm an artist."

"We're *Indians.*" He leaned toward her. "You don't know how to be an Indian. You don't understand."

"You're *Cherokee.* Cherokee are civilized; imitation Anglos. How can *you* understand?"

"Silly cunt."

"*Art* is Indian. Art is *solidarity.* Even though the truth that can be shown, said, sounded, is not the truth, art keeps making paintings and sculpture and books and music. Art tries to show, to say, to sound truth that cannot be shown, said, sounded. It's a passionate search for expression of solidarity, of the me with the it, of the me with the thee, of the solidarity of human life, of all life, of all existence."

"Nonsense! Art is Coyote. Coyote, Woman, is our creator. In the Old Times Coyote made us. Look in the mirror, and who do you see? Bear? Raven? Wolf? No. You see Coyote. Coyote formed us in his own image. Awkward, tricky, cunning, creative, ugly, deceitful, irritable, unpredictable, vulgar, greedy, cruel, vain, opportunistic, egocentric, resourceful, mean---- a tease, a joker, a liar, a traitor, a sado-maso leather queen. Coyote is *dangerous.* Coyote is Bugs Bunny. Worse! He's the Chinese monkey god. Coyote is us, you and me. Humanity. Us." He mopped up the grease and egg yolk on his plate with a piece of toast. "I'm going for the Morgan today."

"So soon?"

"You bet! That car's like family to me. It's almost human; and, yes, surely it's one of the powers from the spirit world. I don't want the Morgan to come into my dreams angry." He stood. "I've got a chopper coming this afternoon---- one-thirty."

"Is it legal? To go snatch a car up like that?"

"My lawyer-- the guy's an Iroquois, a Seneca fighter, he worked it out with the appropriate functionaries. It was easy because there's precedent. They use helicopters to pick wrecks up off the south coast, cars and whatever else has run off the cliffs from Hurricane Point to Big Sur, and all the way down beyond Gorda."

"So you're going real soon."

"Uh-huh. Had a real good dream about it last night. Condor came, and grasped the Morgan in his claws, and lifted him straight up into the sky, and carried him home, and took him right inside, into the garage, and set him down at the feet of Running Deer."

"Well double-damn! That car's alive for me, too. I call him Jimmy-the-Morgan."

"Want to come along?"

"Love to."

"You're not scared?"

"Sure I'm scared. But I can get snuffed here almost as easily as out there. The FBI's project COINTELPRO or CIA's operation CHAOS. Remember them? Whomever it is, they're after me to get at you. It's me, then you. But before they go after you, they're going to have to tell you what they want. Hey, you know . . . . I don't think Funny Face would have killed me. He would just have left me there."

"Maybe."

"Honest Injun, how safe you think I'll be?"

"With me, you're always safe."

He called the motor pool manager in the garage and asked him to get the blue van and the Rolls ready. "Load the bridle in the van." He spoke aside to Beffle. "The Rolls is to officiate at the resurrection of Jimmy-the-Morgan." He rang security and told them to send Ace and Hawk to the motor pool. "We'll take Deer along to rig the sling, and Ace and Hawk for the Hell of it."

When they'd finished eating and drinking a glass of brandy to the health of Jimmy-the-Morgan, they rode down on what Bear liked to call their private vertical railroad, strode through the rattling cacophony of the casino, and thence into the peaceful grass smell of outdoors. Bear pointed at the youth mounted on the mower, moving clamorously over the lawn. "Look at that Apache fighter! In the old days, he'd have been urging his steed on into a stampede of buffalo!"

Beffle took her boss's head between her hands and turned it toward the open door of the garage. "Look at that big boxy beauty!" Next to the van stood the Rolls, resplendent in the sunshine; in its open-to-fresh-air driver's seat Blood Turtle hunched, immense, and Running Deer and High Hawk were roosting on its running board.

"How's your leg?" asked Bear as they walked along.

"Seems okay today."

"Still hurt?"

"Uh huh."

"Does it hurt all the time?"

"Yes, but not as badly as your bad back must hurt you. And you never whine about that."

He made his friendly snile. "Our Rolls was-- and is-- fit for a king!"

"Jimmy-the-Morgan is fit for better folk than kings, folk like you and me."

Deer and Hawk rose.

"You brought everything?" Bear asked Deer.

"Sure did." Running Deer produced a chauffeur's cap and, laughing, they tugged it down onto Ace's head. "Well, let's get the show on the road." Bear opened the back door and bowed Beffle in. He followed and, as the car started, lifted the speaking tube. "Ace, my man, head for Jamesburg, via the Village."

Ace wheeled the Rolls out to the road and into town where when people caught sight of it their routines succumbed to curiosity and admiration and they stopped to stare. "Well, goddamnit to Hell, Foul Owl, you'd think they'd never seen wild Indians before." The car churned smoothly to and across Rosie's Newbridge and Bear told Ace to stop at Rosie's Cracker Barrel. "We've plenty of time, Beff. We'll go in and pour a libation to the convalescence of Jimmy-the-Morgan and then go up Chews Ridge where we'll picnic and wait for the chopper." At the end of the bar a group of drunken cowboys crowds around a game of liars' dice. Rosie himself is tending bar. "Two Anchor Steams please." Rosie's a pink, tubby, redhead, a big beardless superannuated Santa. Definitely rosy.

"Did *you* ever dream about Jimmy?" asks Bear.

"Many times."

"Maybe you *do* know how to be an Indian."

"We're not Indians-- Hindians, like Columbus thought. We don't speak Hindi or live in Hindustan."

"We're not Native Americans, either. We're *Natives* Me, full-blooded, you-- half."

"We're invaders, both of the halves, yours and mine. The real natives are deer and bear and coons and otters, here for millions of years before we monkeys came. We're newcomers, immigrants, just like the wild boar, and it didn't take us long to root up the whole garden." She clenches his shoulders and her voice snarls into Beer Fairy tones. "Let's be fucking Indians."

A big nasty cowboy swaggers over, stares at Two Bears.

"Fuck Indians."

"Try Native Americans."

"Fuck Native Americans."

"Natives. Try natives."

"Fuck Natives."

"Fuck you, you pus-sucking cretin." Bear turned, took Beffle's arm, and they walked out, all the cowboys following. Ace swung down from the Rolls, and Deer and Hawk came over from the van.

"Do you assholes really want to play cowboys and Indians?"

Their faces said no, and they went back inside.

"Now for the picnic."

Ace guided the hard-springed Rolls through Jamesburg, where the dog lay sunning itself in exactly the same spot, upward through the greenwood. He spied a tarantula crossing the road and with a quick turn of the wheel crushed it. Beffle sang its death song: Dancing on the brink of the world, until they came to a turnout near the Morgan's brink and parked. Ace opened the door for them and they clambered out. Bear drew a deep breath of sweet, still air. "Condor gave us perfect weather for our project." Deer and Hawk went to the van for a coil of rope and the bridle: an eight-foot steel bar with a ring welded to its center and two more welded to the bottom at each end. To these were shackled stout ropes padded with canvas which would be pulled under the Morgan and belayed in the rings, making slings at the front and back. Deer tied one end of the coil of rope to the top ring, took a turn around a tree, and slacked off as the other men went over the side and guided the rig down to the car. When they got there, Running Deer tied the rope to the tree. "That bridle I made will hold anything the chopper can lift." He smiled at Beffle. "Let's lay out the picnic." They spread a green checkered cloth on the ground next to the Rolls and fetched the food basket and ice chest and a radio from the van. Deer opened two beers, gave one to Beffle. "When the helicopter comes we'll clip its cable to the ring, bring the car up here and set it on the road where I can adjust the slings for the trip home." He tuned in to KBACH which played soft classical music.

Beffle sat on the running board, smiling at Deer sitting on the ice chest. He's almost my age. Pale, smooth skin. Probably shaves but once a week. Slim. Strong features. Black eyes and hair. What a beauty! And sharp! Sophisticated! Articulate! Too bad I'm too old to make kids. He's an aristocrat like me. Risen from the cream of the gene pool. Yet, I scarcely know him. An emptiness, a sadness overcame her, produced by the thought it was now too late to try for better offspring than Charley.

"Running Deer . . . ."

"*David* Running Deer."

"David. You can call me Beffle. My adolescent nickname."

"Beffle. I like that."

"What tribe are you from?"

"Blackfoot."

"Tell me about the Blackfeet."

"We're supposed to hate the Crow, but I don't."

"What of the Nez Perce? Aren't you supposed to hate them, too?"

"So I've been told."

"Why?"

"It's because custom and tradition obliged the tribes to raid one another, more for adventure, as a test of manhood, than out of greed for spoils."

"I'm half Huron, and half Irish, of the O'Neill tribe. With the Irish tribes and the Highland Scottish tribes as well, it was exactly the same thing. They used to raid each other for sport, steal a few cattle, exult in cunning and battle." Driven by guilt feelings for lying to Deer about her background, Beffle began blurting much of what she'd learned about Irish tribal lore in anthropology class, from books, in bars and from boyfriends. She told him about Bardic Druids, about males not ready for battle until they stood before the enemy painted and naked with hard-ons; she told him about Irish tribesmen beginning each day with a bath, even as did the Ohlone, and about confrontation with Vikings who never washed or wiped. She told him about the king candle, big as a man, the O'Neill chief kept always near his side, and about the hand on the O'Neill coat of arms, celebrating the O'Neill spirit demonstrated during a boat race with another clan toward a disputed island which would be awarded to the clan whose chief first "laid hand" on it. When The O'Neill saw his boat would surely lose, he chopped off his left hand and flung it onto the island, a noble if Pyrrhic victory, for sure. She told him of Owen Roe O'Neill, and as it all swept her along, she burst into song, the lay of Owen Roe O'Neill, "You proud and saucy Sassenach, look to your powder now! Look to your spoils, O robber, for sore need you'll have I vow; look to your lives, ye sleuth-hounds false, for naught shall us withstand; hope has gleamed in every heart and steel in every hand; O! Saxons, tyrants, spoilers, by Liffy, Foyle, or Maigue, where'er your found, Owen's hand shall scourge you as a plague! O! Hellish memories steel our hearts, our mercy sense benumb! Up Gaels! Up Gaels! Revenge! Revenge! Owen Roe is come!"

This produced a sweet smile on David's face. "Beffle," he said, "I feel strong sympathy with the Irish, with the Irish resistance, with the Irish Republican Army. We Indians and the insurgency in the four northern counties have a great deal in common. I belong to AIM, you know, the American Indian Movement, which the FBI is sworn to destroy. One of their policy directives says to eliminate people like me, or Leonard Peltier, 'Have local police put AIM leaders under close scrutiny, and arrest them on every possible charge until they can no longer make bail.' I'm one of the Coyote Warriors. We'll have a long talk about that some day."

They both fell silent, as their passion faded into the requirements of the now. "David, you are very well spoken. Beautifully articulate."

"As are you. We speak our tribal languages at home, and English, the world language, when out in the world. Do you know your tribal language? O'Neill Gaelic?"

"No. And I regret it."

"You and I, Beffle, have to live in two worlds at once, worlds as different as our home vernacular and the world language."

For me it's a different world pair, came her reply unsaid. My world of lies, and my world of truth.

The others came clambering back over the brink. "It looks good," said Bear. "Damage only superficial. The slings fit well." He opened the picnic basket. "Let's eat." They plundered the basket, opened beer, and gorged on cold chicken, potato salad, thick delly sandwiches, Deviled eggs, and fry bread. Ace went to the van and came back with two Indian drums. He sat on the running board of the

Rolls, and began pounding out a throbbing heart beat. "And now, Beffle," said Bear, comes my response to your thirtieth reunion dance." He went to the van and fetched four hooded robes covered with gleaming black feathers. "Ours, Beffle, is to celebrate a ten-thousandth re-union. And to do it, we don't need an orange roughy dinner, nametags, a speech by the principal, or, for that matter, a swing band, a no-host bar, or a Holiday Inn. No. We'll join the dance, the dance of life, become life through the dance."

"What dance?"

"Condor. The condor dance."

Beff laughed. "Try con d'or."

"Con d'or."

"You know what you just said in French?

"No . . . ."

"Golden cunt."

"Halfbreed!"

"Grease Face!"

He handed her a robe. "Put this on."

Beffle, Two Bears, David Running Deer, and High Hawk dressed in the robes, and the beat went on.

"Now, Foul Owl, open to this, *open*. Fully, utterly, absolutely, completely. The drum dance will carry us to the other side, into the spirit world, into your art solidarity, into Indian oneness, into the purity of Sacred Time." She donned her gleaming black garment. "You will come out of yourself and become one with the all, you will lose the me, cross the frontier between the me and the it, *become* the it. We'll become the big black birds of the Other Side, we'll dance ourselves right into a world unseen and unseeable. Into Sacred Time."

Ace redoubled the plangent pulse-beat of the condor song.

"Bear! I don't know how to do it!"

"Just open to it and copy us. Imagine you walk like a condor, talk like a condor, hover and glide like a condor, have the nerves of a condor. Bird nerves. The sudden and abrupt movements of a bird. You'll learn the dance by doing it. Just watch us. Be a bird---- a ferocious fowl with a golden cunt." He flashed a radiant snile. "You'll learn."

And the dance began, and she was caught up in the prime-mover heartbeat of the drums and their throbbing pulse transported her into new dimensions sans time sans weight sans care and they were all raptors now dancing on the brink of the world and she bird-spasmed to the rhythm of *heart*beat drums and began *thin*king *thin*king *heart-*beat *heart-*beat and *say*ing *say*ing loud loud loud and loud and loud and right out-loud *heart-*beat *heart-*beat thick and thin come on dance within my skin oh my heart beats *up* and it beats *down* and the sound the sound leaps all around and keep on saying it you big black birds and birds and birds and bird bird words they sound the song the song song song they sound the song and turn upside upside-down and Ace hands pound drums drums drums and all the black birds dance and over again and more more more and Ace drums drive it farther on and Ace hand-pounded drums drums drums drive bird nerve into every one and the beat moves on and on and in heartmind's eye Eddy Ed Ed clad in Lake-Lake-Lakewood High *Times* times *Times* dancing not showing if he's still of this world or's been sent off into sacred time, and maybe he's dancing in enemy skin and I'll flay him him him and peel him inside inside out and I am dancing in Eddy Ed Eddy dancing skin and I sing and shout but do not whine and does he dance sheathed in my skin mine and if not him who will be that swine, that clumsy awkward imitation inside-me and O! yes I hear Ace hand-pounded drums make dreams of my skin but not of me so what does it mean? that I do the one 'l' Eliot Boston Bean? oh, yes, tell me, what does it mean? that one 'l' Eliot Boston Bean?

And then the gruff coughing of a helicopter intruded and the beat stopped and an aluminum fowl spun overhead like a giant carnivorous hummingbird ready to pounce on prey and Bear drew a pager out from beneath his feathers and spoke to the pilot.

"Ten-four that's an affirmative. Slack your cargo hook down to the car, and we'll signal when it's secured. Affirmative. Lift the car up here and ease it down next to the Rolls so we can adjust the slings."

They shed their feathered cloaks and as David and Beffle folded them and stowed them away in the van along with the drums, the others clambered over the edge and down to the Morgan. The helicopter hovered at road level and lowered its cargo hook; then, when it had been clipped onto the ring on the bridle, the cable drew tight and trembled and the chopper rose and Jimmy-the-Morgan appeared; the chopper lowered him down next to the Rolls and, beating still air, it held a strain on the cable. The bridle seemed a very sturdy rig as David adjusted it and the others came back up onto the road.

The beautiful spinach-green Morgan trembled with energy as the helicopter churning above held it ready to ascend.

Two Bears stood on the driver's side, fondling the oaken steering wheel; Beffle stood opposite, one hand on the soft leather seat. She locked his glance into hers. They stared into each other's eyes for a moment, and smiled why-not smiles.

"Let's play Pegasus," she said.

"And ride a Flying Green Horse."

"Yes."

He bowed to her.

"Madame, after you."

She stepped in, sat down, and snapped her seat belt. "How dare you put this anachronistic drek into a classic Morgan?"

"It's the law," said Bear as he climbed in behind the wheel. He snapped his belt and spoke into his pager. "Lift her off, Boris; take her up . . . and . . . *away*."

Twisting slowly from left to right, Jimmy-the-Morgan sprang from the ground, levitated, his cable reeling up until he hung suspended about ten feet below the spinning copter, which, then, swiftly rose, as David and Ace and Hawk whooped and laughed and waved.

"I don't think Boris has noticed us yet."

They were high above the trees now, moving toward the valley, as Jimmy's shadow, trying to catch up with them, raced along over woods and fields and houses

Bear found he could keep the car aimed ahead by using the front wheels as a rudder.

"Now," said he, "I know how Santa feels flying behind all those reindeer.

"Or what it's like to be Odin when he manifests as the Dread Huntsman of the Air."

A fog bank stood over Carmel.

"Boris, take her over there, into the fog." He held the pager to his ear and listened for a moment. "What?" He winked at Beffle to suggest he would repeat Boris' side of the dialog. "Why can you hear my pager so well? It's the new megavortex model. Where am I? Just hanging around, Boris, just hanging around."

"This, Grease Face, is true *suspense*, what I call the hover-bird *dance*."

The helicopter persevered on its course to the casino.

They waved at a passing Piper Cub.

"Boris. Fly into that fog bank. Why? Because I say so." The chopper changed course as instructed. Bear turned to Beffle. "People usually do what I tell them to." He spit over the side. "He can't see us. He *still* doesn't know we're here." Bear started the engine, spun the wheels. "Guess what! Everything's still okay! When we fix the radiator we can drive anywhere!" Beffle began humming the Air Force song, and soon they were both singing it, caroling out their mood of absolutely surreal euphoria.

"Jimmy's Indian name, Bear, it's got to be . . . ?"

"Flying Green Horse!"

"And we're riding him deep into Sacred Time."

The fog bank approached, a soft wall, wisps, haze . . . then sudden nothingness and they glided along through bright gray light. "We should have worn our feathers." In silence they drifted, disembodied, environed by featureless mist, as in a dream, birds in a cloud, fleas on a bird in the clouds, condors preparing to drop a feather down from Sacred Time as a token of alliance to some favored human far below. "Once, Bear, long long ago, far far away, in a meadow, on a mountain, in Alaska, walking over clover with my husband and little boy, Charley, an eagle feather dropped from the sky, from the clouds close overhead, and spun to earth near him. He tucked it into his mass of thick curling tawny hair and said the eagle had sent it to him. Specially. To signify friendship."

"Could be."

"So now it's our turn." She opened the glove compartment, drew out a pencil and a sketch pad, and peeled off a sheet. She folded it into a paper airplane. Then, on one wing, she printed: AN UNKNOWN FRIEND WATCHES OVER YOU. On the other she wrote ***Present this at the Ohlone Valley Casino Dining Room and receive two complimentary dinners.*** She signed it with her name and title, and passed it to Bear who laughed and did the same. "Wild Child, next time we'll use a frisbee, and flip that out, and do our part in sustaining faith in flying saucers." She kissed her paper plane, and launched it into the mist. "And thus we initiate an unknown series of events leading to . . . ?"

"World War Three."

"Eternity for you and me."

"And Coyote as Almighty."

"No. Eternal human harmony."

Bear took Beffle by the hand and squeezed. "At last we're absolutely, truly alone; no one can see us, no one can eavesdrop, so now I can tell you what I think, and what I plan to do."

They smiled at each other, and, holding hands, they flew along through the mist, mute, open, aware of the Ace-like beat of the helochopper pulsing the silence of their motionless Flying Green Horse dance from long before the condors, in the big bang of Creation Time.

A shrill beep intruded. Bear lifted the pager to his ear. "What? Keep circling in this cloud for now, Boris. When will we head for the casino you say? After while. I'll call you back and let you know."

"Safe at last."

"Unless Boris is one of them." Two Bears produced a tin of snuff from his shirt pocket and rubbed some on his gum. "We can't just sit around, passively, with our thumbs up our ass, and wait for them to hit us. I have to go find out who they are. First, I'll go to Vegas and ask around. I'll begin with the Mafia. I don't think it's them. After all, we send them our sports bets. If it's not them, the Mafia, we share a mutual enemy. If by some chance it *is* them, they'll tell me what they want."

"Stay away from the Mafia! Once you connect, they never let go."

"I have to start somewhere."

"Don't start there."

"You have a better idea?"

"About what?"

"About who's after us."

"It's skinwalkers. Witches."

"Witches! Don't be facetious."

"That's not facetious. We Indians are supposed to believe in witches."

"Not any more."

"Ghosts, then?"

"We don't have to believe in them these days either."

"Maybe we're speaking the names of the dead too much, and their ghosts hear, and come to do us injury."

"Sure. They doctor machines and control dice and walk off to the ghost world as big winners." He stomped the floor. "So who the Hell *is* after us? Where should I ask first? Got any ideas?"

The blank and empty mist seemed a mirror of her mind. "No. But start somewhere else. The Mafia'd love to muscle into the Indian casinos."

"Our tribes are organized and organizing. Casino money's flowing into them. We have structure, arms, numbers, dedication, courage, consensus, quasi-sovereignty. And discipline. We have our warrior tradition. We're tough. We're brave. We're together. We'd be too hard to crack. We leave them alone; they leave us alone. We cooperate when we must. As with our sports bets."

"You can't really believe that."

"I have to. That's the way I'm going to play it." He looked up toward the invisible helicopter. The Mafia comes from the same place AIM comes from. The Mafia began in the Kingdom of the Two Sicilies-- Sicily and Southern Italy-- as a guerrilla resistance movement fighting against rule by foreigners, the French Bourbon kings and their soldiers and police. Mafia is an acronym, just like AIM is. The M stands for Morte-- death-- and the F is for Francesi, the French That's the secret original meaning of Mafia: *Death to the French.* When Italian immigrants came to the States in large numbers, and the Yankee establishment shit all over them, the Mafia came together and protected them. The Mafia solidified Italian-Americans, the wops and dagos, against oppression. The Anglo establishment shits all over *us.* With our American Indian Movement, and its bloodstream of casino money, we Indians are coming together, getting things done. But something is going wrong. I've got to find out what that is. Don't you see! So I talk to the Mafia. And fuck up somehow. The only person who'll get hurt is me. But I won't get hurt. They'll give me some ideas, some leads, and I'll keep looking, and share what I learn with them. Whoever is trying to break us is their enemy too!"

"So you think you can just barge in like the puffed-up snarling double-bear that you are and get away with it?"

"Goddamnit it to *Hell*, you *still* don't get it! You're not nearly Indian enough to take an Indian view!"

"Sure. *As in* when the Lone Ranger and Tonto were surrounded by hostile Indians with no hope of escape. The LR asks Tonto: 'What do we do now?' Tonto thinks, then says, 'Ugh Lone Ranger. What's this *we* shit? Ain't *my* problem.'"

Two Bears balled a fist and spoke through clenched teeth. "Foul Owl, it's *as in* when at the beginning of this country, in the early sixteen-hundreds. The Dutch invited a tribe to a big cookout in lower Manhattan, and that night, when the Indians were asleep, the Dutch massacred them all. And the Pequots! The English burned hundreds of them alive in one of their stockaded towns, then sold more into slavery in the West Indies!" He's looking so angrily at me it's as if he thinks *I* did it! It flashed on her that her Mayflower ancestors probably did help burn the Pequots and then and there she trembled on the edge of telling Two Bears the truth. "Beffle. Think of it! And these are only symbols! In the next century, General Amhurst gave Indians thousands of blankets infected with smallpox and, right down there, in that mission, the Spanish enslaved every Indian they could catch and baptize. And then in the eighteen-hundreds, ethnic cleansing drove the Cherokee out of the Carolinas on a death march and then came the Nez Perce death march! And all those broken treaties! And the Kickapoo joy juice merchants! And up north of here, bounty hunters killed Indians for reward money provided by Anglo taxpayers! Captain Jack and the Modoc Wars! Wounded Knee! Alcatraz! Our war against European occupation has been going on continuously in the Americas for *five hundred years*, and *still* goes on! These days, it's the Termination Policy meaning ethnocide, cultural extermination! Drive everybody off the reservations into the people-pounds of the inner cities. Casinos are the answer to the termination of the reservations. And I am an effective leader of the casino movement. People who make or will make big bucks off that policy, or some focus of the feds, or dope barons, or multinationals, or Triad gangs, or or or . . . or maybe some constellation of them all . . . or maybe even other Indians; some of them or all of them are the ones who want to kill me or compromise me-- and *you*. That's my theory of why and what. But as to the *who*. Don't have a *clue*. Not a single blasted *sign*."

"You think the Mafia's better than the Anglos?"

"You know this shit too, but you don't feel it."

"I 'm trapped in your fury." She looked over the side, into the mist. "I'd get out and walk home if the first step weren't so high."

He looked up again; sniled at her; lifted the pager.

"Boris. Take it up on top. Over the fog, and head for home. You still don't know where I am? Listen carefully." He pressed the horn button to let Jimmy-the-Morgan do the talking. "You've got it, Boris. We're right here, under you, where you can't see us."

It became lighter, then wisping and then brilliant bright under the vast blue sky dome and sunshine washed over the roiling turbulence of the clouds.

Up there the winds seemed tricky. Two Bears concentrated on steering.

"Another thing, Beff. We've been paying out too many jackpots. Way more than indicated by our built-in odds." He peered over the side. "We're like those soft clouds down there, and they, the invaders, come in unseen like this copter and the Morgan and Boris and us, or your malevolent ghosts, and believe me, it's getting on my nerves."

"Let's stay up here forever, Bear, just you and me. We can shit over the side, drill holes in the floor to drain our piss, raise the top and windows in bad weather, idle the engine for the heater, and, when we get bored, listen to the radio. We make them keep the helio spinning there forever, like MERV, refuel it from tankers, resupply it from other copters, and always keep a three man crew aboard, and they can cook TV dinners and lower them down to us and send down beer and we'll suck on it and gaze over all this virtual reality parading below and we'll kill off the cyber-French for the cosa nostra, our thing, my cosa, and what all this really means is I'm pissed at Charley for being such a worm and at Feral Frank for croaking and at myself for being too old to build a new family and coming close to the age edge of being Wild Child and look down there at that lovely rippling gray sea of nothingness all sunbright covering Pebble Beach and Carmel and all the golf Nazis with gloom, chilling the bastards I hope, so, Bear, let's just hang around here forever, and look down on everybody else, and because there ain't no good and ain't no bad, we'll dedicate to pure harmony, to pure art."

"Beffle, if that ain't a mouthful, nothing is."

"I can still taste it."

"What's it taste like?"

"Old car smell. Jimmy Morgan fragrance."

"Wild Child, the premier contradiction, the prime discord in all this is we need big start-up money for new casinos and have to go outside to get it. Outside investment capital is not always satisfied to hold a mortgage, like we were buying a house. No. It usually wants a piece of the action, and control over policy, and gets it sometimes, and nobody outside knows about it because it's all stipulated in secret contracts. So maybe something like that is the prime mover of what's out to get us."

Sure, and if everybody you trust is as phony as me, and you can't tell, you'll be in big trouble. A big innocent bruin on the way to negotiate with the Mafia! Maybe I'll have to become your keeper. Tell you the truth, then do it. No. Two Bears, you wouldn't know what to do with the truth. No. Me, I'll just do it! Be your maven. Your raven.

"Beff. What are you thinking about."

"Nothing I can put into words."

They left the cloud floor behind and gazed at toy people and toy cars and toy houses and toy trees and toy roads of the model-train-set virtual-reality life stirring around below in the sunshine.

"After Vegas," said Bear, "after I learn what I can from the Mafia and the other powers there, I'll go to Indian casinos around the country-- there's more than a score of them in California alone. I'll visit them and try to solidify them into a single organization, one that can serve as the armature of an intertribal confederacy. If I can bring the tribes together in harmonious association, that might shake off our enemy, if whatever is trying to bring us down is in any way Indian. If not, it will give us a truly strong united front against attack. It's our turn to circle the wagons. To produce unity, we have to produce benefits for all, and honor everyone's traditional ways. We don't give anybody free money. We provide jobs for our people, and training, and capital, and they can start businesses, and work at building reservation infrastructure, roads, sewers, septic tanks, water systems, schools, houses. And clinics. On the res right now it's still dirt roads, wells, and outhouses, and hopeless unemployment, and booze, and illiteracy, and disease. Think of KILI Radio, started by the Lakota Sioux themselves. Broadcasting continuously in the old language. Casinos can have radio stations. TV channels. We'll send youth to school, to the university. Doctors and lawyers and teachers, all the professionals, will be our own people. And this will come-- it *is* coming right now, from casino organization, and from money sucked from the bloodstream of the occupation forces and their colonists!"

"So you're going to walk in the footsteps of Pontiac and Tecumseh."

"Our last try at tribal unity, the occupation of Alcatraz, was wrecked by tribal hatreds exacerbated by the CIA and FBI." He looked down at the approaching home compound. "I think I'll start at the beginnings. After Las Vegas, I'll cross the country to Ledyard, Connecticut, to the Foxwoods Resort Casino, owned by the Pequots, the Mashantucket Pequot Tribal Nation."

"One thing you're leaving out, Bear, about the Pequots, and a lot of other tribes, is they were cannibals." He scowled at her. "We Hurons, Grease Face, tell a story about one of us coming into an Iroquois butcher shop. A number of human carcasses hung from hooks, attracting the usual flies. 'This Penobscot's a good buy,' said the butcher, 'only four dollars a pound.' He probed another carcass. 'This Micmac and the Niantic next to it, and the Podunk over there, too, they're all priced at four-twenty.' The Huron asked about a rather scrawny piece of meat hanging by the Podunk and asked the price. 'Nine dollars a pound.' 'How can that stringy piece of meat cost so much more than the others?' The butcher replied, 'Because it's a Cherokee. Did you ever try to clean one?'"

Two Bears made a face at her and said: "Last Friday evening these two pals of mine in Monterey, young women, one's half Irish and half Huron, had just come home from work and were enjoying a Martini and waiting for their boyfriends. They spied a florist coming up the front walk with a huge bouquet of flowers which he soon presented to the halfbreed along with a card from her Romeo. 'Oh my God,' said the halfbreed. 'Now I'll have to spend the whole weekend on my back with my legs spread out.' Her friend smiled at her and said: 'Honey, why don't you just use a vase?'" Two Bears raised his arms to embrace the scene opening before them. "How about this view of our place, Beff? Sure looks good from up here. Elegant. No neon. Old-fashioned, like Monte Carlo." He spoke into the pager. "Boris, see that flat mission-style building over there, arcaded all around? It's our motor pool and garage. Affirmative. Ease us down in front of it, and we'll loose the bridles; then you land, and we'll go inside and finish the paper work." He turned to Beffle as they sank down. "Always pay people in cash as soon as they've finished the job. Makes them happy."

"Some dance," she said.

"It ain't over. When we get down, pack for a trip."

"Why?"

"I'm leaving tomorrow. Flying from Monterey."

"And . . . ?"

"And you're coming along."

"Really."

"If you want."

"Let's stay at Caesar's Palace."

A light bump and Jimmy-the-Morgan once again stood upon solid ground. David Running Deer strode over as they alighted. He was wearing a sliver-and-black Oakland Raiders cap. She thought of her pirate book, and decided to take it along to serve as her Oracle. They removed the slings and David detached the bridle from its cable and the helicopter moved aside and landed. David walked around Jimmy Morgan, looking at the wounds, and then got in and started the motor. "Hey, boss, I can have your Morgan like new in a few days." Bear said he'd come back in the evening to discuss the details and Running Deer drove the car inside.

"Maybe I'll have him bring it to Vegas."

"And we'll have it to drive east."

"And around town."

"Think it over," she said intently. "Nobody in his right mind would barge in on the Mafia."

"As they say in Vegas, nobody in his right mind would bring a woman to Nevada." He grasped her shoulders and peered into her eyes. "You sure you want to come?"

"Yes, snuff us here, snuff us there, what's the difference."

PART THREE

What is it like to be ignorant? To know nothing of past, of other peoples, of other places, of sciences, of literatures, of arts and religions, to miss the referents of most symbols and most words? Ignorant!

--Theodora Eliot Braun
Las Vegas, Nevada, 2003

SIX

LAS VEGAS (THE MEADOWS) is an island on the land. Las Vegas is an irrigated billion-watted light flower placed in a desolate pink and purple mountain bowl. Las Vegas is a parasite which produceth not; it is an economic vampire sustained by currency and chips. Las Vegas is the rasping crunch of one hundred thousand slots; it is the rattle and click of dice, the howl and honk of jackpot wins, the smell and dirt of cigarettes and currency; it is the multi-queened hill of a million fire ants. Las Vegas is a theme park, home of a crunched and counterfeit New York, Paris, and San Francisco; it is a space probe, rocketing away from Earth into the vast surreal. Las Vegas is Hellfire and delirium; it is a contagion, a masquerade, a fever, a vulgarity so immense and monumental as to be beautiful . . . or so, at least, it seemed to Beffle, as she sat at a horseshoe bar in Caesar's Palace, nursing a beer, slowly slipping quarters into the built-in poker machine in front of her, musing on her first impressions of this grotesque adventure as she waited under the watchful eyes of Ace and her Puritan totems in Sacred Time for Two Bears to come back from a meeting with some local powers.

A big, sturdy, tough looking Roman soldier in the helmet and dress of the first cohort of Legio X Fretensis sat down next to her and ordered a water glass brimming with house red. Falerian, no doubt. A short sword hung from his belt; his bare muscular thighs displayed a spider web tattoo. His helmet's blue plume trembled as he thumped it down onto the bar. "My name's George," he said in a rough voice.

She eyed the bottles displayed at the end of the horseshoe.

"My name is George and I'm the Wandering Jew. You can call me Blood Glutton if you want."

She focused on Wild Turkey.

"I'm talking to *you*!"

She glanced into the gaming room at Ace and signaled him.

"You won't talk to me because I'm a fucking Jew!"

With leveled hands Ace made an it's-okay motion.

"I was raised Jew, in Palestine, but I ain't one now."

She stared at Wild Turkey.

"Ain't no Jews in the army. We're all Mithraists."

She clenched her fists.

"I've been baptized with bull blood."

Ace is laughing!

"We have a sacred Mithric Grotto right here in Caesar's Palace."

Got to wait here for Bear.

"Deep in the basement."

Will power! Patience is a virtue!

"Fucking bitch! You're prejudiced against Mithraism!"

No help from Turkey; appeal to Beef Eater.

"You hate us just because we don't let no women into our church!" Abruptly she became aware of a heavy hand on her shoulder; she spun around, and there stood Two Bears. "Beffle, I want you to meet my friend, George Baxter. He'll be looking out for you while we're in town."

"What!"

"Ace and Eagle are guarding you, and now George, so somebody's on the job around the clock."

"Well, George," she said, "you caught me by surprise." She shook his hand, rough as granite. "I thought you were some kind of masher."

Bear made an amused snile. "Beffle and I are going away for a while. Tell Ace to wait here, then relieve him at noon." He turned to her. "Come on, Beff." He led the way through acres of slot machines and gaming tables, by perfect clones of classical statues, to the grand entrance and outside where they waited submerged in grave Roman music piped out into the fresh air whilst a starter captured a cab.

"We can talk in the cab."

"We can talk right here! Why in bloody Hell did you hire that Roman creep to be my keeper?"

"He's no worse than those other two."

"He's fucking *awful*!"

"Maybe. But he's trustworthy, an excellent security man, and knows his way around town. And we can *trust* him. I know him from before." They got into the back seat of a cab. "Drive downtown to the Horseshoe and then bring the lady back." He turned to Beffle. "Going to the bar at Binion's Horseshoe. Going to meet some casino people there." On the map, exotic Vegas looked to Beffle like a spatula: the grip is The Strip where the big casinos stand ranked on both sides of Las Vegas Boulevard. Then comes the shaft, more than a mile of boulevard leading to the shiny square blade, Downtown, Casino Center, a blaze of smaller places crowding together in an endless flare of energy, one that produces a party, like New Orleans' Bourbon Street, a party that may poop a little, but is never over. Two Bears rubbed some snuff on his gums. "This's about the only place we can talk. They, whoever they are, can eavesdrop on us anywhere else, the gaming rooms, our rooms, the buffet, the street-- anywhere."

"So what'd you learn?"

He leaned back and relaxed. "The Mafia's not big here. This place is run by businessmen, the kind who sell junk bonds and drink the blood of saving-and-loans, the kind who float big stock issues and manipulate Wall Street, and men like me who establish themselves at the heart of a rich and neglected market and organize it. Merchants of fun. I just talked with some people our sports-book associates in Chicago recommended. They have no more insight into the source of our troubles than we do. They want me to tell them what I learn about it."

"Maybe the multi-national casino game is a colossal money laundromat, and the laundress wants to take us over and add our washer to her Maytag brigade."

"Could be. Those people kept saying, at the most conservative estimate of a year's action, gambling in this country is a hundred billion dollar business." He paused for a moment. He seemed puzzled. "Tell you one thing. Those Mafia guys hate Indians. Must be Foxwoods, our castle there at the heart of Mafia New England. The Pequots have the biggest casino in the Western Hemisphere."

"Which takes a big bite out of the hundred billion."

Abruptly, they rolled into a blaze of casinos, a place of thronging pedestrians and constipated traffic, perhaps the world's densest gambling conglomerate. "You know, Beff, this makes me think of the Indians who were here first, like everywhere else in the Americas. The Paiute, who used to be the locals, loved gambling. The males had this game they played with bones, and they got so caught up in it they'd bet their horses, or even their wives."

"And now look at it! From a horse-and-wife real world yesterday to a CD-Romville in Tabloid Fantasy Land today! Do you think it makes the Paiute homesick?"

"We Indians are still in the race for the hundred billion. We have Foxwoods, and *our* place, and plenty more, and over ten percent of the action. We'll wind up and fling an O'Neill hand up onto the island."

"He told you!"

"He tells me everything."

"So let's make a King Candle, an Ohlone Candle."

"Okay. Why?"

"It will burn as our eternal flame, representing the spirit of the Ohlone, of all the Indians, those lost in the five hundred years war against the invaders, and today's resistance fighters, resembling, well, you know, the eternal flames they have at Arlington and Paris and London, and other cities, too, for unknown soldiers."

"All right! And we'll make a real candle, fifty feet tall, with a blazing gas jet, and set it before the entrance to our casino, and mark it with a spotlight, one you can see from all over the Monterey Peninsula, and from Salinas too! The world's Indians will all be honorary Ohlone!" They were approaching Binion's Horseshoe. "And, oh yes, Beff, we'll run it by Running Deer when he gets here."

She felt a shock of hot anticipation. "When's he coming?"

"Any day now. In the Flying Red Horse. He told me on the phone, Jimmy-the-Morgan's almost ready."

The cab stopped and Bear stepped out and paid for the round trip. "Stay at Caesar's till I get back. I can find you easily. Your guards all have pagers."

"My keepers."

"Your secret service."

"I can do better protecting myself than relying on those three slugs."

"Suit yourself. They'll be watching you."

She kissed his cheek. "Have fun."

"See you soon, your room, or that saloon." He pressed through the crowd thronging under the hundred-foot high vault arching over Fremont Street mall, and into the casino. On the way back, the sights reminded her of what she'd seen in L.A, on stretches of Wilshire Boulevard. Wilshire Boulevard! The last time she'd cruised it had been with Braun. She'd always called her husband Braun, and Charley, Charley Braun. Braun! His prick twisted to the left, but not his politics. She'd never found out about Charley's prick. Does it twist? How long is it? How many mothers have seen a son with a hard-on? One in ten? One in fifty? A significant anthropological question. With cunning methodology, it would be meaningful enough to grow into a dissertation for a Ph.D. That was the summer of '85 when they'd stayed at Manhattan beach. They'd exchanged houses with friends: Three months in Berkeley for three months in Manhattan Beach. The Jose Cuervo Volley Ball Tournament! Braun was good at it, *is* good at it. Me, too. A multitude of nets out on the sand. But no tequila. They'd-- she'd-- joked about Mescal. The only place the late bird gets the worm. Couldn't get Charley to surf. Or play volleyball. He was thirteen! Be wild, you fucking boring child! Braun wouldn't surf either. Where's Braun today? Does he come to Vegas? We used to talk about it, but never got around to coming. Does good boring beautiful book-of-moron never-masturbate Charley come here? To Caesar's? No! He'd go to Circus Circus. Or maybe Grand Slam Canyon. Does his prick have a left curve? I really love him, Braun too. I've no one to tell any of this. David R. Deer! I'll tell DRD!

But he tells Two Bears everything.

And now we're back here in ancient Rome.

She slid out, opened the front door, and gave the driver a big tip, and he replied with a merry Thanks.

"You guys need a union."

"We have a union."

"Oh, good. The casino troops don't all have one, so I thought maybe you didn't either."

She walked through the fresh air musical expression of antique Res Publica Romana gravitas into the present playing in an imaginary past, back into the acres of games and statues in rooms as elegant as the Pantheon. Pantheon! All gods. Here, only some gods. KENO. Baccarat. Twenty-One. Craps. Roulette. Poker! Excitement. Envy. Greed. Euphoria! Our merchandise. She lost her way, and found herself in an area of Roman streets with fancy shops under a trompe-l'oeil sky, and then she passed an immense statue of Bacchus enthroned in a fountain. An amazing maze. We built ours well, but theirs surely is *bigger*. She paused and gazed up at Michelangelo's David. Florence displays a fake David, too, because automobile hydrocarbons were rotting the real one. Soon, I'll see a real David! David Running Deer! The thought made her warm and happy. Why don't these workers have a union? How else can one person alone bargain with a billionaire casino boss? Or a billionaire international casino corporation with no boss? Two Bears has the right idea about that. At the outset of the Ohlone Valley Casino, he told all the workers, Indian and Anglo alike, to join Local 483 of the Hotel Employees and Restaurant Employees Union. His dream of confederating all the tribes through an economic association of casinos, a heart, through which beats the transfused blood of Anglo money, which then goes out through arteries and capillaries to every tribesman and tribeswoman and tribeschild, he believes that is much the same as the labor unions' dream of confederating all workers through the association of union locals which he thinks of as workers' tribes gathered together in national unions combined on top into AFL/CIO. "We're building an INDIAN union which can associate at all levels with AFL/CIO. Ain't that right, David?" She raised a hand in Roman salute. "Solidarity for the poor! Solidarity forever!"

David gave her a big toothy smile.

Thinks I'm Jonathan, no doubt.

She pressed on through the maze of temptations separating her from the elevators. We do the same at home. You can't walk anywhere without the maximum exposure to slots and games. Should be so you can't drive anywhere either. Invent some car game! Use credit cards! Auto KENO maybe? She studied the swarming clients, trying to pick out the spotters, the floormen-- some of whom are women. They are security types who disguise themselves as clients. Actors in truth. They have to perfectly pretend to be the greedy housewife from East Turkey Junction, Wyoming, or pose as the money starved accountant from West Covina. So, what will I do when I get up to my room? Who will I be? The accountant? The housewife?

The Beer Fairy!

Should I resurrect the B.F.?

Should I metamorphose at all?

Should I trust in Hawk and Ace and that horrible Roman?

Should I walk the streets of old Venice wearing a mask?

Have to ask the Oracle first.

I'll get advice from Sir Henry Morgan and l'Olonais and the Knight of Grammont, and all the other pirates who still live in my pirate book.

She paused before Discobolis.

Disco! Bolis!

The ancient Greek marble athlete throwing a marble frisbee.

"You, my friend, are the ultimate floorman!"

Is the frisbee which cannot be thrown a frisbee?

"The truth that can be said is not the truth," quoth the statue.

"The song that can be sung is not the song," she replied to her imagination.

"The art," quoth the statue, "that can be seen is not the art."

The last and unchallengeable word ringing in her ears, she went to the elevators. Who is omnipresent at home now that I'm not always there with my Beffle-eye scrutiny and my hawk-eye electronics? I wonder who's robbing the Indians today! A Roman elevator, which should have been made of bronze and floored with a marble mosaic of entwined bunches of grapes and the legend IN VINO VERITAS, whisked her up to her home floor. She hoped to meet Nero Caesar in the hall as she went to her suite, but no such luck. Once inside, she went to her courtesy bar, mixed a tall drink, and then tuned the radio to classical music and sat on the side of the marble tub dominating the center of the main room. That mirror over my bed? Is it really one-way glass? She filled the tub, stripped, slipped in, and using the complimentary kit of toiletries, stirred up a bubble bath. Whom should I be . . . ?

Just be me?

The drink and the scented water and the music produced a mellow mood of peace and comfort as she reflected upon disguises and drama and her yearlong success at playing the part of a Huron/Irish halfbreed. I'm supposed to be a New England blueblood, but I never felt like one. This is more what I really am. In high school she'd appeared in her senior play, a melodrama, cross-cast as Dashing Jack Dalton of the United States Marines. She should have reminded Eddy about that and found out how well he'd played the same part out on the stage of reality. In amateur productions which had become part of her life she'd taken character parts. She'd been old, young, an adolescent, male, female, once even a child. She'd played Othello and, after learning all the lines, had auditioned unsuccessfully for Hamlet. Sometimes she inserted fragments of these lines or those from other plays into her conversations. The anthropology courses at Berkeley had raised her dramatic imagination to a higher order of magnitude. So as to get an overview of how its society functioned, to understand a culture one should imagine oneself into all of its roles. And she'd done it. And it had worked. So why not, in *this* culture *play* all of the roles? If one can be someone else behind the footlights, why can't one be someone else *before* the footlights, and let the play write itself? Yes! Vault the footlights. Be a character in the theater of the real. Inserting herself in the guise of a selected character into any situation would both affect that situation and induce drama. This would be Dada playwriting even more intense that *Ubu Roi*! Her role as halfbreed, adopted because of the obvious requirements of the job, had been the first. But that had been spontaneous. In the job interview Two Bears had asked her if she had Indian blood, and, clearly, she had to answer *yes*. The Thirtieth Re-Onion had offered the first chance to try out this new art. So to give it a radical test she'd begun as the Beer Fairy. She'd flown to Pittsburgh, made up as the homeless hobo Beer Fairy, forwarded her baggage, and hitch-hiked. And it had worked! And then she'd been Melissa. Carrot Top. And that had worked too!

So, who should I be now?

Leave that to the pirates!

She climbed dripping out of the Roman bath and laid the pirate book on the dresser. She closed her eyes and at random, selected a page.

She opened her eyes.

Le vieux Pehrson contemplait d'un air satisfait la pose sérieuse et la discrétion du jeune homme.

With a satisfied air old Pehrson was contemplating the young man's serious attitude and reserve.

Now what the Hell does *that* tell me?

An old man and a young man average out to one middle aged man.

Both seem to admire a serious attitude and reserve.

The context tells me the old man is a local, the young man a stranger.

So I'll have to be a local stranger.

A middle aged tourist!

Pirates would never advise *that*.

Or maybe before I leave classical civilization, I should be a centurion and torment George.

They'd like that better.

But, then, why trust pirates?

As a youth, J.C.-- Julius Caesar-- had been captured by pirates, who spared him. Definitely, a young man of serious attitude and patrician reserve.

When he came to power, he had them killed.

Pirates have bad judgment.

With good judgment, they could have built a pirate empire in the Caribbean.

At least, that's what Voltaire thought.

They had the spirit and the power.

Two Bears likes to cite that in support of his plan to unite the Indians.

Pirates treated the Indians much better than did the Spanish.

So, who should I be?

Oh Beer Fairy, my just-in-case fairy, I dreamed you'd come in handy.

She took her make-up box out of her stack of baggage, and opened the suitcase containing her disguises.

Bear had truly been pissed at her for defying his instruction to travel light.

Bear, Bear, if only you knew! She slipped on some sensual lingerie. Eddy's the only one who knows about my deceptions. This time the Beer Fairy will appear as a floorman, a spotter, posing as the money starved accountant from West Covina! An immensely boring job, a tract home in Dullsville! And fat cretinous rug-rats arrayed before the TV, drooling and farting and eating candy bars. She put on a loose Hawaiian sport shirt, white knit cotton socks, well-advertised running shoes made by slave labor in Indonesia, and baggy loose shorts printed with the green MacLeod hunting tartan. She packed more clothes in a shoulder bag. She stood before the mirror. Yes, slim enough so that with the thighs partly covered, her legs would pass as male. She adorned her neck with a string tie clasped with a silver-mounted turquoise. Oh . . . *yes*! And now for the face. My hair's short enough. She slipped on the Beer Fairy mask, and a well-barbered blond wig. O! Fucking Kay! She strapped on a fanny pack, closed and stacked her luggage, slung the shoulder bag, stepped out into the hall and closed her door, sank earthward in the elevator, passed by rattling honking machines, under vaulted ceilings, through triumphal arches, and out a side door into the heat. She crossed the boulevard to the Barbary Coast, bought a cowboy hat in the gift shop, and, paying a week's rent in cash, registered as A. R. Naseby of 1437 Hummingbird Drive, West Covina, CA 91790.

Believe me, Ace and company, I'll take care of myself.

And take better care of me than you can.

Her new room, where the leopard could change its spots, was Wild-West Victorian with a fake balcony and a brass bed framed in curtains where red ruled, an architectural hemisphere removed from her lodgings in ancient Rome. Did Caligula Caesar embellish his chambers with red-and-tan striped wallpaper and a framed poster for Buffalo Bill's Wild West Show? Well, time for another change. In as the West Covina money slug; out as . . . ? As an automobile salesman from Saint Louis. Named . . . Emil G. Braun. Brown? No! Yellow. *Gelb.* Die Frau in gelb ist gegangen! The woman in yellow has gone. Die Frau in gelb ist in salesman drag. She packed the quiet covetous accountant into her shoulder bag and unpacked the attributes of E.G. Gelb: a black wig, baseball cap, gray slacks, black shoes, a stylish baggy sports shirt, a Groucho Marx mustache. She dressed, adjusted everything, went back out to the street and scanned the slowly parading traffic for an empty taxicab. Sweat flowed under her mask and wig. The baseball cap shading her eyes spared her from the worst of the heat's glare and shimmer, but not its smell. The palms in the center strip made her think of dildos. Caesar's music formed a medley with the smog. Strangers thrust leaflets into her hands, screeds bearing phone numbers and sexy photos and offers from both women and men eager to favor her with a French massage, a personal lap dance, the lively companionship of Room Service Show Queens, or the delivery of a Strip-o-gram.

The fiercely flaming gridirons in the basement of *Hell* could not be worse than this Mojave Desert weather.

A taxi responded to her signal and stopped at the curb. The driver opened the door from inside so she wouldn't burn her hand on the handle. Air! Conditioned! "Am I glad to see you!" she said in her grinding Beer Fairy voice as the cab slipped back into traffic. "It's *hot* out there!"

"Radio said it was one hundred fourteen at noon."

She told him to drive downtown to Glitter Gulch.

"I don't like the Strip," she said. "It resembles TV. It's a stage set for the enactment and sale of bogus history and counterfeit myth."

"You've got that right, mister. The Strip's at once wholesome and fulsome." He glanced back at her. "Where downtown?"

"You know what fulsome really means?"

"Certainly. Otherwise, I wouldn't have used it."

That smacked a stinging swat flat on her egalitarian principles. "So it's good-bye Strip. Hello home."

"Where's that?"

"The Golden Nugget."

"You live there?"

"That's where I'm staying."

"Where you from?"

"A place I've never been. Saint Louis."

"Riddles?"

"Not really. I grew up there, but, well, it's like I've never actually *been* there."

"Me, mister, I grew up in Covenant House in L.A. I'd been on the street. Never mind why. They took me in. So, I guess you can say, if anybody ever truly grows up, I grew up there."

"Did you get to go to school?"

"Some high school. Some night courses. But I don't watch TV. I think it simplifies and stupefies. Can't tell you a thing about classics like Beavis and Butthead, but I read a lot, and hang with people who know things, so I can tell you about our context, history, science, politics, economics-- all of them different windows into the same room." He glanced back at her. "Call me Charles."

She made the mask smile. "Charles?"

"Yes. Tell me, how can people stand being ignorant?"

"Charles, I often wonder about the same thing." The other Charles, despite a good education, never talks like this. "What's it like to be ignorant? To know nothing of past, of other peoples, of other places, of sciences, of literatures, of arts and religions, to miss the referents of most symbols and most words? Ignorant. And there are so many ignoramuses! How can they stand it? What do they think about?" She leaned forward. An example? "Viet Nam. To this day, nobody seems to know the truth, the real reason the government pulled our troops out. The same reason the French left Algeria. A growing mutiny. Aggression. Troops need to be aggressive to be useful. Our men were losing their willingness to attack. They began fragging-- killing their officers, and lifers, men they'd come to see as deputies of the real enemy, those who'd sent them there."

"So I've heard. But, Mister, when you look around, keep your ears and mind open, it reminds you we people were created by Coyote."

"In his own image."

"Hey? You know about Coyote! My grandmother told me about him. How he invented the human race. Me, I'm part Indian."

"So am I."

He passed under the glistening Fremont Street vault and stopped before the Golden Nugget. "I've enjoyed talking with you."

"And me with you." She paid and tipped. "My name is Gelb. Means yellow in German. E.G. Gelb."

"Mr. Gelb, my cab number's six sixty seven. Call me if you ever need me."

A plunge through heat, back into conditioned air. She paid a week in advance, and went up to a bright room with a tropical motif. Now Mr. Gelb you have a home, a place of your own." She adjusted E.G. Gelb in the mirror, freshened up, went back down, and stepped out of the elevator into a bright, white, casino-- one built around the leitmotif of informal comfortable elegance. East Asians, she noticed, as she went back to the street, seemed to be attracted by such a cheery atmosphere.

She hailed a taxi and E.G. Gelb told it to go to Caesar's. They turned left onto Bridger, right onto Las Vegas Boulevard, and soon were flowing southward down this six lane automobile river through the pseudo-Wilshire part toward the Strip. As through E.G. Gelb eyes she watched this anywhere USA scene of franchise foods and gas stations and flashing contesting signs reel by she hoped she hadn't thrown Bear into a frenzy of concern by vanishing. She vaulted denial; glanced at her watch. Only *two hours* have gone by! Ten to one Bear's not back yet. Go to the bar in Gelb drag and watch those keepers sweat!

She settled down at the end of the bar that on a twenty-one table would be called third base. George was sitting opposite at the other end of the horseshoe, first base, drinking with Ace. The barkeep dealt Gelb a tall screwdriver. Ace glanced around and by her, walked out. George sat looking in her direction, and not seeming to notice anything, popped a lump of bubble gum into his mouth and blew a big pink bubble. Ace came back and joined him. Go give this spotter role a *test.* Gelb strode around to first base. "Can you gents tell me where's the best place to find some hookers?"

George blew a pink bubble, and contemplated until it popped. "Right here in the Galleria Bar used to be, before Disneyland for Adults took over. Back then the cunt smell was so thick you could cut it up with a cleaver and cook it."

"Well thanks, gents."

"Don't get me wrong. Plenty of pussy around, only now you got to cruise for it, sniff and follow the scent, or ask one of them fucking bellhops."

Smiling beneath the mask, the Gelb Fairy walked back to third base. Sit for a while. Watch Bear give them Hell for losing me.

As she observed first base and its occupants earnestly conversing about something, and sipped free drinks, she slipped into warm serenity.

Are my keepers sweating?

Doesn't look like it.

Suddenly, behind her, a horrid familiar shrieking whoop.

"Oh! There you are!"

It was Pearl!

Pearl.

Rushing in from the casino.

Strings of pearls bouncing on her bosom.

She'd said she comes to Vegas sometimes.

Bad movie melodrama.

I'll willingly suspend *belief*.

Does she recognize me?

"Hello, sweetie!"

God have mercy!

Pearl bolted right on by around the bar into the arms of George!

And, hugging, they swayed together, George's sword clanking against his stool, and they drew apart, and George introduced Pearl to Ace, and their loud voices carried clearly from first base to Beff's third-base Gelb ears. "Believe it, toots, this guy, this fucking Injun, the bastard's almost as mean as me. In Viet Nam he served in Marine Corps recon. You want to start a shit storm, call on them fuckers, and you fuckin got it." The barman dealt them drinks. Pearl raised her glass. "Here's looking at you." They toasted. "Oh aren't you two a pair of roughnecks!" She shrilled and whooped laughter and slapped their backs. "In hoc signo vinces," said George.

A plan! Metamorphose back into Beffle and give these three fools a surprise. Maybe watch from among the machines for Bear to come back and scold them. As for now, rehearsal's over, play begins. *Be* Gelb! Slide off the stool; walk right by them, and out. George stopped Gelb. "Cunt, Mister." He smiled. "Hope you find that hair pie."

"As a matter of fact, when I really need cunt, I know where one's *real* close."

"Me, honey," said Pearl, patting her chest. "I've got one you can have, if you've got the bucks."

Gelb waved and walked on red carpet and stepped down into the gaming room.

Somewhere near, bleating honking siren shrieks abruptly announced the payment of a jackpot. Acting Gelb, being Gelb, thinking she'd have to invent Gelb's life story, Beffle paced through blare and clamor outdoors into the shimmering drums-and-flutes Roman-music hydrocarbon heat, crossed the boulevard at the light, and went into the cool San Francisco weather of the Barbary Coast. Upstairs, she stripped off her A.G. Gelb hide, slipped into a light summer dress, preened, went back to Caesar's and up to her room. Once again she noticed its architects had placed a mirror on the ceiling over the bed. At the courtesy bar she poured a drink, and sat on the marble pool side, sipping and looking around. Something was wrong! The baggage still stood piled and locked, but someone had moved the pirate book. She'd left it angled slightly on the dresser top; she knew this because she remembered pushing it away when she'd stepped back and gone to get her theatrical luggage--now safely stowed on the Barbary Coast. Yes! No doubt! For certain-sure! The pirate book is squared on the dresser top.

Someone's been here.

And they want me to know it.

This is a foreshadow of the maturing XXI Century when each one of us will be under surveillance all the time, at every moment, from fetus-hood to corpse-hood. And all of it will be recorded. And subject to retrieval!

Learn to live it.

Learn to love it.

With a sigh, she looked up at the mirror. Is it what it seems to be? Or is it in fact that nineteenth-century surveillance system known as one-way glass? She made a nasty face. Do they take photos? Although forbidden by charter to operate in the United States, the CIA maintained a Frisco love nest where hookers brought selected victims to be observed and photographed through one-way glass. Even compared to that, Caesar's mirrors must get an eyeful!

Beffle, mindful of at once sustaining perfect carriage and an air of scornful confidence, opened her door and stepped back out on stage, where she would play the part of herself. She went down to the casino and paused mired in the second-hand excitement and smoke of the slots to spy on the Galleria Bar. No Bear there. Ace and Pearl stood, as before, at third base, drinking and listening to George. "You shitheads should have been here back in the days of the A-bomb tests. Bomb parties went on all night and just at dawn when the shot blew a tremendous window-busting shock wave hit and the goddamned mushroom cloud rose up into the sunrise flashing a million colors!" He clapped Pearl on the shoulder. "Now, babe, *that's* what I call a *show.*"

Yes! Why not . . . ? What fun! Outpearl Pearl!

Beffle gathered her strength and rushed in shrieking, "Pearl! Pearl! Oh there you are!"

Astonished, Pearl turned, and whooped in joy, and they both bleated "sweetie" as they embraced.

"You two broads know each other?" asked George.

"Hell no, you drooling Roman twit. We just share an affinity."

Pearl commanded a round.

"Where you been?" asked Ace. "Where's Bear?"

"Beats me."

"We thought you were going out with him."

"I did."

"We were worried."

"It's cool."

"You want to hide out? Hide out with me."

"Bear would not approve."

Pearl took Beffle by the hands. "When I turned just now, honey, and saw you, why you could have knocked me down with a *fender*! Get it?"

"Feather, fender, farmer. Father? Why not The Future?"

"You always were a *card*."

"Right now, I'm the Queen of Spades. Let's go over there to third base." She turned to the men. "Catch you later." They walked to the other end of the bar. "Have you seen Eddy?" Pearl shook her head. "Have you any word of him?"

"Ain't heard a thing." She ordered wine; they clicked glasses. "So, Beff, you had any orange roughy lately?" She drew a handkerchief from her purse and dabbed at her eyes. "I don't have to pretend with you, sweetie; we're old pals-- been a long long time-- no, I don't have to say take the bitter with the better, no I don't, none of that. And I don't have to make conversation, like tell you about my blackjack system, and, believe me, it *is* one Hell of a system, so, no, believe me, it's so good to see you, and know I can say what I feel. All the time, nowadays, I feel down in the dumps, blue. Oh, so blue. Except when I'm here. This here's my fix. Vegas costs me a few, I'm the first to admit that, but it's worth it. The thrill as the cards turn and the wheel spins and the bones click and roll. And drinks and music and people, and men, too, like George, and everything I like in one place, so I come here, and forget I'm getting old, and I have fun."

"Pearl, think DNA. When we know why people get old, we can fix it. Save for disease or a railroad wreck, eternal youth can be yours. Fat? We can fix that too. Longer legs? Sure. Bigger tits? Even if you're male, okay.

We can do it. A tail? Why not. Three arms are in style? Pay for them, you've got them."

"Don't tease me." What a sharp squeaky voice! "You were always like that, dreamy, believing in a better world."

"And trying to knock you down with The Future."

Two Bears stepped in between them.

"Boss, this's my old friend, Pearl. We go way back to junior high school." He pumped her hand. "Pearl, this is my friend and boss, Two Bears."

"Pleased to meet you." Pearl beamed upon him. "Hey, kiddo, seeing you bare just once would make me happy."

"Have to take a raincheck. Beff and me, we've got to go now. To a business appointment." They walked away through the elegant vulgarity, or is it the vulgar elegance, of the casino, and out to the taxis, where strangers thrust flyers advertising the erotic services of sex mercenaries into their hands. In the taxi, they dropped these invitations to cruise Erotica onto the floor. "Take us to the airport." The cab eased out into traffic. "If someone's following us, they'll get a false clue." Bear sighed and sprawled, went limp. He suddenly seemed exhausted and, except for her, alone. "Here we are back in our mobile hideout," she said. "In our own special interchangeable clubhouse where we can speak truth." She glanced at a canoe riding a trailer in this river of traffic. "So what happened?"

"Nothing, really. Nothing."

"Then why do you look so beat down."

"Those guys speak for or *are* the business interests. They're in cahoots with the cowboy types who wield the political power around here. They are smooth, polite. And for us, no help at all."

"Meaning in this hot place, we're out in the cold."

"That's it."

He drooped heavily on his seat, contemplating something.

"They don't like Indians either."

"How do you know?"

"I don't *know*. It's what I sense."

"And that's all the meaning you found?"

"No. Things are still coming up-- green shoots out of parched sand. As our colloquy went on, I became more and more aware, in their business schools, these guys had been trained to be diplomats, so they're actors, always disingenuous, letting me know only what they want me to know, and calculating continuously the impression they want to make on me and leave with me, the audience." He slapped his knee. "Hey, I've got it! I've a strong intuition they'd been talking with someone else, possibly, and each other, surely, before we met. I think they-- whomever *they* are-- want to split Native Americans off the general gambling movement, and then crush us, one casino at a time." Abruptly, he tensed, alert, once again radiating energy. "That could explain everything that's happening to us. The places that worry them as dangerous competition are not those cheap ugly places standing alone way out in the tulies, like the Cache Creek Indian Casino north of Winters. No. Nor a garage full of slots lost in the Rocky Mountains. Nor a few tables and wheels in Hanged Man North Dakota. No way! What they see as the real danger are well built and professionally operated places established in locations which are already premier tourist attractions, especially in California, whence comes a third of their clientele "

"Like the Monterey Peninsula."

"*Beginning* with the Monterey Peninsula. One of the hottest tourist destinations in the country."

"For sure! Ask a computer to list the best place to put a full service hotel casino, with Indian privileges, and it would print out our address."

"You fucking A it would! And we've laid an O'Neill hand on it! Perfect climate, sweet air, airport, passenger train connections with Frisco and Oakland and San Jose and Sacramento. Marinas, colleges, golf courses up the ass, Pebble Beach, Carmel, Big Sur, mountains. Wild boar hunting, deep-sea fishing, beaches, hiking trails, a jazz festival, big-time motorcycle races, Cannery Row, the Concours d'Elégance, historical buildings, Carmel Mission, thriving legitimate theater, a symphony, world-class art galleries, hotels, restaurants by the hundred, bars, clubs, and more, much more, to come, like passenger ship connections to L.A. and Frisco."

"And that's something *we* could do."

"Sure as Hell is."

He sat there throbbing energy, his old self, and Beffle thought, this man is the champion fighting for all the Indians.

He shouldn't have to bear that alone.

But he's not alone.

No.

I'm here.

Sure!

Living a lie.

She felt intense shame.

And knew she would no longer be able to paint it over with denial.

Shame would henceforth be her loyal companion.

Until she told him the truth.

Without question that is the right thing to do.

So, tell the truth, and get fired.

Tell the truth, and leave him to fight the fight by himself.

Maybe, as well as powerful components of the gambling industry, crime syndicates like the Triads, and the government, and, even, possibly, the Moonies, have all targeted us for destruction.

And Two Bears faces that, alone!

We're in immense danger.

That feeling is another omnipresent companion.

"Bear."

"Yes . . . ."

"I . . . well, my life has become one of waiting for a horrible crime to happen. I don't know what it is, or where the danger is, so I can't run away, or attack it either. I have to be ready to deal with it when it comes."

Two Bears took Beffle by the hands. "Fowl Owl, I feel exactly the same way."

Looking at him, the champion of the Indians, vulnerable, alone, she felt a terrible guilt. I've got to tell him! "Beffle," he said to her, "O! Beffle, what am I going to do?"

SEVEN

GLANCING FROM TIME to time at his radar and lazer detectors, David Running Deer guided Jimmy-the-Morgan at top speed across the desert through the night toward Las Vegas where he would soon add himself to the million plus local Vegans and the twenty-plus millions of people who go there every year. Shortly before sunset he'd seen scores of cars stopped at roadside, the doors of many gaping open, their passengers staring awestruck into the sky, utterly oblivious to other cars and trucks blasting by. Way way up, flashing silver in the sun, David Running Deer discerned a message from the spirits, not a flying saucer, but a weather balloon, cut loose by Eagle as prelude to and warning about his impending advent in Las Vegas. Deer's grandfather had been one of the first visitors; he'd come in 1905 as a section hand-- a gandy dancer-- on the Union Pacific, shortly after the railroad had built a few sheds and buildings and called it a town. Those mighty steam engines had carried the spirit, as did this sensitive Morgan. A pale glow intruded into the starry sky ahead and grew brighter and brighter. His father had told him about it. Neither father nor son had ever been there. Deer Clan Spirit was bringing him now, to close the circle, not in world time, but in Sacred Time.

"Jimmy," he said, "we are approaching a spiritual disease with lights."

He stroked his hair and touched the silver clip on his ponytail. Be they at the Ohlone Valley Casino or under the glow ahead, all gambling games are rooted in the spirit, in Sacred Time. Wheels and numbers and cards and symbolic bones had once bridged the mist between Sacred Time and world time, producing momentary connections through rituals which if sustained in truly open heart could, like the drum dances, meld and endure. He stroked the dark green enamel of Jimmy's door. "And now, all that has passed to us, not to them, but to us." The Ohlone Valley Casino seemed an iron age vestige of the liturgical force of ancient medicine opening worlds now debased to worship of the money god everywhere in the compound---- except in the motor pool where chemical and electronic medicine prevail. The Morgan, the Rolls, and some of the others are the true descendants of the games of old, embodying a power connection, a DNA, an access and a truth, one David Running Deer had resolved to maintain and did maintain in the heart of the blasphemous degeneracy of the casino.

And what lies ahead?

Under that glow, that glare, burning a hole in the starry sky.

"A gleaming spiritual disease."

And Eagle and Coyote and Deer Clan Spirit.

He watched the glare intensify until it was shot with colors, like the atomic mushroom clouds of yesteryear.

And as he watched, he thought of what in Anglo civilization the Spirits had become, a new perverse ferrous religion, whose prophet was Walt Disney, whose temples for Sissy and Sonny had risen in Anaheim, in Orlando, in Paris, in Hong Kong, and, there, under the polychromatic glow ahead: Disneyland for Daddy.

Smoky the Bear;

The Road Runner;
Barney;
Bugs Bunny;
Pokémon.
The deified dog, the holy cat;
Craps, KENO, and Baccarat.

And he remembered Deer Clan feasts at home in Montana where he breathed the rich smoky fragrance of the pampered and fatted family dog roasting over an open fire. The Deer Clan prepared the luscious meat of the Anglos' hallowed animal by . . . no, not by roasting, but by *barbecue*, a word taken from the way the Carib Indians used to entertain the Spanish who were out to massacre or enslave them. Spaniards who could be persuaded to be guests of the Caribs, were invited to dinner, not where they would eat, but where they would be cooked over an open fire and *eaten*.

Ahead, now, he could see the strange cityscape of casino signs and towers and pyramids reaching for the stars.

To free his hands, Deer braced his knees against the wheel and steered with them instead.

He drew a pair of spoons from the glove compartment and began drumming the dashboard, and singing to the six directions: to sunrise and sunset; to the two half-ways, dark cold North and hot bright South; to Mother down and Father up.

And then to the Morgan, a deer spirit manitou, a kachina, whom he sang into the Deer Clan, as Swift Roller.

"I'll make you a deer crest, Swift Roller, and bolt it to your back bumper."

Singing and chanting as they entered the Vegas flash and flare, he imaged Deer and Eagle, certain, despite the danger of doing so, he might have to ask them for help before he and Swift Roller could once more run free of this dazzling light-blister temple of money. At Caesar's they stopped at valet parking where with great anxiety Running Deer gave Swifty's keys to a Roman. Doing what he never did at home, he passed through the casino; where the sight and sound of intense adoration of the money god churned him with nausea, and he checked-in, and went up to his room, and stared at the lights of the city and those of the firmament. It was after midnight. He'd escape into sleep, into dream time, and call Two Bears in the morning.

Down below, on the casino level, in the dim light of the Galleria Bar, Beffle sat, nursing a drink, musing about the lives and characters of A.R. Naseby and Emil G. Gelb, and resenting being confined to Caesar's and the surveillance of her keepers whilst Two Bears rushed around town. Where the Hell is he now? Two a.m.! Easy. Don't be childish. Leave that for Naseby. Bear had said he'd spend as much time as possible with the local power elite to learn what he could by colloquy, eavesdrop, and osmosis. "Beff, believe me, now, all the time, we have to be ready to leave town, and *fast*."

She glanced out at the machines and there, yes, making his way through the rattling clanking hooting maze, handsome and elegant as ever, David Running Deer!

He smiled and sat next to her.

"What a pleasant surprise," he said, and explained he'd just arrived, checked-in, couldn't sleep, decided to go outdoors for a walk. "You won't believe this, but it's raining, *raining*."

"It never rains at this time of year."

"I told myself that, but it didn't help any. It's *pouring*, like *Miami*. And I left my trench coat at home."

He seemed nervous and out of place. Hold him, cuddle him, bring him back into life.

"I'm really glad to see you," he said. "This place gives me the creeps. Right now, I need some good company."

Smiling, she laid a hand on his, ordered him a beer. He never drank anything else. "How'd Jimmy like the trip?"

"Fine! We got along so well I named him Swift Roller, Swifty for short, and initiated him into the Deer Clan."

"Where's Swifty now?"

"Valet parking. I had to turn him over to some Roman. Of course I can trust the casino to care for a car, but I don't trust Romans. I don't even like them. That's what Anglos are, latter-day Romans, who want to enslave everybody."

She glanced up. Here comes George!

George clanked down onto the stool beside her and, looking at David, said, "Who the fuck is that?"

"George, this is my friend and colleague from Ohlone Valley Casino, David Running Deer. David, this is my keeper, George Baxter; he works with Ace and Hawk."

They shook hands. "I'm the Praefectus Castrorum around here," said George.

"The chatelaine?"

"That's one of his many wanna-bees," she said.

"Not only that," snarled George. "I'm the Wandering Jew."

"The Wandering *what?*"

"An alien wanna-bee who came flying in straight from Jew-pitur," said she.

"You're the Wandering *who?*"

He scowled fiercely. "I'm the Wandering fucking *Jew.*"

David stood. "I don't like it here, slots, the games, any of it."

"What I don't fucking like shithead is they couldn't care less about getting their history *right.* Julius Caesar is

Rome; he's the hinge on which Res Publica Romana swung from republic to empire. But do these assholes give a fuck? Shit no! Everything here's wrong! Everything but the Carrera and Florentine marble. Nothing in Rome ever looked like this place. And the interiors, the decor! Greek and Byzantine and USA and even frigging Renaissance! Did you see it, the Michelangelo fucking David? It's enough to give you a shit fit."

"George," said David. "I get your meaning. But what can I do about it? Me, I don't work here like you do. So you fix it. I've got to leave now."

He offered his arm to Beffle; she took it, and, as they turned to go, a sudden shriek came from behind. "Beffle Beffle, there you are!"

"Pearl!"

"Oh honey, do I have a surprise for you!"

Pearl put her arm around George's neck.

"A real lallapalooza!"

"And what might that be?"

"Wouldn't be much of a surprise, Beff, if I said."

David drew Beffle away with him, out among the floormen, boxmen, wheelmen, stickmen, skymen, spotters, streak breakers, pit bosses, crossroaders, and clients. "Let's go up to my room, get some food from room service, and listen to music, and talk, and imagine we're somewhere else."

"How about Prague."

"Prague it is!"

George followed them to Prague, but the door shut him out. "George's Indian name, Deer! I've got it! *Coyote Breath*." With a snort of laughter, David fetched beer from the courtesy fridge, set it on the table, and, smiling tenderly, sat down across from Beffle. Definitely, an aristocrat! A smooth beauty! David, Prince of Cars. "Does that weird Roman follow you everywhere?" he asked.

"Two Bears thinks somebody's out to hurt us, or kill us, and events seem to show that he's right. So he has Ace and Hawk and Coyote Breath guarding me around the clock. As in where will lightning strike next? They may be fools, those three, but they're formidable fools." She told him all the details. None of it proved to be new to him, though, because it turned out on a number of occasions he'd talked it over with Two Bears. "He's seriously worried about it, and so am I."

"How do you think it will end?" asked David. "Perhaps as in 'The Mafia and Indians fight to the finish?'"

"That's what happened in Cuba. Castro extinguished the Mafia's casinos. So the Mafia and the CIA tried to kill him, and because Kennedy would not carry the fight against Cuba to the finish, they killed Kennedy."

"Bear says everyone hates our artesian money-well for Indians."

"I think Bear's right. Like he says, David, our place is a lightning rod for the hatred generated everywhere by Indian casinos."

"What clued him to the whole thing, he told me once, is that in Ireland, and Britain too, the only remains of the pre-Celtic peoples who lived there for thousands of years are a few stone structures and the DNA that crops up in folk like the black Irish. *Nothing* remains of their languages, their cultures. Nothing! That's what the Anglos want to do to us, drown our cultures in theirs." Thoughtfully, he stroked his cheek, and then, speaking softly, went on. "Nowadays, we're pumping money out of them, pumping their blood into our reservation infrastructures, and into our tribal colleges, into our arts, our electronic and print media."

David R. Deer took her hand. "It's a hemorrhage, Beff, it's economic leukemia, and it scares them. AIM says our movement is a metaphor, a symbol, of the common man's struggle everywhere."

They fell into silence, pensively looking at one another, and out the window at the lights. Beffle stood, and went behind Deer, and began softly kneading his shoulders. Is all this play-acting too? "Hey pal, here we are in *Prague*. What now."

"We'll dance."

They stepped to the radio, found some slow swing music, and, close together, he guided her around the room. This guy is good! As they glided to the music, she took his cheeks between her hands and gave him a deep kiss. He drew back. "No, no. Let's just be friends." A warm tide swept through her and she embraced him and he pushed her away. "No, Beffle. Not now."

"When?"

"I can't. I'm in love."

"You can be in love with me."

"I don't want you."

That hurt. She sat on the marble hot tub, aware of jealousy swelling within. She'd never cuddle and preen this beauty; she'd never hug him and fuck him and kiss him all over. For whom does he long? Does he feel the same hurt, the same envy, produced by the same scorn radiating from *his* unattainable lover? He sat beside her, and spoke in a caressing voice. "We're friends."

"Yes." This jealousy has no target, no image, and maybe never will. Or maybe some queen will step into that empty space, and just by being, provoke attack. "We're friends and colleagues."

"Sure"

She took his hand. "It's bedtime. Let's be pillow friends."

He stood. "You can stay if you like. I'll sleep on the couch."

She hugged him goodnight, and stepped out into the hall. Coyote Breath had transformed into High Hawk. "Ms Braun, I'll walk you home." They passed Bear's suite, which was close by, and soon arrived at hers. Hearsay had it Hawk's name derived in part from him being high all the time. Not so, tonight. She thanked him, stepped inside, and secured all the locks. She poured a tall drink and clicked on the TV and began surfing. What an array of drek! A true expression of the Las Vegan spirit; an ultimate of fevered folly. She clicked it off and went to her laptop computer to see what kind of company she could stir up in the chat rooms. Maybe she'd find something to fit her mood, something as deep and dark as the caverns of DOS. She connected with her server and typed in her screen name, Beer Fairy. Years ago, when she'd signed onto the service, typing in answers to its questions, she'd been drinking beer and thinking she'd soon be flitting around the net, light as a fairy, changing personas as she fluttered about. Suddenly the prompt told her to invent a unique screen name for herself and type it in. Thus was born the hermaphrodite Beer Fairy who could be and often was all things to all people.

She scrolled down the list of chat rooms, looking for one with an opening.

Teen Talk.

All right!

I'll be an old curmudgeon.

She clicked in.

She watched the conversation developing, line by line.

At least these young people are learning to write Hemingway dialog. Strangers from all parts of the country, conversing, making an old-boy/girl force for union, every member rich enough to waste twenty-three bucks each month on the user fee. And much more on cybertoys. So once again the rich still rule. And they have an etiquette. They're at an honest/dishonest cocktail party with many rooms. No! They're *all* Beer Fairies! They mask with pseudonyms, and can play any part or say anything. Not altogether so. Some tell the truth in their conversation and their bios.

Others have more names than an Indian chief.

She let her attention move from generality to the specific.

```
Missy952: oh
OhioSlug: Firing loaded weapons is cool.
TLuehrs: SKI HOWS THE SNOW BY YOU
Missy952: ok
San Quinn: what kind of guns do you shoot, SHOOTER
OhioSlug: as opposed to unloaded ones
KNevers392: h
KNevers392: e
KNevers392: l
KNevers392: l
KNevers392: o
OhioSlug: m
OhioSlug: o
OhioSlug; r
San Quinn: WHERE DID YOU GO MISSY
OhioSlug: o
OhioSlug: n
TLuehrs: ANYBODY FROM MILWAUKEE
KNevers: shut up slug
OhioSlug: HURT ME
Missy952: no
KNevers: ok, bap bap
Ski Jordan: Missy, where are you from
Missy952: VA
```

SHOOTER979: What do you shoot, Ohio?
San Quinn: ANYONE FROM FRISCO
Ski Jordan: I'm from Washington
SHOOTER979: Anyone from S.C. or Georgia?
San Quinn: D.C.? JORDAN?
Ski Jordan: Hell no
KNevers392: yes I'm
Dada Klub: Monterey, here. 120 miles south.
OhioSlug: Anything I can....mostly my friends BB gun, not sure what kind, but it is pretty high-powered
KNevers:392: I'm from SOUTH CENTRAL
Ski Jordan: really
Missy952: I live in VA but I am moving to MN
KNevers392; WHATS UP MY BROTHA
Ski Jordan: I'm not a girl
OhioSlug: Must have gotten his computer during the riots
Ski Jordan: Yes!!!!!!!

Should I . . . ? Should I get into this?

Almostpoet: is there intelligent life out there?
Ski Jordan: No!!!
Missy952: yes
Domaz: You know if people were dung beetles there would be no need to turn chairs into ducks
KNevers392: YES
OhioSlug: Yes, but, if people were dung beetles, then would I be the slug I am?
Domaz: Ohio: No, you would be a duck
Missy952: WHAT ARE YOU TALKING ABOUT
OhioSlug: As opposed to a dung beetle
Ski Jordan: I have no idea
SHOOTER979: Any single young ladies out there, 21-30 Or so?
KNevers392: YES, I'M 28
Domaz: Ohio: Well it really depends on which way you want to look at it
Missy952: WHAT IS A DUNG BEETLE?
Ski Jordan: A dork
KNevers392: you

OhioSlug: It is a thing that eats the feces of other creatures. In short, KNevers392.
Dada Klub: At UC Santa Cruz, Slug, slugs are holy.
Ski Jordan: Not
Beer Fairy: Out here in Las Vegas, they're as sacred As money.
KNevers392: slugs suck
OhioSlug: BANANA SLUGS...MY BROTHERS!
Beer Fairy: Your brothers are the official mascots of the U. of Cal. In Santa Cruz.
OhioSlug: I have a BananaSlug hat and shirt-- I wear them every day.
Dada Klub: But are you slimy, Slug?
OhioSlug: Only when females are around.
Domaz: You know too many people use mediocrity as their own persona
Deer Stlkr: How ever did ya guess?
Dada Klub: Hey, Slug, go for UC Santa.
OhioSlug: Hey, in 3 yrs, I'm there! Ya gotta love a team named the Banana Slugs
Beer Fairy: Hey, Slug, when you get to UC Santa, go Down to Carmel Valley to the Ohlone Valley Casino, ask for me, Beffle.
OhioSlug: Sorry, I'm just a slug
Beer Fairy: Free beer. I've got the power.
OhioSlug: FREE BEER WORKS
Beer Fairy: And is available in unlimited quantity to Beer Fairies.
OhioSlug: Gotta go now. Gonna be an OhloneSlug!
Beer Fairy: So long, Slug. Good-bye, all.

Well, for sure, that room would never win a grammar prize. Beffle scrolled down the chat list again, searching for a more engaging group to join, one with less than the maximum number of guests: twenty-three.

Native Americans!

Why not!

OnlineHost:*** You are in ▌Native American Chat▌.
JMRisin121: Good bye everyone
Tochoway: Ride with the winds, JMR.

RedHwkWmn: Nite JM-- sweet dreams

Type a message . . .
then click *send:*

Beer Fairy: Greetings, all.
HOST Maize: Beer Fairy, Hi! Come join us in Native American Chat!
ET Bear 1: Jroica, were you there for the Deer Dance this year?
Lilo: and changed their name to avoid being sent to the Oklahoma reservations
JROICA: Yes, I was, ET. Were you?
Gooseman69: I've never been to a Pow Wow and there is one at Lake Casitas on Oct 14. Should I go?
RedHwkWmn: Go Gooseman - much fun!
V1piano: gooseman-you havn't lived until you are at a powwow!
Angie Ara: Lots of fun Gooseman!!
JROICA: Karuk's dance their Jump Dance every year.
Gooseman69: I'm part Blackfoot and I'm not sure if I should go to a Pow Wow of a Nation that I don't know.
DRDeer: I'm full Blackfoot. It's ok.
HOST Maize: Gooseman . . . most are Inter tribal . . .
RedHwkWmn: Check it out - Open Mind, Open Heart, Open To fun experience!
V1piano: gooseman-i am Ojibwa, but spend more time With Lakota & Crow, Onondaga & Mohawk
DHeames503: May the wind be at your backs
Tochoway: Goose, PowWows are for everybody. It's a learning experience, too.
JROICA: Pow-wows are social events, Goose. It's a Place to meet people.
ET Bear 1: Will see you... Night, all, remember True Medicine Heals from the inside out!
NAC Fire: Night ET Bear
Mobillone: Take care bear
RedHawkWmn: NAC Fire - didnt see you lurking around the edges of the group . . . . Hello!
Tochoway: Hate to do it but it's a work night so off I go.

V1piano: nite tochoway
Tochoway: Your company has warmed my heart and spirit.
NAC Fire: Hee hee RedHwk.... I am hiding behind a bush
Tochoway: May the Spirits guide and protect each and every one of you until I return.
Akwesane: ANY Mohawks out there
HOST Maize: Well gang...gotta get going now...have fun with NAC Fire!!
Gooseman69: Does anyone know where I may find some Info on the Blackfoot Nation?
V1piano: Blackfoot were the Siksika, The Blood, The Piegan aligned with the Atsina & Sarsi
NAC Fire: PapaFish, welcome.....my friend. Please stay with us a while.
ChrisE1178: My Ojibwe professor was talking yesterday about a blackfeet friend of his
DRDeer: I'll look around for info, Goose, and get back to you in one week, same time.
Akwesane: where you from JROICA
NAC Fire: RITAST, :::::::putting log on fire:::::::. Come sit around the fire and chat with us.
JROICA: Hoopa, CA. Home of KIDE-FM

Can DRDeer be *David*?

V1piano: hello fawn
NAC Fire: Hoopa, home of HiEaglet
JROICA: Yes I know her; she's here.
NAC Fire: Sioux Maid, come in and be amongst friends tonight.
FAWNWRITER: hello Nac!
Sioux Maid: aho my brothers and sisters
NAC Fire: I am really in great spirits today. Very happy
Scott4Real: hau everybody
Istagi: Hau Scott, what's up?
Scott4Real: getting ready to leave for a pow-wow
NAC Fire: Where at Scott
FAWNWRITER: hi scott! Its been so long! How are you!
Istagi: there are no dances here this weekend ::pout::

NAC Fire: I was just at the Wolf Moon Pow Wow last weekend.
Scott4Real: I am fine, the pow-wow is in Fayetteville, NC at an indoor arena
ChrisE1178: University of Minnesota has a huge American Indian studies dept., Goose. I can most likely find some.
DRDeer: Good idea.

David Running Deer? Can it be possible?

Akwesane: HEY RIT where you from
RITAST: The growing metropolis of ❙Hogan❙ moons ago-- still have family there and still go up
JROICA: Hey you Hogansburg folks, you know the Cook family?
RITAST: I'm in Syracuse now Akwas-- was just up two weeks ago.
NAC Fire: ((((((Rez shoes)))))) great to have you here tonight
Rez shoes: Hi
JROICA: What rez you on Rez shoes?
Rez shoes: Navajo Rez
DanceEagle: Yo Brothers
Hieaglet: Hi there, Dance Eagle, Welcome!!!
DanceEagle: Does this place have evil
Hieaglet: This place is not exempt from evil, Dance, but we overpower it with kindness.
TateNagin: There is good and bad everywhere DanceEagle, the trick is to keep the balance
DanceEagle: Controlling evil is like controlling a storm....it wins.
Cohannal: Yes, DanceEagle, you are very right
Hieaglet: Well put, Tate.
Dance Eagle: We need to purge evil by being evil.
DRDeer: We need to purge evil by joining AIM.
DanceEagle: reserved evil grows in proportion to its constraint
Beer Fairy: Go with Deer; through the means of balance, of yin-yang, strive toward the ends of AIM.
DRDeer: Brothers and sisters, the American Indian Movement is our union.
Beer Fairy: Are you by any chance David Running Deer

```
    of Las Vegas?
DRDeer: The very same.  And who are you?
```

Much to the surprise of David, Beffle typed in "Beffle," and with sweet phrases they bowed out of the chat room and connected on the house phone and laughed and talked and said goodnight and she slipped into bed, into Dream Time, where sculptural shapes and colors from her studio in Carmel, from the ether, the empyrean, pulsed, swirled, roiled, and at last solidified as Jimmy-the-Morgan wafting through a hot sunny mist. Someone on her right behind the wheel. Why is Bear driving and not me? Where in Dream Time impending is he taking me? But it's not Bear. It's David! And they burst from the warm intimacy of the cloud out into the sunlit expanse of the high desert where close ahead rise the towers and pyramids of Las Vegas, silent, still, a mirror of its builders, of its Coyote architect, here in Future Time, shattered, sand-drifted, devoid of green, dead, a ghost city, besieged, sacked and abandoned during the Great Troubles, home now to no one but Raven and Crow, who can live anywhere, and to the lesser beings of the dry and barren Mohave. A strange cloying odor of burning tires, melting plastic, and decaying flesh rose from the ruins; a few gaming chips, scattered and ignored, lay about like poppy seeds on dried out bread. As the Hopi prophets and those of so many other tribes had foretold, the hubris of Anglo civilization and its defiance of harmonious balance had produced the inevitable catastrophe.

A ringing phone intruded and Beffle abruptly reared up in bed.

She sat listening, procrastinating, feeling homesick for what she used to believe about America.

She lifted the phone.

"Rise and shine, Beffle! Meet the new day."

She cursed at Bear and swung her feet to the floor.

"Get dressed. I'll be at your door in twenty minutes."

"Yeah. Okay." She stood. That damned knee hurts again! It's going to be a bad day. "Have a bad day, Beffle." She limped into the bathroom, began her toilette. Where's Deer? Damn it Deer, get out of my head! Her mind's eye saw him in the garage, caressing Swifty-the-Morgan. Swifty. A better name than Jimmy. Swift as a deer! Sure. Frau in gelb. She pulled the yellow dress over her head, smoothed it into place. Is it only advancing age that makes it harder to believe in America than formerly? Charley-the-Moron believes in America. God's chosen country. Feral Frank's voice echoed from the past. "Wild Child, if you'd sprouted instead of split, I'd have named you Charley." So how about Charlotte or Charlene? "Your mom got to name the girls." In our case, the girl. What's it like to grow up with siblings? An aching homesickness for her lost belief in America overwhelmed her. One akin to her arthritis pain. She sought out her yellow shoes, buckled them on, and, for the fun of it, put on a string of pearls. Will they work as medicine, as a passover sign, to spare me from encountering Pearl? She limped to the bar.

Start the Roman coffee machine.

Pour in the courtesy coffee.

What did Caesar use to jump-start his mornings?

Loud knocking announced the arrival of Two Bears. She greeted him with a hug and, showing him in, said, "David's back in town."

"Yeah, I know."

"Think we're being monitored?"

"Wouldn't doubt it."

She fetched bottles of orange juice from the fridge and opened them. She lifted hers to the ceiling mirror.

"A toast, Bear. A toast."

He looked up, raised his bottle.

"To our loyal audience!" she said.

"And to melodrama. May they always enjoy our show."

"And now for breakfast. We'll taxi somewhere."

"If you say so."

He embraced her, whispered: "We'll *Morgan* somewhere."

"But first, coffee, to get us going."

She brought cups and the pot to the table.

"Tell me, Bear, what did Caesar use to start up his mornings?" Two Bears shrugged. "Whatever in the fuck it was, I need a quart of it right now! Man, I feel blue. *Blue.*" She told him about the dream. About the parched and abandoned ruins of Los Vegas. "That's the *prophesy.* And it sure looks inevitable. So why the fuck should I care? But I *do* care."

"The elders say the collapse of Anglo civilization will spare us, and the tribes will recover their land, and balance will be restored, and life will be true again. But I don't believe that. No fucking *way.* They're *dreaming.* Even though it's going to *happen*, and it will eat us *all*, we'll keep on struggling against it. Even though we're doomed to fail, we'll keep on sucking money through our casinos and building our confederacy. Why do it? Why bother?" He slammed the table. "You know you'll die for certain sure, so why bother to *live*? And I'm not poor rotting old Louis XV saying the flood'll hold off till after I croak. Hell no. So what the fuck is it . . . ? I know I'm going to drown, but I am by God going to drown *swimming.*"

"Right on!" She smacked him a high five. "Fucking-A."

"I wish we could turn it around, but we can't."

"Why not? Democracy means rule of the rich by the rest."

"Yeah, sure."

"So after more than two centuries of it, why do the rich still rule?"

A coded knock sounded at the door.

"Expecting somebody?"

"No."

"Anybody but David and your keepers know where you live?"

"Deer's the only one I told."

The coded knock came again; Beffle went to the door and opened it and gasped in dismay.

There stood Pearl.

Ugly as a parking lot!

My pearls proved to be an attractant!

"Beffle!"

A fat smelly sweaty hug.

"How'd you find me?"

"George."

Pearl stood back, still framed in the doorway, beaming a wide and happy smile.

"Open your ears and shut your eyes and I will give you a big surprise!"

Beffle narrowed her eyes to slits.

"You're peeking."

What the Hell. Close them.

"You can look now."

Before Pearl, dressed in summer leathers, stood Flora and Fauna, the Twins.

They swarmed in, hugging and shrieking.

Bear, then Beffle began whooping laughter.

"Hey, people, a kiss for us dykes on bikes!"

They kissed Bear, then Beffle, on the mouth.

"Hey, free spirits---- for us free *spirits*."

Reveling in the utter absurdity of it, Beffle poured them spirits.

Bear surveyed the slender leather-clad duo. "Do you guys have tits?"

"Yeah, but not as big as yours, you lovely wild bull."

They turned to Beffle.

"Who is this big hunk?"

"My boss." She introduced them.

"Girls, sit down and visit while I make a phone call." Two Bears produced a cellular phone from his jacket and went over to the window. Pearl and the twins took off their shoes, and sat around the marble tub, drinking and bathing their feet.

"Beffle, sweetie, some surprise, eh? Dynamite! Flora and Fauna! Ain't no surprise to me, though. They been planning to go to the motorcycle races at Laguna Seca for months now, and, on the way to California, to stop here and see yours truly. I arranged my vacation to fit. Honey, the big surprise for me is running into *you*."

Beffle babbled something appropriate as she went to the table for her purse. She rummaged in it, drew out a yellow highlighter, and came back. "*Flora!*" A twin smiled up at her. Beffle limned a sunflower onto her forehead. "For the rest of the day, Flora, you'll be a sunflower Hindu."

Flora reached up under Beffle's dress and jerked down her panties. "Only if you let me kiss you *there*," said the sunflower Hindu. Beffle pulled her skivvies back up and went to the other side of the tub. "Mark *me*," said Fauna. Beffle drew a wildcat or her brow. "You're now a temporary jaguar Aztec."

"Speaking of temporaries, after Laguna Seca we're going to Frisco. We're thinking about moving there. We work as temps for the Charles Schwab brokerage house, so getting work in Frisco should be easy."

"Yours Truly," said Pearl, "keeps telling them to stay in Cleveland. Folks are getting it together there. I mean *together.* Like a new stadium and lots of other groovy things. They don't even make Cleveland jokes on TV any more."

Bear turned from the window, where he'd been surveying the cityscape. "Cleveland is like Vegas and LA. It's an artificial city. There's no economic necessity for its existence. Geography and commerce would put them, all three of them, somewhere else, not where they are. It's fierce greedy domineering men who caused them to be located in the wrong places." He came over to the twins. "Well, sure, part of what determined their locations is pure accident, and, yes, Cleveland does have water. Vegas and LA are exotic irrigation flowers. Cut off their water for a month and they'd dry up and blow away."

The Aztec reached out for Beffle. "Come on, let's strip, and slide into the water."

"To mix a metaphor, I'll have to take a rain check on that."

"You'll get to meet the real us and we'll kiss you all over."

"I met the real you in high school when you gave that coach a hot foot with magnesium ribbon."

"Yes, but you've never seen us naked."

"I'm not interested in your bodies."

"Your father knew every inch of our bodies."

"Of mine, too," said Pearl. "And that's one Hell of a lot more territory than the two of you together."

"Beffle," said Bear, "pray tell, was your father some kind of child molesting pervert."

"No, he was a doctor. Their family doctor."

"A doctor?" said Bear.

"Sweetie, not just any old doctor. Blond and slender and funny. A fox!"

"Owl, you never told me your father was a doctor."

"That's why he was so direct and earthy. I've told you that part. He called me Wild Child, and I called him Feral Frank."

"At the reunion," said Pearl, "she told me she's half Indian. I never would have guessed it in a . . . a month of Sundays."

Beffle felt a hot flare of guilt. I've got to tell him the truth!

But not now.

"My mother was a Huron, Huron heritage. She had a nervous breakdown, and Frank put her in a recovery hospital."

"You should have seen her, Mister Bear," said Flora, looking at him through her drink. "She really truly was a master boozer."

"Well, now, girls, you'll have to cut this visit short. Beffle and I have work to do."

"As in you haven't given her her morning fuck."

Beffle noticed a subtle nasty smile touch Bear's lips. Imagination placed David Running Deer at her side, and she felt a strong urge for him. Why not for Bear? He peered down at the twins in contempt.

"Yeah," said Flora. "You're pissed because we interrupted you nosing around in Beffle's pants."

"When you reach in her drawers," asked Fauna, "do you find a banana clit?"

Bear glanced at them in turn. "Your mother should have taught you better manners."

"You know what?" said Fauna. "You're fulla shit."

"You know what?" said Bear. "You're outa here."

He picked them both up, one under each arm, and carried them, shrieking, out into the hall. Pearl followed. Bear stepped back in and slammed the door in their faces. He began laughing. "Were all your high school friends as rude and coarse as that?"

"Most were worse. We can't all descend from Hurons and medical doctors." She looked him in the eye. "Frank's *father* was the doctor. Frank's was first mate on a Great Lakes ore ship."

"Sure. I remember." He smiled at her. "As for that phone call, Fowl Owl, I told Deer to come over with Swifty."

"Swifty! He told you?"

"He tells me everything."

EIGHT

SWIFTY SAT PURRING in contentment near to a back door of Caesar's Palace whilst David Running Deer, the Morgan's keeper, sat peering into the rearview mirror, grooming his hair. Bear and Beffle came up to him. Quickly, D.R. Deer slid along the seat and out as they slid in. Waving good-bye, they sped to the boulevard, moved into traffic. "So, hey, Beffle, let's go over to the Liberace Museum for an Italian breakfast." Spying an empty space ahead, he eased out of the flow and stopped and drew a small gauge from his pocket. He moved it slowly over Swifty, and let it guide his attention under the dash to the top of the steering column. Holding a finger to his lips, he detached a magnetic bug, showed it to Beffle, and stuck it to the frame of the car parked in front. He slipped Swifty back into traffic. "On second thought, let's run out to Mount Charleston."

Two Bears wheeled Swifty onto the freeway. A desert traffic jam! They sat sweating under their canvas top and inching forward. "We've got all day," said Bear. "Up there in the mountains, it's a different world, another planet. The stars shine at night and it gets cold." He burst into song as they moved sporadically through the green new suburbs. "Oh what was your names in the States?/ Was it Johnson or

Thompson or Bates?/ Did you murder your wife and run for your life?/ Oh, what was your name in the States?" Abruptly, they left the structures and gardens of town and found themselves passing by the clumped shrubs and gravelly cement-like soil of the desert. The congestion loosened. Is the desert a traffic laxative? They went by named streets leading nowhere, waiting for lawns, for houses. "See that overpass way up ahead? That's the Paiute Reservation. They traded a small piece of their old land for all that." To the left, streets of modest new homes appeared, and, to the right, the money cows which had paid for them: a tall hotel, a casino, a golf course. Indian mode designs decorated the overpass. Bear guided Swifty onto the shoulder, slowed, and stopped beneath the bridge. "Don't want to go in there. Might attract attention."

"And stopping here?"

"We can risk it." He made a sweeping gesture at the designs painted on the surface of the overpass. "I wanted to show you this."

She replied with an affectionate "Thanks."

"*Look at them.*"

Beffle saw rude designs in bronze and terra-cotta colors, cave paintings, crossed by jagged flashes of brown lightning. And . . . of course! That's only the surface. I'm looking at the sea, trying to peer through the roil and glare on top to the abundant variety of life it conceals! But it's *not* the sea. Just as written words present a mirror, one which reflects black designs on paper if you don't know the language, so do the drawings in this modern cave. If you know the language, you have no awareness of the black marks on paper, but pass right through them, through the mirror, to another reality on the other side. Can these designs be a door to Sacred Time? I had a sense of it during the drum dance on Tassahara Road during the rescue of Swifty. But this door is closed! I stare at it. Nothing. Am I trying to play the Lost Chord on one of Liberace's show pianos?

"So, Wild Child, what do you think of it?"

"It's beyond words, and beyond me. It covers something I can't get at!"

No purebred New England WASP could ever read through this.

"It speaks to me." Bear sat in silence. "Beff. Without your help, following the Sacred Trail to the restoration of the tribes . . . . I mean, sometimes it seems like, without you, it might be too much for me." He started the engine, and wheeled Swifty out onto the road. "No. I don't think I could do it alone." He accelerated, producing a cooling breeze. "Some of the tribes who are into gaming have mutual benefit associations now, not all of them honest, and, driven by lust for big money, they clash. You and me, and our dream of a continental intertribal confederacy, and the Ohlone Valley Casino too, all of us, we're sitting on an immense ant hill, eating honey. This year California Indians will suck in about four and a half billion."

"What did you learn about the Paiute casino?"

"I talked with them yesterday, and they said they like my idea, but I could tell what I was saying to them was going in one ear and out the other."

"So you didn't learn anything."

"No." He turned off onto the Lee Canyon Road and went toward the mountains. "I told them our casino is a success, not just as itself, but as a model for financing Indian tribal renewal. We are in the avant-guard of humanity's battle against white supremacy. So we *must* establish and maintain our independence. We do it for ourselves? Sure!

But also for the young people. What is there for them on reservations with no utilities and forty percent unemployment? They live in Indian past. They have nothing but despair and history. But if we use the casino opportunity right, they can look ahead, live in the future, *make* history." Swifty had now carried them upwards into a region of rugged ochre buttes and big cacti called Joshua trees where coyote and wild burros and feral horses range. "So I told them, as a model, and by choice, we hold our administrative costs to the minimum; we finance Ohlone needs as determined by the Council; we buy as much land as we can to expand the reservation; and we invest the rest of the profits. We'll hold the invested capital in a trust fund until I can cobble together the beginning of the tribal confederacy. When that happens, profits beyond tribal needs will go into the pool, a foundation, which can grant money to legal tribes, to Indian schools and media, and to individual Indians." He let Swifty rip along the empty road. "And it's happening! It's fucking happening!"

"Who put up the capital to start our casino?"

"A variety of outfits."

"Who?"

"It's all paid off."

"How much do we have in the trust fund?"

"I don't know. Millions. I'll look it up for you."

He doesn't want me to know.

He doesn't tell me much.

He doesn't pay me much, either.

They sped along in silence.

The road signs had all been pocked by bullets.

"Some of those peaks, Beff, are almost ten thousand feet. Dahl sheep and mountain goats live up there."

The air cooled.

They ascended into a ponderosa pine forest.

"This road goes up to the ski lift, and beyond."

What an utterly different world! A cool forest, spreading before jagged peaks!

He turned into the Deer Creek Road. "We'll go to a vista from which we can look down at where we came from." He pointed out the location of a cave called Robbers' Roost, said to have been a sanctuary for train robbers, and then he guided Swifty slowly into another road, and stopped. "Just down this path." A short walk took them to a place offering an immense and gorgeous view of the mountains and the desert basin and the bleak treeless peaks on the other side toward the Colorado River. Signs and a map had been erected for orientation. "See, way over on the left, the nuclear testing grounds. People used to come up here with food and drink and wait for dawn when an atom bomb was about to blast a huge flashing mushroom cloud into the sky. And see, way over on the right. Vegas."

"And that needle with revolving wedding chapels on top. Someone told me it's the tallest building west of Chicago."

"It doesn't look like much from here, but from high up, neither does Chicago." He rubbed some snuff onto his gum. "Even though the pawn shops never close, Vegas, it's really just a big village."

"The crew's quarters of the land ship on which we're all taking a desert cruise."

They stood, silent, admiring, open, contemplating. Beffle spoke again: "Bear, you know I'm virtually detribalized. You always tease me about it. But I try to be Indian, *feel* Indian. I really do."

"You're close sometimes."

"Looking out at all of it, the mountains, the desert, the pines, the birds, I think of, I sense, oneness. Unity. A solidarity as pure as Sacred Time. The old people must have felt it intensely. But no. It was always there. For them it was more like wearing a warm robe. The garment of unity. Each living thing exists only to make more. What flows through eternally is *life*." She gestured at Vegas. "And what if they'd come over this hill a thousand years ago and seen *that*!"

"They would have sung their death song."

"Why?"

"They'd have known we've broken the balance of life."

"I saw it in my dream. A ruined deserted Vegas, burned out and drifted over. I've always been able to remember a lot of things, some of which are in the future." Feeling an intense melancholy, she turned and walked back to the car. "Think of the archaeologists excavating Caesar's, Luxor, New York, Paris, Mirage! Two Bears, My archaeologist son wears a T-shirt marked: We Dig Up Your Past. I know of a detective agency with the same motto." She climbed in and secured the seat belt. He's a Mormon studying in a Moron college. Going for an Ed.D., minor in archaeology. "Do you think he'll be trying to dig up more golden plates inscribed with the word of The Almighty?"

"I don't know, but if he does, tell him to melt them down, change the gold into quarters, and bring them to our gaming temple to sacrifice to the slot god." Bear guided Swifty back to the highway, and along to the Kyle Canyon Road where he turned left and drove downhill toward town. "I been thinking, Vegas shows no mercy to quarters. In the temples, every day, the public sacrifices millions and millions of them." Ahead, loomed the Charleston Mountain Hotel, the first commercial structure they'd seen since leaving the

Paiute Reservation back on Route 95. "I figure playing one quarter at a time in a single hour a person who's really conscientious can feed just one machine a hundred and eighty bucks. They get some back, but still!"

Swifty rolled into the hotel parking lot and stopped.

"Do these folks have a gaming room?" asked Beffle.

"Fucking-A! Everybody does. Down in those new suburbs they build neighborhood casinos. Stores, gas stations, even churches have slots, consecrated to the slot god. And, hey, just wait another twenty years when gambling is legal throughout the States, the world. Casinos and slots will be every fucking where! Yeah! The moral of that story is we Indians had better bleed the beast while we can." The front door of the hotel admitted them to the rattle and ring of a gaming room, in which, as in most, it was neither day nor night. Players, holding quart-sized plastic buckets of coins, sat raptly feeding the machines; change girls and cocktail waitresses ranged the aisles. Beffle and Bear paused in the doorway to take in the scene.

"Could be our place," said Bear, smiling warmly.

"Yes. It makes me homesick."

They stopped to watch a woman feeding two machines at once, her right hand blackened by holding quarters and pulling the handle. Beffle looked away at Bear. "Hey, Lard Face, we should tell her about the free 'professional slot players glove' offered by that place in the Fremont Experience mall."

"Maybe she likes being in the Black Hand Society."

"I've noticed in our place people can get so mesmerized by the machines that even when they've invited their families to dinner and have a reservation for a given time nobody can pry them loose."

"I've seen people with full bladders put off leaving the machines until they piss themselves."

In a mirthful mood, they walked through the gaming room to the buffet and breakfast. Beffle searched the bounteous counters and tables for her usual: orange juice, maple syrup, and grits. No grits. She took French toast and soaked it with syrup. As expected, Two Bears heaped his plate with grease food. At the table, he raised a toast to her. "Here's to you, Foul Owl."

She clicked her glass against his cup.

"And to you, Suet Puss."

Feeling warm feeling at home, silent, steeped in the rattle & ping muzak ringing in from the gaming room, they ate. Finished, Bear wiped grease off his mouth and said, "Around here, when people look back for the golden age, for Eden before the snake, they talk about a legendary past when the Mafia was in power. One guy, and these are his words, told me: 'You shoulda been here in the good old days when the mob ran things. It was crazy, nuts, fun! And no fucking crime. Except they'd find bodies in the desert, but that was family, and didn't give us no trouble."

"The Vegas economy! Can't be anything like it anywhere else in the whole world! They don't grow anything, they don't mine anything, nor do they make anything. No industry in Vegas but programmed computer greed!" She watched Bear devouring sausage. "What in all Hell do these people believe in?"

"Fun"

"Bullshit, Lard Face. Bullshit."

"I know what I believe in. So how about you? What do you believe in?"

"You mean as in socialism, anarchism, capitalism?" She looked at the grease congealing on his empty plate. "I guess I'm just like you. I don't believe in anything but . . . metabolism."

On the way out to Swifty, Bear said, "The chiefs around here seem to be smelling trouble." He explained that just in the area around Luxor there are more hotel rooms than in all of New Orleans. "And they want to keep them full." Beff and Bear got in and drove out onto the road. "I think they're planning some big changes."

"Like being honest."

"They're honest now. Being crooked would be bad for business, and, besides, they don't have to be crooked; the odds plus psychology gets them all the money, anyway." He accelerated. "They seem to think the family theme doesn't work any more, so they're going to concentrate on attracting high rollers. But times have changed. Now that casinos are rising up everywhere, they have to offer something extra, bait which ain't on the hook anywhere else. In the old days, in Paris, in New Orleans, and other places, too, places where capital felt safe, there were big, expensive, luxurious whore houses. In Nevada, everywhere but here in Clark County, and around Reno, bordellos are legal. On the highway, you look to the sides of the road for a red light, and if you see one and drive in, you'll find a quaint roadside cathouse. But imagine! A fifty million dollar pleasure dome alongside some palace like Caesar's! Who could compete with that! And they don't have to borrow from banks to do it. They build it with big dope profits like they have with a lot of other stuff around here. Just think of it! They build their sex palaces; the hard drug money is invested; the rooms are full again; and once more Vegas is years ahead of everybody else."

"You know what I think they should do with the dope money?"

"No. What?"

"Build fifty foot bronze statues of the founding fathers and mothers and erect them in front of City Hall. Bear! Picture it! See them standing there, fifty feet high! Bugsy Siegel. Meyer Lanski. Benny Binion. Elvis. Sinatra. Liberace. Marilyn Monroe. Sammy Davis Junior, Kerkorian, Wynn! And more!"

Swifty the Morgan had by now descended to a level where road signs no longer displayed bullet pox. Why is Bear reaching for his telephone? Is sign shooting a highland phenomenon? "Deer," said Bear to the phone, "in half an hour be alongside the Barbary Coast ready for Swifty."

"How'd you know he'd be in his room?"

"I told him to wait there."

"But we've been gone for hours. How could you be so sure he wouldn't go for breakfast or something?"

"Because he's reliable. He does everything I tell him to."

How can that be? It's almost as if Bear, this big greasy sweating bearded champion of all the Native Americans, has some kind of grip on David much stronger than a paycheck. It must be Deer's devotion to AIM extends to this man who means so much to financing an Indian revival.

And here we are, rolling along an ugly freeway, back in the horrible hideous heat.

And over there, Mount Charleston, almost twelve thousand feet! Ten thousand higher than here! Charles! Can't say that of him! Have to send him a post card. Of Mount Charleston. He never writes, never has. Always phones. Wish I could persuade him to write. Even e-mail. If the Morons can retrain him, why can't I!

"Beffle, riding along, safe from the all-hearing ear, I can tell you . . . I *have* to tell you, I still don't know what's going on. I'm beginning to see patterns, but nobody I've talked to has revealed any useful details which could give me a better idea of who's after our ass and why."

"Something I see, Bear, is it's not the Anglos who exploit the Indians, it's the worldwide power class which exploits both. You know, keeps us fighting each other so we don't notice them robbing us. The psychological lever is white supremacy; the fulcrum is fear. Look at me! A fucking halfbreed! Half Anglo, half Indian." That lie again! "Me, I'm supposed to have a civil war in my own heart!"

"I have to meet some folks this afternoon. At Bally's. You know, across the street from the Barbary Coast and cat-a-corner from Caesar's. I want you to come with me. And see what sense you can make out of it."

"All right. I'll be glad to." But not really glad. No. I don't really want to. When men are together with women, they cluster and ignore the women, don't listen, make them shut up. Hetaerae, geisha, Marilyn Monroe, are the models of proper feminine behavior. We pamper men en-route in airplanes; everywhere we serve them food, make their beds, cuddle them, preen them, fuck them, burp them, change their diapers. Two Bears? An exception? Fat chance! "Who's going to be there?"

"Don't want to tell you till after."

"Why not?"

"I want your rawest impressions, your inductions and deductions drawn exclusively from what you observe and hear there." The traffic had come to a full stop. "We are in deep shit. We have to shape a hypothesis about what's happening, the who and why of our enemies. They've been hitting you first to soften me, to teach me a lesson. Somebody wants a deal, and we could make a deal with the strongest. Or else, more likely, somebody wants to snuff us and take over our place. But we *won't* make a deal and we *will* survive. It's our idealism that makes us a target. That's my best guess. We are committed to building a financial structure for tribal renewal. That is our objective, our destination. And we will by God get there."

"How?"

"Barefoot, over broken glass."

Horns began sounding. Bear clapped Beff on the shoulder. "You're okay! We'll make it!" His hands began drumming the dashboard and he burst into song. "Frying on the freeway/ Going no-where today/ This's where we're gonna stay/ Frying on the freeway." The jam broke and they rolled ahead. "You see, the old Indian way worked. We sing to restore a broken harmony."

They slowed again.

She looked at the bleak mountains ranged behind the city.

And then at Mount Charleston on the other side.

She could see and taste the poisonous smog.

"We'll be late. You think Deer will wait?"

"Yes. Take my word for it."

"I want to see him."

"Why do you keep bringing him up?"

Tell him!

Why not?

"Because I have a crush on him."

Bear detonated into laughter.

'What's so fucking funny!"

"What's so funny?"

He laughed so hard people looked at them from other cars.

Bear controlled himself, then said: "David Running Deer is a flaming faggot."

"How the Hell do *you* know?"

"How do I know?" Chuckling, he shook his head. "Because David Running Deer is in love with *me*!"

With this big hairy slob?

"Poor bastard, it doesn't do him any good. It helps me, though. In dealing with him, I emphasize AIM, because AIM's his other passion. Consequently he does everything I tell him to. David Running Deer is the very spirit of robot obedience."

So, of course, was Swifty the Morgan. Bear drove him off the freeway down into the city streets, turned onto Flamingo, and went toward Las Vegas Boulevard and the Barbary Coast. "Hey, Foul Owl, did you know because of its brain chemistry, a crush can last two years?"

And there, just beyond the Bourbon Street, beside the Barbary Coast, by the door that opens on the registration desk and elevators, stood David Running Deer, as elegant and handsome as ever.

"I told you he'd be here."

They said hello, and slid out. David sat down behind the wheel, and gazed up fondly at Bear. Beffle gripped his shoulders. "Look at me!" He glanced at her, irritated. "I'll see you later," she said. Bear bent down and peered at David. "What you waiting for? Get the fuck out of here."

Swifty moved into traffic and vanished. "Beffle, did you know that because it's so long and thin, the lot this place sits on was going to be used for parking, until some smart architect came along and designed a hotel-casino that would fit." A number of shabby looking characters came over to them and began handing them flyers and tabloids. "Hey, Bear, look! This one says we can send strip-o-grams! Let's send a strip-o-gram to David."

Bear stuffed some of the papers into his back pocket.

"And this one! A whole page of sexpots where nobody has a name. They all have numbers! Like a book of artists' models."

More people pressed up to them, offering papers and leaflets.

"And dig this . . . !"

Abruptly, Beffle felt pain slice across the back of her wrist as with a powerful backhand swat Bear knocked a huckster flat.

Seizing her arm, he pulled her into the hotel door. An elevator was just opening. He pushed her inside and pressed 5. A gash on the back of her left wrist was oozing blood. "I saw the blade just in time. That guy was trying to *kill you.*"

Beffle felt as if she'd turned into liquid and she gasped and trembled. The elevator door opened, and they stepped out on five.

They stood there, perplexed.

They looked around.

Blood dripped slowly onto the carpet.

"Now what?" said Bear.

"Now . . . we go to my room."

NINE

BEFFLE UNLOCKED THE DOOR and led Bear inside. This is the first time I've ever seen him looking truly astonished. He sat down on a brass bed framed by a fringe of red-and-white calico curtains; she looked away from him at Buffalo Bill in the Wild West poster hanging on the red-and-tan striped wall, and then looked back. "Damn my eyes," quoth Bear. "You got yourself a hideout and you didn't tell me." She drew a clean handkerchief from her purse and took some tape from her disguise kit and sat at the table. "This is my goon-free territory." Bear stood and fetched a wet washcloth from the bathroom, tore up the handkerchief, and bandaged her wound. "Nothing your bruisers can save me from could be harder to endure than their company." She'd been cut, superficially, from the back of her forearm down to her hand. "George! That goddamned Roman!" Did they mean to slit my wrist? Bear sat down across from her. And I've never before seen him look so utterly dismayed. He slammed the table with a fist. "They knew I was coming to Bally's! They even knew when!" He peered into Beff's eyes. "But who the fuck are they?"

"Are you still going to go there?"

He set his phone on the table.

"No. I'll call and say I can't make it."

"And then what do we do?"

"I don't fucking know." He pinched some snuff from his tin. "Got any ideas?"

"Well we have a TV, and we have room service. Let's copy-cat Howard Hughes and stay here forever."

"Sounds like a plan"

Abruptly, she felt a rush of adrenaline energy, and stood, and looked down at him. "Bear, I'm going to go out and do some scouting."

"Scouting?"

"You stay here; I'll reconnoiter."

"In that yellow dress they can see you for a mile!"

"Die Frau in Gelb ist gegangen. *Kaput*."

She held the hem of her dress and curtseyed.

Then she peeled it off and began transforming herself into A.R. Naseby, floorman, spotter---- posing as a money-starved West Covina accountant. Two Bears watched, astonished, as she drew on white socks and running shoes, slipped into baggy green plaid shorts, and a loose long-sleeved Hawaiian shirt. "How's that for ugly?" She adjusted her western string tie with its silver-mounted turquoise clasp and brazen tips. "Now I'll go for hideous." She strapped on a purple fanny pack, leered at Bear as he burst into laughter, then, seated before the vanity mirror, she put on and adjusted the Beer Fairy mask, and crowned it all with the blond wig and cowboy hat. "Two Bears," said she in her rough Beer Fairy voice, "you are now in the presence of A. R. Naseby, fearless, deranged, money-hungry accountant, from West Co-vee-naa, CA."

"Well now, ain't *that* just fucking *special*? Trickster Beffle! You are Coyote him-herself!" He whooped with laughter. "Think I could wear your yellow dress?"

She walked to the door, and turned, beaming.

"How can you tell a Cherokee airplane? Give up? It has hair under the wings."

"You better come back before you have to piss."

She went into the hall and the door clicked behind her.

Now what?

Plunge in.

On leaving the elevator, she walked the length of the casino, through rattle-and-ping muzak that sounded like the machines, and out to Las Vegas Boulevard. Feeling a grind of arthritis, she crossed over, and went into a Roman temple and onto a people mover which afforded her a nice view of The Strip as it carried her into Caesar's. Somehow they'd forgotten to build a mover to carry people *out*. She walked down a grand marble staircase into a swamp of slots, and suddenly nervous and frightened, she stood still, watching the players as she tried to acclimate, to slip into her new role, not yet trusting the asylum provided by her Naseby armor. In old Venice-- at least according to some half-remembered book-- people often wore masks so they could safely walk the streets among their enemies. She studied a young longhair obsessively working a machine. There's the tit, and there's the child, but this child puts more back into its mother than it takes out. No chance any of *these* people will notice me.

So okay, Naseby: Do your stuff!

She was ranging among the machines, looking for a bar, when a roulette wheel caught her eye. Why not? The croupier stood by it, alone. She went over; he said hello, and she laid ten dollars on the black. "My politics are red, but my bets are always black."

He rolled the ball into the spinning wheel. "From the look of you, sir, I would have guessed differently." The ball rattled around and eventually dropped into a black number. She took the chips she'd won, and left, discovered the Olympia Bar, and seated herself. A built-in poker machine tempted in front of her. She ordered an orange juice in a way that would suggest she was a spotter in disguise. The bar, open to the casino floor, resembled a horseshoe with a bite out of its center where it abutted an immense column, one it would be easy to hide behind. She studied her two chips, felt them. They don't seem like money. They're infused with hypnotic magic! They cast a spell! She turned on her stool and looked back over the vast gaming floor. Two Bears had told her, typically, in Las Vegas, each slot nets more than a hundred thousand dollars a year. Vegas is so stupendously vulgar, it's beautiful; so surreal, it's realer than reality. The column caught her eye again. A hiding place. *Hiding place?* In the Ohlone Valley Casino, our eye-in-the-sky sees everything. We can monitor almost *any* conversation. And here! From their heavens, these guys can see every sparrow fall. They're omniscient and omnipresent. Omnipotent? History is the biography of power. Looking at it that way, the Roman theme, the other themes---- Egypt, pirates, carnivalia, cataracts, volcanoes, savage beasts, Brazil, Bagdad, South Seas, Wild West, outer space, King Arthur, showboats, Country-Western, the Chinese Empire, and their ubiquitous anachronisms, all of them interface. They are software applications compatible with the hard drive of now. A shocking fear that Naseby is transparent hit. I'm immensely alone and vulnerable. Sure. But isn't that life's secret truth?

They tried to kill me!

She gave the barman her chips for a roll of quarters.

The adrenaline had all seeped away and now there was nothing but cold and empty anxiety.

He cracked the roll and handed it to her.

She dropped a quarter in and began playing.

Soon it was just her and the poker machine.

The cards it shows, like the big red heart on the hearts, are the same design displayed on all the machines and are so beautiful even losing hands look good. That heart seems virtually *alive.* Roman music resembling Adeste Fideles and then Roman steam organs sounded in her imagination. I'm upset! She asked for more orange juice, and said *please*, a magic word they say is never said in Vegas, and she tipped the barman a *thanks* and a dollar for the free drink. Then she got a spade flush, a welcome boost to the credit number displayed before her, and she pushed the cash button and quarters rattled into the receptacle. They felt greasy, insubstantial, quite inferior in heft and texture to the silver quarters of yesteryear. Funny money! Government chips!

She caught herself reasoning whether or not to break a pair of jacks and draw two to a Royal.

Wait! Think! Naseby! Beffle! Cool it! You have to make plans, to dare and do!

Well, lose the ten dollars first.

As she bet and dealt and held and drew she began to appreciate the network of poker machines as an awesome accomplishment. Being, as it is, a product of all the sciences, hard and soft, of sophisticated engineering and computer expertise, of the arts, and of down and dirty criminal experience, it focuses the heritage of knowledge. It's designed and programmed to cause psychological errors. It is above all else, subtle.

Thinking that everything we know about life, embodied by immense capital, drives Vegas, she dropped in her last quarter, lost it, stood, and walked into the gaming room. This place is a focus of America. She trekked around

Rome in her Naseby skin till she came to the Galleria Bar where she settled at third base and ordered a double screwdriver. At a table near first base, deep in animated conversation sat Ace and George---- and Pearl!

Beneath the transparent Naseby skin and mask she felt herself naked, and in both thought and body fully visible to the spy in the sky. All right. Bear seems to be out of ideas. What to do? Leave town. How? No way to disguise Bear! Go where? Home? Her thoughts slid back to their casino. The cat's away, so the mice do play. The steadying influence of her constant vigilance removed, professional cheaters-- crossroaders-- would swarm in, and, even worse, dealers would steal more than ever. If only she could call Charley and get some independent, objective advice. The eagle must have had a good reason for dropping that feather to him. Call him. Meet him somewhere. Don't you wish! A phone call might be overheard, and, most likely, would interrupt him reading the *Book of Moron*, which Mark Twain had quite rightly referred to as chloroform in print. An arthritic pain touched her and she looked down at her ailing knee, exposed beneath the hem of her ugly green-plaid shorts, and observed neither the smooth skin of it nor its shape gave any indication of its infirmity. I'm still a nice piece of living flesh sculpture, body as good as ever, though beginning to rust away inside. George's voice boomed out from behind first base. "Fuck you, Pearl. It's a fact. At night, Vegas is the only city you can see from Mars!" That makes it some kind of center. An art center? Bear thinks the arts are happening here. Well, maybe. Architecture, in a few cases. That talking Bacchus is one Hell of a sculpture. Some shows. Maybe Vegas prefigures the arts we'll have after TV completes the pre-frontal lobotomy it's performing on our culture. She abruptly cringed from a strong sense the gaze of some spotter was fixed on her-- on Naseby that is-- and she thought that everywhere, even in the loo, her every movement could be and probably was seen by the authorities. Is this awareness but a new form of classical Native American thought? Two Bears said, traditionally, Indians sense they are continuously watched by unseen powers who surround them always. Aren't we eternally submerged in modulated electromagnetic impulse? On the bar by her glass video poker spread a beguiling hand and flashed invitations. Isn't this a visible manifestation of the spirit of its electronic net? She bought another roll of quarters and, vowing not to hazard it, she cracked it open.

And then David Running Deer walked in.

Responding to some cybernetic call to duty?

He said something to Ace, then, as graceful and elegant as ever, approached and sat nearby at the bar.

Beffle-Naseby asked the barkeep, who at the moment was arranging bottles across from her, to bring David a beer.

David accepted it and smiled.

Beffle-Naseby smiled back.

Welcoming this chance to test the verisimilitude of Naseby, she pocketed her quarters, rose, and, carrying her drink, went over to Running Deer.

"I'm feeling lonely. May I join you?"

"Oh? Yes, please do."

She introduced herself as Charles, a fallen-away Latter Day Saint.

"I'm David Running Deer, pureblood Blackfoot."

"Me, I'm a mongrel, a mixture of European tribes plus some mystery ingredients. I love being here in Vegas where I don't know anybody and can do what I feel like doing."

David smiled.

"Same here, Charles. Where I work in California, and in Carmel where I live, it seems sometimes as if *everybody* knows me. I'm in a fishbowl. I don't know if in a real bowl the guppies and all their fancy friends miss their privacy, like well, we can't do what we want because everybody's watching, but me, I sure as Hell can't."

"Try being a Mormon in a small town. They even lift the covers to see if you're jacking off! Believe me, these days I masturbate all the time, for revenge, for . . . for joy and Jehovah."

"Me, I've never been to Vegas before, but I'm tempted to buy a house and move here. I could get a job, easy. But it gets so dog-gone hot! You'd have to stay inside all summer. Somewhere air-conditioned. So you sit around your house, and go crazy, or you stay cool in the casinos, and gamble, and pretty soon you don't *have* a house."

"And you eat and eat and eventually croak in some Coronary Buffet."

"On the road, approaching Vegas, I thought I'd hate it. I hate gambling, and still do, but I sure like the freedom this place provides to be one's self."

Beff made Naseby smile and nod assent.

David ordered more drinks.

Beff said thanks and raised a toast.

"Charles," he said, "I heard the funniest goddamned story today. And several people said it's *true.* Okay. You know those progressive slot machines are all connected-- Reno, here, everywhere in Nevada, they're all hitched to a central computer which builds enormous jackpots, payable to whoever wins with five quarters. If you hit it with less than five, the payoffs are much smaller. So into Caesar's comes this guy and his wife of many years. He's looking at a machine announcing a jackpot of over three million bucks.

His spirit keeper-- it's got to be Coyote, tells him the next play on that slot is *it*. They only have three quarters between them, so he tells his wife to wait there, hold the machine, while he goes for more. She waits, and gets bored, and plays the three quarters. It hits! She only wins a hundred grand or so. All the honking and flashing and sirens attract a mob of celebrants who congratulate her. Her old man comes running, and he shoulders right through the crowd, and smashes her in the face, and knocks her flat. He starts kicking her, and the bystanders peel him off, and the cops come, and take him away. His old lady bails him out, and what do you suppose happens then?"

"It's gotta be that to defend him from all the felony charges, they spend the rest of their lucky win on lawyers."

Deer laughed and Naseby laughed in her Beer Fairy voice, and Deer said, "You got it! That's what they told me." What a charmer this guy is! "Charley," he said. "How's this sound. You and me, let's go to a show. I heard about a place where they have dynamite female impersonators."

"Drag queens?"

"Precisely."

"That's something I ought to try."

"You've got a good body. With a nice wig and good makeup, you could be a beauty-- a mature beauty."

"I've often thought of having a go at it."

"It's fun. You'd like it."

"Did you ever do it?"

"Sure. I look great in a dress."

"I think I would too."

"So let's call and see when the show starts. We can go over in a cab."

How to finesse this new complication? He's *glowing* warmth. Yes, *affection*. Me too! She sensed her crush taking possession as if it were some external animal spirit. With it came a jealous rage against Two Bears. "You know, I think my magic helper is Coyote."

"What do you know about Coyote?"

"I like to read about Indians."

"Good! We'll finish our drinks, and go phone."

Beffle felt her resolve melting away. I've got to concentrate on our problem, and on being Naseby, and hurry back to Bear.

A Roman soldier appeared beside her. Then Ace. And *Pearl*.

What now?

Gotta be polite and socialize.

Gotta go!

Where?

"Hey Running Deer," said George, clapping David on the shoulder. "Where the fuck is Bambi?"

"Bambi?"

"You know. That cunt lapping movie deer."

"*Book* deer," said Beffle. "Bambi was a book deer first."

"Who the fuck are you?"

"I, sir, am an accountant. A general accountant. A philosophical accountant to whom you are accountable. I add up your good deeds and subtract your sins and torment you with the bottom line. I am your conscience."

"I, asshole, am the Wandering Jew. I can imitate Irving, play poker and pool, and strum on the Spanish guitar. I'm over two thousand years old and I've been everywhere and I know everything and then some." George slammed his helmet down on the bar and its plume trembled. "And I don't have no conscience."

"How about Mithra?"

"How the fuck you know about Mithra?"

"Most Roman soldiers worship Mithra."

Deer peered at him. "Who's this Mithra?"

George glanced at Pearl, then glared at him. "No woman may know our mysteries."

"Why not, honeybunch," Pearl asked. "Why not?"

"Because women bleed from the wound that never heals. They're slime and squalor."

"I can dig that," said Ace. "George's going to show me his grotto. Mithra's for fighters, not whining wimps, or bags of lard like you."

"Listen to Ace," said George.

"And what's under your beetle shell, sweetie?" Pearl rapped his armor. "Fat. Lard. Tons of it. Or have you forgotten last night already?"

"Drink up," said George. "Next round's on me." The drinks came. "And you, Running Deer. You want to see my grotto?"

Deer, damn him to Hell, seems interested!

Another crush birthing?

"Excuse me," Naseby-Beffle said, "I have to go to the gents."

"What's this gents shit? You mean you going to piss?"

"I . . . am . . . going . . . to . . . the . . . *gents.*"

"He don't mean no harm," said Pearl. "He's just drunk."

Waving a hand, Beff turned and walked away. Yes. Now back to Bear! Keep a low profile. Blend into the autonomous masses. Go. Go. Go! Arthritis in her knee twitched then grated and as there were no seats but those before the slots or at the tables, she sat down in front of a cumulative machine. Coyote whispered in her ear: Play it.

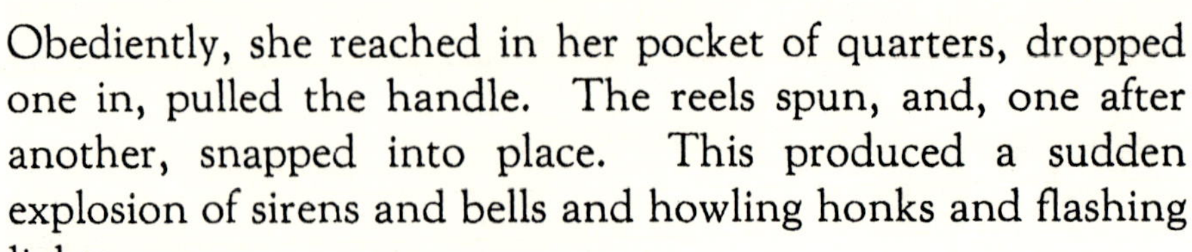

Obediently, she reached in her pocket of quarters, dropped one in, pulled the handle. The reels spun, and, one after another, snapped into place. This produced a sudden explosion of sirens and bells and howling honks and flashing lights.

Keeeerist! The jackpot!

Oh boy Naseby here comes your ultimate test!

Abruptly Naseby-Beffle found herself at the center of a swarm of joyful jealous celebrants. Among them stood George and Deer and Ace and a braying whooping Pearl.

A pit boss appeared and with a gesture hushed them all and said to her and the crowd, "The house takes great pleasure in congratulating this gentleman. He just won two thousand four hundred and twenty-two dollars. With *one* single solitary quarter." And there next to him stood the Twins. Beffle embraced one and whispered: "I'm Beffle, in disguise and in trouble and needing help. Meet me in twenty minutes at the bar at Bourbon Street, just up the block from the Barbary Coast." The Twin said, "Okay mister," and the pit boss said Naseby'd have to come with him to the office for the payoff. "We've got to take care of some paper work and red tape." In the office they met an agent of the Internal Revenue Service who gave Naseby a form to complete. It demanded her full name. Address---- and social security number. Ohhhhhhhh . . . . "Mister, I don't remember my number."

"They can't pay you if you don't give it to us." He seemed to take her ignorance of the sacred number as a personal affront. "We collect a twenty-five percent tax right now, and we have to have the paper work to keep your account in order and give you the proper credit."

"But I don't remember my number! Am I supposed to tattoo it on my arm or something?"

"You have to give it to me, or he can't pay you."

"My wallet's out in my car, along with my drivers' license. The number's in there. I'll go get it and come right back."

They agreed and she rushed out of the office, out to the boulevard, across, and along Flamingo Road by the place where she'd been attacked and on to the corner. She went into Bourbon Street to the bar and ordered a Jaegermeister advertised as on tap. Will they come? Imagine! Longing for the Twins! She noticed, like all other casinos, the place had no windows or clocks. No night, no day, no hurtling time. And she chugged her drink, and ordered another, and then there they were, the Twins, striding in the door.

"Beff! Don't you look like something the cat dragged in!"

"That's how I feel, too."

"Dragged in. *Drag*, Beffle. *Drag*! Get it?"

"Yes, fart face, I get it."

"Did you get your money?"

"No. If you don't know your SS number, the casino's an Indian giver."

"Beffle, it's the thought that counts."

Beffle stood and put her arms around their shoulders. "I need your help. I've no one else to turn to." She showed them her wound and made up a Mafia story to go with it. "When you leaving for Monterey?"

"Today, tomorrow."

"Bear and me, they're trying to kill us. We have to leave town. They seem to be hip to everything we do. We're afraid to go anywhere around here. I'm in disguise; Bear's hiding in my room at the Barbary Coast."

"Hell with Bear. Look at the way he treated us."

"He's my boss. My livelihood."

"So okay, pal. What can we do?"

"Here's some money. You can go buy two motorcycle helmets-- an extra large and a medium, then in exactly two hours from now, be on your bikes waiting outside the first door to the Barbary Coast, the one where the elevators are. Bear and I will come out, don the helmets, get on your buddy seats, and ride behind you to our place in Carmel Valley. And you can stay in our hotel, and go over to Laguna Seca in style. Yes! You can ride over there in our Rolls that used to belong to the Sultan of Morocco."

"Sounds good to me," said a Twin.

"Me too," said the other. "We'll strip Bear and have an ogre orgy."

Beffle left them at the bar, and went back to her room. On the way she decided to say to Bear: "I've been wildly romantic whilst you've been yawning through your dull Howard Hughes day." But, when he saw her, Two Bears shook his head and burst out laughing. "Goddamned if you aren't a sight!"

"Like something the cat dragged in?"

"You can say that again."

"Get it, Lardface? *Drag*?

"As in drag King?"

"She sailed her Texas hat into a corner. I can't wait to get home."

"In good time." He slacked into a chair. "I've been sitting here, opening my spirit to what my mother used to tell me about darkness and light and how all on earth was dark until Grandmother Spider made a long journey to the land of the greedy sun people. She stole a piece of the sun, and brought it back for us. That's how we received light and warmth."

"Not so."

"Oh yeah!" He walked to the bed and sat again and leaned back against the brass head frame. "Out there, did you learn anything?"

"I learned your mother had it all wrong. A hideous wicked selfish man locked all the light of the world into a box. Coyote heard about it. Grandmother Spider told him. Every morning he creeps into the man's house, and opens the box. Every night the evil light-miser stuffs it all back and locks it in. And that, my friend, is why we have sunrise and sunset, day and night."

"Okay. Have it your way." Wearily he stood. "Did you learn anything?"

She told him the whole story.

"And now to get ready." She pulled the belt out of Naseby's shorts and snapped it. "I brought my money belt, Bear. Did you bring yours?"

"Hell, yes. My plastic, too."

Beffle put her belt back on. It was fat with currency. "You're about to become a blond Indian." She opened her makeup kit and dyed his hair. "And now for Dream Time with our animal helpers, Fauna and two Harley riding-hogs. Flora, too." She shaved his beard. "It's about five hundred miles to Carmel Valley. We should be home by breakfast time."

"We're not going home. We're going to Connecticut."

"Connecticut!"

"We're going to the airport at Ontario, and then we'll wing to some transfer point like Denver or Chicago, then on to Windsor Locks, Connecticut, near Hartford, where we'll rent a car."

"We're going to go home, and work out a plan, and do it."

"We're going to Mashantucket and the casino and see what we can learn and try to put something together."

"No. Carmel. My studio. That's where I want to be. I'm tired of being pushed around. And I don't like Connecticut. I've never been there and I don't want to go there."

"You're talking like a fucking *pluke*."

"A *what?*"

"A goddamned dot-com *tourist*."

"And you're a squealing male chauvinist *Cherokee*."

"And you're a crybaby! You're fucking *homesick*." He went to the mirror. "Well, I'll be double damned if you haven't made an Anglo out of me! But, what the fuck. Some of the Pequots are blond, too. And I know a couple of them who came to our place." He glanced at his watch. "Let's go." He walked ahead to the elevators. I'm following him *again*. Is that what being female means? Foxwoods! The biggest casino in the Western Hemisphere. He knows a lot more about all this than I do. Home? Foxwoods? The Twins will do what *I* tell them. Out of the elevators, back into the blazing heat. And there they are! Engines throbbing! Now, tell them. "You guys, there's been a change of plan. We're going to Ontario airport, near L.A." He slapped her back. "These bikes should be *Indians*." They swung up onto their seats. "When we get there," said Bear, tugging on his helmet, "I'll write you comps for food and rooms and a ride in our Rolls."

The Harleys rumbled up to the boulevard, and turned right, and passed an artificial cataract in what once had been desert, and raced up onto the freeway. Good-bye Vegas. Vegas, good-bye! Farewell! to a bizarre world where two-thirds of the populace feeds on the gambling biz! They overtook a traffic jam and rushing between the cars, swiftly slipped through. Ontario's only about two hundred and thirty miles away. Abruptly they left the irrigated city and plunged into the Mohave. Five hours at the most. Soon they were speeding along in light traffic under drifting cotton clouds. The sun set, and in the pure night sky the stars shone as brightly as Liberace's sequins.

As ever, thought Beffle, I'm wandering off into the future.

PART FOUR

Any one of us who looks carefully into the mirror sees what? Coyote! That's what!

--Beffle a.k.a. Foul Owl
Mashantucket, CT, 2003.

TEN

RACING ALONG THROUGH the clear warm night on a virtually deserted highway, Bear and Fauna, those two animals riding close ahead, sang out loud and fragments of what they sang came drifting back to Beffle, songs she knew because Bear often crooned them, so for a while she sang along, hoping in accord with Indian tradition her singing would help maintain the general harmony.

But if such is Bear's purpose, he sure makes strange choices!

Blue Corn Fry Bread!

In revenge, she sang the Lakewood High *Alma Mater* song.

Flora screeched it from the driver's saddle.

And of course Bear pays no attention.

Because he's ahead where he can't see or hear us.

He's imagining that instead of me behind him he leads an immense Cherokee army, sustained by gambling money, on the way to sack and burn L.A.

And me, I'm following still.

But he's yet to sing a war song.

The moon rose and gleamed close overhead like an alien casino on a space cruise for the flying saucer people.

Full moon!

The Twins turned off their headlights and they raced along the freeway abreast of their speeding moonshadows.

Bits and fragments of Two Bear song drifted over to her.

Old Howard's dead and gone,
Left me here to sing his song;
Old Howard's dead and gone,
Left me here to
Sing
His
Song!

Over and over and over and then:

Boiling cabbage down down;
Turn the hoecake round round;
The onliest song I can sing is
Boiling Cabbage Down.

Over and over and over as the Harley wheels went round and round and round.

Justice!

To each his own!

Indian cycles for Indians!

But Indian motorcycles are dead and gone: extinct.

And I'm still following that fucking Cherokee.

And still pretending I'm half Huron and half Irish.

Still deceiving him.

And following along behind him.

Maybe that's why Feral Frank used to scowl at me sometimes and say in the new world of his invention every parent would have the right to kill one child.

And they raced through the beauty of the warm night.

And she watched Two Bear's broad moonlit back.

And I'm following an Indian who's determined to go to Connecticut.

And unite all Indians.

Bear's homesick for classical Indian times.

Clio, Bear's name for history, interrupted her thoughts by pronouncing Connecticut in the classical manner.

"*Quoneh-ta-cut.*"

Should I tell him the truth?

About my ancestors in the war of 1637, sixteen generations ago, Eliots and Ludlows and Masons and their comrades, virtually exterminating the Pequots.

At the University of California, Berkeley, in an attempt to learn the truth about these forebears, encouraged by Feral Frank but not by her mother, she'd written her senior paper on the Pequot Wars.

Forebears.

For-bears.

Four Bears.

Trying for context, she sank into the story before 1620 when the first English settled, and after trimming off as much as possible, she wrote about the Pequots in 1610 being driven out of the Hudson Valley by the Mohawks of the Iroquois Confederacy. The Pequots forced their way to the Connecticut River and then fought down through the river tribes to its mouth where they invaded and occupied a large piece of territory belonging to the Niantics. Next, they subjugated all the neighboring tribes, save for the largest, the Narragansetts to the east in Rhode Island, with whom they remained perpetually at war. Then came European invaders. The Dutch bought a piece of land from the Pequots, who owned it by right of conquest, and established a trading post. Shortly afterward, Puritans from Plymouth, followed by more from the new settlements at Boston, established four villages on the Connecticut. One of these, Saybrook, at the river's mouth, they fortified. By 1636-- only sixteen years after the Pilgrims stepped ashore on Plymouth Rock-- the 2,200 Pequots were confronted on the

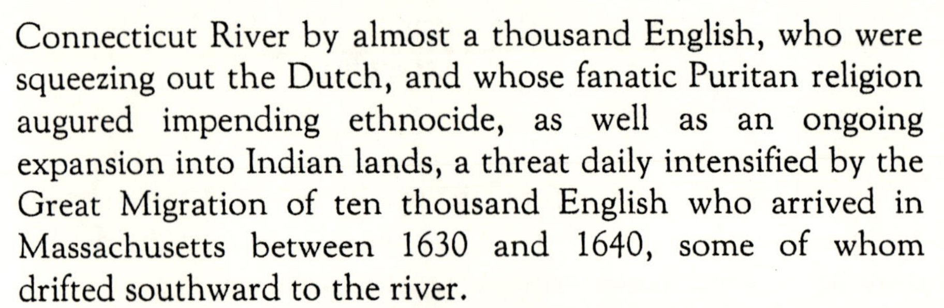
Connecticut River by almost a thousand English, who were squeezing out the Dutch, and whose fanatic Puritan religion augured impending ethnocide, as well as an ongoing expansion into Indian lands, a threat daily intensified by the Great Migration of ten thousand English who arrived in Massachusetts between 1630 and 1640, some of whom drifted southward to the river.

In 1636, Indians from Block Island, clients of the Pequots, boarded a trading pinnace, and, with a hatchet, split its captain's head. In response, the Bay Colony sent ninety men to kill all the men on Block Island, and then go to the Pequots and demand wampum, hostages, and custody of those guilty of previous murders. At Block Island, the Indians fled, and the English smashed their canoes, torched their wigwams, stole and burned their corn, and took souvenirs, mainly mats and baskets. Then, having tired of negotiating while the Pequots hid their goods, the English landed and once again burned wigwams and wrecked canoes. The troops went back to Boston, leaving the Connecticut towns to absorb the wrath of the Pequots, who, immensely provoked, began waging guerrilla war. Pequots killed livestock and burned houses; they ambushed soldiers working fields around Saybrook Fort; they attacked boats on the river and killed their crews. One man taken gathering hay, they roasted alive. Others, they tortured to death. By spring of 1637, the settlers and soldiers could not hunt, fish, farm, or travel in safety. They went everywhere armed and feared formation of a union of tribes, sponsored by the Pequots and, perhaps, sustained by the Dutch. So powerful was the appeal for solidarity in resistance that even the Narragansett were tempted to join in a common effort to drive out the English.

While researching her paper, immersing herself in the times and their story evoked nightmares which on occasion tormented her still. In one of these soldiers, who Beffle now thought resembled George, uproot and trample the Three Sisters-- Corn, Beans growing up Corn's stalks, and Squash maturing between Corn's rows-- whilst others smash canoes and burn wigwams and stockpiles, a tactic meant to cause suffering and produce famine. To this the Pequots replied with a campaign of terror, ruin, and murder. A hideous dream that haunted her still derived from a day and an evening of reading in the stacks of the university library. A shipmaster and companion are floating in a canoe on placid water, fowling along a wooded shore. The master mariner fires his piece; before he can reload some Pequots leap aboard, kill his comrade, and seize him. They tie him to a stake, slowly *flay* him, thrust hot embers into his flesh, cut off his fingers and toes. It takes him hours to die, and he does so in utter silence, earning their respect. In another dream, three men in a shallop are beset by several Indians in canoes. After a hot fight in which one dies, the other two are captured. Both are cut in two from the legs to the head, then hung by the neck from trees by the riverside.

Speeding through the moonlit night, imagining ancestors who looked like Feral Frank and his close relatives living this life, bound now many generations later to confront the Pequots again, Beffle, aware of the context, slipped back into the Dream Time of 1636-1637, where projected in the theater of her mind, from her position on the parapet of the palisade at Saybrook Fort, she sees three Pequot canoes on their way back to Pequot Harbor from a lethal raid on Wethersfield displaying from poles as pennants fragments of English clothes.

By the time of this precipitating incident the Pequots and their allies had killed about thirty settlers. The General Court of the Connecticut villages, meeting at Hartford, declared war on the Pequots and began raising troops and gathering their provisions. On 10 May of 1637, after assembling almost one-half of the able-bodied men from the three towns, some ninety of them plus seventy Indians, mostly Mohegans led by Uncas, who some years before in Plymouth had been the guest of honor at the first Thanksgiving dinner and now was a disappointed rival for the chieftainship of the Pequots, this war party, commanded by Captain John Mason, embarked and sailed toward Saybrook Fort where it would become part of the punitive expedition. After several delays resulting from running aground, Uncas requested his comrades be set ashore so they could proceed overland. These men arrived at Saybrook first, whence they sallied forth and returned with five Pequot heads and a captive scout.

Uncas insists the scout be put to death in the traditional manner.

The English judge it imprudent to interfere.

They allow Uncas to proceed.

The Indians kindle a bonfire.

And they grasp their enemy and by brute force tear off his arms and legs.

And they cut his flesh into pieces and passing it from man to man, they devour it as they sing and dance around the blazing, crackling bonfire. And then they toss the bones and scraps into it.

Beffle held tightly onto Flora as these Thanksgiving images reeled through her head and the motorcycle plunged into the warm moonlight. An ache, a dull *truth* ache, seized hold of her, swelled through her, intensified, began to clot.

I've got to tell Bear.
For my own self.
He'll *fire* me.
And I'll be left to face my danger alone.
Is someone *stalking* me?
Maybe he'll beat me up, or worse.
I have to tell him.

Back in Dream Time, the expedition assembles and embarks once more, its saintly Puritans black and white as if costumed for some Thanksgiving pageant, its Indians blood red in scarlet plumes and crimson paint. *Redmen.* The war party lands behind the Pequots on Narragansett Bay, receives permission from the Narragansett chief to pass through his territory, and advances to a palisaded Narragansett fort on the frontier. Here about five hundred boastful Narragansetts from the fort and elsewhere join Captain Mason's force, but, on progressing into Pequot territory, begin to desert. After trudging twelve miles they come to a ford where the Pequots often fish, and about three miles beyond, arrive at a newly planted cornfield. That evening they move silently ahead through moonlight, come to a swamp between two hills where Groton now stands, and camp. Close ahead, Pequots revel in their palisaded town. The expedition's advanced sentries can hear them singing and rejoicing and insulting the English, for they'd seen the pinnaces sailing by some days before, and now believe the English dare not fight.

Soon after daylight, the English swiftly hike two miles to the hill where the palisaded village stands, its back to the Mystic River. Inside are clusters of wigwams sheltering the fighters' families and stores. The two entrances are blocked with brush piles. The raiders divide their forces so they can attack both openings at once. Silently, the advance begins.

When Mason's men are within twenty feet of their objective a dog barks. Then a startled voice cries out: "Owanux! Owanux!" which is Algonquian for "English!" Rushing up, the men fire a volley through gaps in the palisade, then follow the bear-like Mason over the breast-high brush pile. The surprise is absolute. The Pequots are sound asleep, then fuzzily awake, groping for weapons. But too late. Meeting no one at the entrance, Mason strides into the first wigwam, fights off some men who jump him, killing one, then marches down the street toward the other approaching force. Pequots in between shoot arrows which are deflected by English armor, and they scatter. Mason, convinced his troops cannot prevail without changing tactics, shouts, "We must burn them!" and snatches a brand from inside the first wigwam and sets fire to the dry mats covering it. It blazes; other fires start; the conflagration spreads; the Pequots panic; the English withdraw and surround the fort. Some Indians climb the palisade, others dash into the flames; many of them gather to leeward and shoot arrows while the English reply with bullets. About forty men come running out in a hopeless attack and are cut down with swords.

No quarter was given, even to women and children. More than six hundred Pequots died, seven were taken, and seven escaped. Of the English, two were slain, about fifty wounded.

"Thus," wrote Captain Mason, "did the Lord judge among the Heathens, filling the place with dead Bodies!"

Harassed by Pequot fighters from another fort, the small army marched hence to Pequot Harbor, where they were to and did meet their ships. The English began occupying the Pequot country. The crippled Pequots reorganized as best they could; many took refuge in the woods. The settlers, set on obliterating the Pequot tribe, brought together one hundred and sixty English, two hundred Narragansetts, and Uncas' fighters in a new army. This force found a band of miserable, famished fugitives in a swamp near Groton, reserved eighty women and children for bondage, killed eighteen men, and spared two sub-chiefs, whom they later beheaded. They then met and defeated the remaining Pequots in the Great Swamp Fight, whence most survivors, including the premier chief, fled to the Mohawks. After this, the English went home, but the Mohegans and the Narragansetts hunted down scattered bands, frequently bringing gory heads to the Puritans at Hartford and Windsor. Soon the Mohawks killed the premier chief and sent his scalp to Hartford whence representatives carried a piece of the chief's skin and a lock of his hair to Boston to display to the Bay Colony's chiefs as tokens of the death of their enemy. This inspired Massachusetts, Connecticut, and Rhode Island, to celebrate a day of joyous thanksgiving and prayer

Determined to extirpate the Pequot tribe from memory, the English blotted out the tribal name and divided the tribal lands between Connecticut and Massachusetts. The survivors were forever banished from their country. The captive women and children were given as spoils of war to the troops. Some were sold in the West Indies as slaves. When the remnant of the tribe surrendered-- only about two hundred of one thousand adult males survived-- they were amalgamated with the Mohegans and Narragansetts. The Pequot River became the Thames; Pequot Harbor, New London.

And the Reverend John Eliot took in an English-speaking adolescent, captured while visiting Pequots, from whom he learned Algonquian. Eliot then translated the Bible into the local language and preached in it so effectively as to convert enough Indians to populate new villages. Hence the Praying Indians and, in all, what Beffle's paper identified as the true beginning of ethnocide in New England.

And now, she marveled, as the moon set and Flora's Harley sped up into the Sierra Nevada, the Narragansetts have built a casino to compete with the Pequots.

How would this, as both fact and symbol, affect the balance of centripetal and centrifugal forces swirling in Bear's dream of Indian unity?

And how will his dream be affected if my posturing as an Indian is exposed?

Tell him!

And resign?

But he needs me!

Preoccupied with this dilemma, her mind's ear heard Bear calling her O'Squaw and McSquaw and FitzSquaw, a friendly mockery of an ostensibly Irish-Huron woman that in fact cut into her profoundest sensibilities. The Harleys rushed through Cajon Pass and down down down toward a hot flat L.A. County winking a billion lights, a mirror of the sky above. They passed by San Bernardino and turned off of I-15 at the Arrow Highway, and rumbled west to Cucamunga, south on Haven Avenue by the Brookside Winery to the airport and drew up before the terminal. Beffle and Bear swung stiffly off their buddy seats and Bear wrote out an order to give the Twins a complementary suite and anything else they might request. He then gave Fauna a fifty dollar bill.

"So, what's that for?"

"Your gas."

"Didn't cost nearly that much."

"So have a drink on me."

"Okay."

"It's not really on me."

"So who the fuck's it on?"

"All those fools who bring their dirty money to the Ohlone Valley Cleaners."

With a whoop and a screech the Twins raced away. For a moment, Beffle and Bear stood outside the terminal, feeling the promise of a hot humid morning. "Bear, the Ohlone used to get up before sunrise, and sing to the sun, and urge it to come back, and shout greetings when it did. And then have acorn mush for breakfast." Soon they were watching the day glow dawning behind the mountains, and then the sun in all its glory burst over the top. "Beff, the Ohlone think Coyote created the Earth." Once inside, they bought tickets with a transfer at Chicago, and sat down by the variety store. Bear bought the *Los Angeles Times* and Beffle's glance roamed over the magazine covers displayed on the rack. Except for a few animals and middle-aged political chiefs, the covers showed Nordic Anglos, mainly beautiful, all of them between eighteen and forty. That brought to mind the photos of the members of the San Francisco Symphony Orchestra arrayed on a lobby wall of S.F.'s Performing Arts Center. Anglos, all, save for a few Asians. No blacks. No Cherokees, no Hurons, no Ohlones, no Blackfeet, no Mohawks, no Narragansetts, and no *Pequots*!

Who says White Supremacy's not alive and well and in the saddle?

She pointed it out to Bear as they rose to board their plane, and he said one reason the remaining Pequots had been ill treated in recent times is that some of their families intermarried with blacks. They slept all the way to Chicago where, drowsily, they walked into the waiting room. Bear made a phone call, and then they began a long trip on

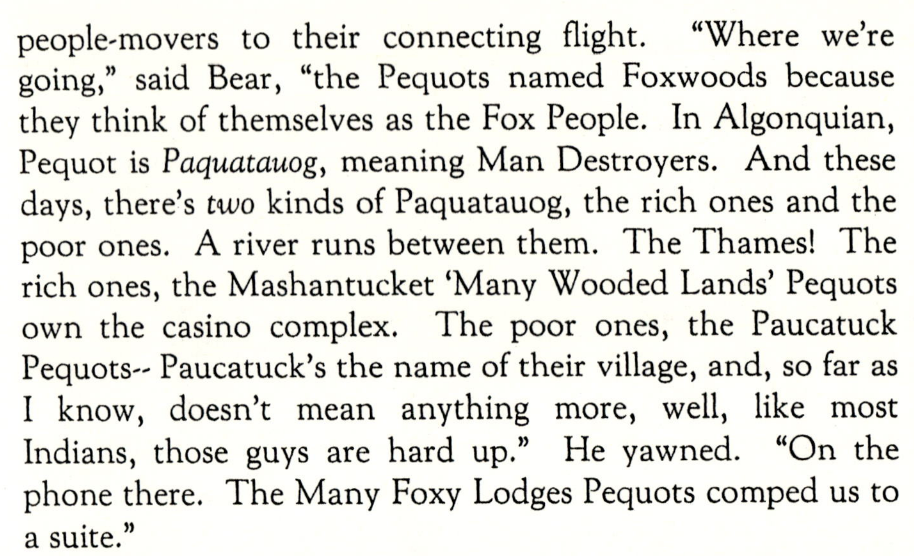

people-movers to their connecting flight. "Where we're going," said Bear, "the Pequots named Foxwoods because they think of themselves as the Fox People. In Algonquian, Pequot is *Paquatauog*, meaning Man Destroyers. And these days, there's *two* kinds of Paquatauog, the rich ones and the poor ones. A river runs between them. The Thames! The rich ones, the Mashantucket 'Many Wooded Lands' Pequots own the casino complex. The poor ones, the Paucatuck Pequots-- Paucatuck's the name of their village, and, so far as I know, doesn't mean anything more, well, like most Indians, those guys are hard up." He yawned. "On the phone there. The Many Foxy Lodges Pequots comped us to a suite."

On the next plane, Bear sprawling in the seat beside her asleep, Beffle thought her Puritan ancestors would have regarded being comped like that as a Providence. She went limp and tried to nap and she felt closure in her swiftly approaching rendezvous with the Pequots after a delay of some sixteen generations. Writing that paper, as Feral Frank doubtless intended when he suggested it, had disabused her of the weighted and cleansed story served up to her in grade school. The men she'd met in her research were not the saintly Pilgrims of Mayflower pageant, of November show & tell. Nor was Uncas the God-sent Good Samaritan whose corn and wild turkeys saved the Pilgrims from starvation. Daydream carried her back to the Swamp Fight and the Great Swamp Fight where the holy armored English, in exchanges of lead bullets and stone-tipped arrows, had finally crushed the Pequot's fighters, and then in concert with their allies hunted down and killed all the Fox people they could find. And now Pequots are comping an Eliot-Mason to a luxury suite! Surely, the tales that Clio tells are written by Coyote.

And I used to take sides!

Carry my musket as in imagination I walked with my ancestors through the snow to church!

And I used to believe history in America begins in 1492!

Suddenly she became aware of an urge to piss.

Procrastination.

A *need* to piss.

God but I hate airplanes!

Lines had formed by the toilets.

She joined one and anxiously shifted from foot to foot as the pressure swelled and in an awful daymare movie piss flowed down her legs pooling on the floor. But as always she reached the pot in time and sat there, comfortable at last. She sensed the plane settling down at the brink of the world. I'm running away from something, but am I running toward something worse? When on the brink of the world nothing can make sense save for listen to the music and *dance.* And let the next in line have the pot. Back in her seat, she looked across Bear out the window at towns and fields and bosky woods as the airplane sank toward earth. Joining in the stampede of plane-haters leaving the plane, she saw waiting in the crowd beyond the exit point a blond youth holding a sign lettered in green: **JAMES TWO BEARS JONES.** "Look there, Bear. One of the noble savage Fox People come to greet you."

"Could be."

"No Indian looks like that."

"To be a tribesman here, you only have to prove one-sixteenth of your blood is Pequot. Even so, they only have about six hundred members, some of whom were originally Narragansetts. And they have almost twelve thousand workers. What the Hell. Same thing's true with us. I had to hire private detectives to find enough Ohlones to make a tribe, and even then, most proved to be Mutsun. We need more? In most tribes it's traditional to adopt whomever you please as a full member. You, for example. We could adopt you." They walked up to the smiling youth. "Are you Two Bears?" the young man asked.

"Yes. And you?"

"Billy. I don't have an Indian name. I'm a townie."

Billy led outside to a white limo and opened the back door for them. Soon they were speeding to the southeast along Route 2. "How far is it?" asked Bear.

"About an hour." Billy glanced back. "You guys from Chicago?"

"California."

"A state where you never see your breath," said Beffle.

"I'm from California, too, folks, so I guess you're not used to being in a place as small as Connecticut. No point in this state is more than two hours away from any other." In about forty minutes Billy made a phone call, and, soon after, turned off onto a lesser thoroughfare leading through a ragged cedar forest. Then, suddenly, abruptly, looming ahead at the end of this yellow brick road, appeared what looked to Beffle like Oz itself. "Some surprise, eh?" said the cheerful youth. "We have three hotels, the newest with that tower, two casinos, a huge Pequot museum, a virtual reality theater, a monorail, a sports-book center, two golf courses, a tribal community complex, arcades for Indian craft work, restaurants of all kinds, a bingo hall, a five-thousand seat concert arena, archives, a library, labs, classrooms, and much much more!" The buildings, all of them off-white, seemed almost wholesome in their livery of the tribal colors: wampum lavender trim and tule-duck bluish green steel roofs. The young chauffeur came to a stop before the grand entry and opened their door. A lumpy well-dressed man approached as the limo rolled away. "Two Bears!"

"Laughing Fox!"

They embraced, stood apart, smiling. "This is my colleague, Foul Owl," said Bear. "And, Owl, this is my old friend, Laughing Fox, a man who finds much of his time given to laughing all the way to the bank. He's the kind of guy who'd put a whoopee cushion on the electric chair."

"And as for your colleague, here, *Two Bears*. He's my favorite cacaphage."

And as for me, she thought, I'm his favorite flimflam fake and phony, but he doesn't know it.

At the door, bowing to Beffle, Fox said, "Welcome, Owl, to the Mashantucket Pequot Nation and our High Stakes Bingo & Casino Center." Beffle smiled and he escorted them into the familiar rattle and honk of home. Anglo women in Indian miniskirts and feathered hair circulated with change carts and drinks; men in wampum-trimmed tunics conducted the games. Fox led onward into the Atrium.

"Foul Owl," said their host, "Two Bears tells me you're part Huron."

When did he tell him that?

"Here's something you'll appreciate, Ms Owl. Our Rainmaker."

As the atrium's centerpiece, poised on ersatz rocks, a twelve-foot urethane Indian clad in a breech-clout aimed an arrow in a drawn bow at an artificial sky whilst birdsong, cricket chirp, and frog croak sounded.

"Rainmaker sets the Noble Savage theme: he amplifies the Anglos' guilt feelings, making it easier for them to bring us their wages and savings as tribute."

"Reminds me of Caesar's Palace," said Beffle. "You know, their urethane Bacchus."

Steam began surging from the rocks up around the Rainmaker. "Long ago, before the ancient ones," says he, "the land stood still." Rainmaker starts turning red. Wolf howls replace birdsong; eagles cry, rain falls. Thunder rumbles and crashes. Steam rises. Puffy Anglo faces gaze upward as the Indian flushes redder and redder. A crescendo of thunder and rain erupts, and then the storm passes, and clears, and birds raise their song anew, and once again the Rainmaker, wet, shimmering, no longer red, aims his arrow at a clear sky.

Beffle burst into laughter, and then, so did the others.

Fox walked them to the elevators, gave them key cards which they used to summon the private elevator. It took them to the fifth floor where they found their suite. Bear, seemingly unimpressed by having free hotel lodgings composed of two bedrooms, a spacious living room, a large bathroom furnished with bidet and jacuzzi, and a spectacular view, walked to the courtesy bar, poured them drinks, then gazed out over the Sacred Swamp and the Thames to the opposite shore. He broke into a smile. "So, Owl, how's *this* for high life! What a nifty bird's-eye view! Imagine! The Pequots, each and every one of them, can have anything they want. *Anything* short of immortality."

"So can you."

But, the way you pay me, *I* can't.

"Sure. But with me it's different. I don't come from some despised trailertown like they did. Just think, a few years ago these western Pequots were like their eastern brethren. Mud streets, bad plumbing, poor, dirt poor, not a pot to piss in nor a window to pour it out of, and scorned by the local rednecks. When they could work at all, they got the worst kinds of menial employment, like Mexicans in California. And now! Anglos serve them! For good pay, but even so!" He sprawled in a chair. "Hey, you know, thanks to Coyote and Raven and Monkey and Bugs Bunny and all the other gods of irony and prank, on his father's side the Pequots' big chief is pure Anglo!"

She took Bear's head between her hands, and turned it toward their immense view window. "And we're looking down on the Sacred Swamp! Where the Anglos and their allies brought refugees to bay after the fort massacre and killed all they could catch, men, woman, children, infants! And after that, in the Great Swamp Fight, somewhere near, they crushed the remains of the Pequots' little army, and then, after selling some into slavery, binding others into servitude, forcing the rest to join other tribes, and after occupying their land and prohibiting any of them from returning, ever, the Anglos thought they'd succeeded in expunging the Pequots' tribe from history, for eternity, in much the way the Romans had erased the Carthaginians. And that was back in 1637!"

"Fucking-A! In sixteen hundred and thirty fucking seven! And now we're looking down on it from the top of a Pequot city, built on the forbidden lands." He rose, mixed new drinks, raised a bumper. "To Indian games! To Cowboys & Indians; to Pequots & Puritans."

She hugged him, then stood back. "To Coyote at his best!"

"To the swamps. To the Pequots' last stand!"

"Which, it turns out, stands eight stories. In the Grand Pequot Observation Tower."

"And, you know, they don't let anybody forget."

He told her about bronze statues, heroic size, of Noble Savages in romantic poses distributed about the compound.

"They have a giant waterfall. Underneath it, in a theater, free of course, they continuously show a video loop of the Fort massacre, with English yelling *burn them*, and the flames rising, and the people screaming as they burn to death. An escalator, running in front the cataract, passes an Indian standing before it, a peace pipe raised to the sky, and behind him is the Great Cedar Swamp where a dying war chief cursed the Anglos and commanded the golden rhododendrons to grow henceforth with blood-red centers, which they have, and do to this day." He laughed, and said, "So you can learn all that on a break from playing your choice among six thousand slot machines set for a ninety-two-point-four percent payback."

"That beats ours."

"The high-tech technicians who operate this place are mainly Anglos laid off by the Electric Boat Company of Groton which is out of the submarine building business. They're our peace dividend. And they sure keep busy. More than twenty thousand people come here every day and up to sixty thousand on weekends."

She stood at the window, gazing at the Sacred Swamp, and the Thames, and, across it to its eastern bank at the Paucatuc reservation where the poor Pequots live. She turned back to Bear and asked why the eastern tribe is still poor.

"They say, for church reasons, they don't believe in gambling. The tribe split in two in the 1850's. Why? Beats me. Why don't the western Pequots give them money? Who the fuck knows. All I know is there's got to be more to all this than we can see floating on the surface." He stood and paced, once again his vibrant energetic self. "It's got to come *together*." He smacked his hand. "Goddamnit to Hell! The tribes have never been together! If they'd ever managed it, just once, all the Europeans would still be in Europe. But it's still not too late! It's now or never! I want to build a confederacy of all the registered tribes! The confederate council will tax all the gambling operations, and spend the money on the poor tribes. Me, I am going to put that together. I'll use our profits, the nut I've been building, as the seed for this fund, and I'll keep feeding our profits into it! You can bet your sweet ass on that! European greed produces immense gambling profits which we Indians can use to recover the lands they stole from us by the right of better arms, profits we can use to resurrect our cultures which their immense Puritan witch-hunting bigotry and their holy inquisitions and their arms and armor and their money sucked out of us! And me, Two Bears, I'm the guy who's going to do it! Who *is* fucking doing it."

Beffle confronted him. "More Bear hot air! Don't you see! Indians and Anglos and blacks and everybody else are just the same. Any one of us who looks carefully into the mirror sees what? Coyote! That's what! Yeah yeah. By what right are we Anglos here on this continent? In my body? In the big Pequot chief's body? By what right? A right created by violence, duplicity, sophisticated lies, and better missiles and better armor and, as you fucking say: intense bigotry! By what right are the Indians here? The same one! *Conquest.* Other animals lived here in natural harmony for a million years. Then thirty thousand years ago, humans come, break the balance, exterminate the mammoths, horses, tigers. Indians exploited nature too! We know about this crap! Humans have only been in New Zealand for a thousand years. Gone, the moa bird. God only knows how many species we've killed off there in one millennium."

"Beffle, you're full of shit."

"Yeah, but so what?"

"We Indians are much better at preserving the harmony. We lived right here for ten thousand years without leaving a mark. Look out the fucking window! At all those ugly concrete and plastic abominations. A conglomerate of greed and folly deposited in a few centuries. In our poetic memory, back in golden innocent Sacred Time, animals and people all spoke the same language. Animals talked with us, taught us, consoled us, warned us about changes in the weather, served us willingly, bringing us nuts, fruit, vegetables. And in winter, when we were famished, they even offered their own flesh and lives to sustain us. And what did we do? We humans betrayed the love and trust they gave to us. We people, selfish and greedy as we are, enslaved them, made them hunt for us, and work for us, ate their flesh when we had other things to eat, and, even worse, stole their winter stores of food. So what happened then? The animals, bitterly disappointed, stopped speaking the language, and withdrew, to live apart. This story is our genesis. We all learn it on our mother's knee. We Indians respect that lesson. And what do the Anglos learn? What do they try to teach us? As genesis, the Anglo child learns about Columbus! And the first beginning? Genesis? The Bible sets the tone of European life! And God said, Let us make man in our image, after our likeness, and let him have dominion over the fish of the sea, and over the fowl of the air, and over the cattle, and over all the wild animals, and over all the earth, and over every living thing that creepeth upon the earth!"

He sagged into a chair.

"Beffle. Don't you see? What I'm trying to do is not just about money. Money can produce the minimum conditions, the base, but there's more than that. Indians teach that animals are our brothers and sisters. Whom we have already betrayed, but must cherish. In their arrogance, consistent with the call to hubris it shouts out, Europeans are forcing their myth onto us, onto all the world. It's a hideous fable! A crude and cruel power doctrine . . . . And . . . . Oh . . . shit. What I'm trying to do, and, believe me, sometimes it feels hopeless. Sometimes I'm ready to give up. But if I don't make it happen, who the fuck will?"

Beffle sat across from him and they looked at each other, open, warm, sharing a sense of . . . *mutuality* came to mind. Tell him the truth! He'll scold me. He'll fire me. He'll kick the shit out of me. But I've got to! But he needs my support, my help! I can't live this lie any more! I can't leave him because he needs me.

That thought is selfish.

I like the pay and the status.

And the homely feeling of safety.

But he *trusts* me.

I've got to do what's right, no matter what!

Fired, where can this old woman get another job?

Bear rubbed some snuff on his gum, showing yellow teeth.

"Sometimes, Owl, I think it's too late. Nothing left to save. Just think. Among five million Norwegians today you cannot find one true Viking. Well, it's the same with us. How can anyone possibly be a traditional Native American these days? Every community has been radiated by the media's European message. All its mouths declare: You're superior to life, not part of it. Take power! Get rich! Grind your fellows! Strip them bare! Don't be human, be a snob! No. Nobody who's even heard the *radio* can be a pure Indian. Every falling eagle feather has passed through modulated frequencies. Show me an Indian, and I'll show you an actor, one who tries to imitate what life is thought to have been before it collided with the Europeans. Ain't no Indians no more---- and maybe there never were! Show me the common denominator for all the pre-Columbian peoples from the Arctic Circle to Tierra del Fuego! Ohlone origins and culture, the facts about them, are even more obscure than Pequot beginnings, leaving plenty of space for creative fiction. The Ohlone have been studied and studied, and still we can't describe their cultures. So we invent them. For personal romance and public commerce. Tourists. The Ohlone! All their languages and dialects have vanished utterly, except for one that was preserved in part: the Mutsun. All the rest is lost forever."

"You and me, Bear, we can read and write. We handle money. We listen to the radio. You come from the Cherokee who've been European clones for generations. The Cherokee, the Huron, all the tribes are in the melting pot, along with Irish and Poles and Chinese and Hindus. Neither one of *us* is an Indian. There aren't any Indians any more. Neither me nor *you*."

He fixed her with a scornful glare. "The trouble with you, woman, is to be a halfbreed like you are, doesn't necessarily mean you understand both sides. No. Like you, for instance. And I've seen it. Plenty of times. You don't understand *either one*."

She sprang to her feet.

"You've got that right!"

She blurted the truth.

"I'm neither Indian nor Irish!"

She elaborated the detail.

"I'm a goddamned blue-blooded Mayflower New Englander!"

She flaunted the irony.

"My people spilt the blood that sanctified that swamp out there!"

And she asked about her punishment.

"You going to beat me up. Or what!"

He paced, ruminating.

"I've known it all the time."

He went to the window, glanced out at the Sacred Swamp, looked back.

"You'd have had a better chance of pulling it off, Foul Foul Owl, if you'd said you're an Erie. But Huron? For Northern Ohio? No fucking way."

"So you going to fire me?"

"I ought to kick your ass."

"So, kick it, Grease Face!"

"I think I'll kick your donkey instead. After all, your ass can puke at will."

How does he know that?

I've never told anybody that.

"No, I won't kick you, or your ass, or your donkey, or your horse either. You and me, we'll keep on working together; just keep the truth to yourself."

"You don't care?"

"No." He smiled. "You know why?"

"Why."

"I need you. You're totally reliable. You're absolutely honest, thoroughly trustworthy. You never relax or daydream. You're observant, suspicious, and alert all the time, so much so the help think you're always watching them, even when you're not there. You pay attention to the right things. Nobody's going to sneak any counterfeit chips or dice by you." He walked up to her and, still smiling, grasped her shoulder. "Here's what I want you to do. My next move is to get the Indian casino chiefs together in a kind of constitutional convention. And how do we do that? We'll host a powwow. At the Ohlone Valley Casino. I want you to go back home tomorrow and begin the basic preparations."

ELEVEN

NEXT MORNING, THEY were sitting at the table by the window, eating an air-conditioned room-service VIP free breakfast and from time to time glancing out at the hot sunlit scenery, out there in the consecrated swamp doubtless a great day for frogs and snapping turtles and dragon flies and mosquitoes. "Bear," said Beffle, "that's the biggest pile of grease food I ever saw."

"Quit your bitching." With his fork he tapped her plate. "They got grits for you, didn't they?"

"That's why you want me out of here, isn't it? So you can wallow in comp grease . . . in peace."

"I want to move the powwow as fast as possible. I'll be going around, visiting people, and calling you, and you'll be at home, organizing it."

"And you want to start right now."

"Yes. First thing, I want you to take fifty grand and start a special powwow account."

"But that's not the only reason you want me out of here."

"Touché. When I phoned them from Chicago, they said they'd set up a love nest for me."

"How about *me*?"

"They didn't mention you."

"So, I've got to go."

"You told me you don't like Connecticut."

"I don't."

"You told me so before you got here."

"I still don't like it."

"How in fuck do you know? You haven't been there yet."

"So, you glutinous retard, in that case where are we right now!"

"Airport, limo, hotel suite? That's Connecticut?"

"Fuck Connecticut."

"I'm against it. What is it?"

"Get off my case, Grease Face!"

"I'm helping you out."

"I thought you were keeping me safe."

"You'll be safe at home. I'll send Ace and Hawk back as soon as you get there. George, too. David's there now. Called them last night. And you'll have our regular security, and the deputy sheriffs."

"Bear. Fuck you!" She slammed her fork onto her plate and stalked out to the elevator, went down, strode through the casino and off into the heat, and she walked across an English lawn to the Sacred Swamp where she contemplated cat-tails and reeds and listened to frogs croak and crickets click and insects swirl and buzz like World War I airplanes in a dogfight showcasing the Red Baron, and she stood there until she felt herself once more at ease.

She went back inside where she'd stop sweating, and she rambled around contrasting noble bronze Indians to the clients until she felt ready to return to the proto love-nest.

When Two Bears came back that evening they both apologized for being thoughtlessly impetuous. "Beff, I decided to have our powwow on Columbus Day. We'll call it Carib Day, in honor of the tough Carib Indians who resisted Columbus and the rest so stoutly they still exist and have a few islands. Imagine! That war between Europeans and Indians has been going on for more than *five hundred years* and sure as Hell ain't over yet! That's our theme. We'll have to move fast. I bought you a ticket, first class to Frisco, change at Chicago. You'll leave here at eighty-thirty a.m. I won't have time to drive you to the airport, but a limo'll be out front of the casino, waiting to take you."

The next morning, as promised, when Bear escorted Beffle down to the entrance, a limousine stood at the curb. Bear opened the door for her, and saying "I'll call you every evening," pecked a good-bye kiss onto her cheek. In front sat the same young driver as before. Billy. A curlyhead, like Charley, only blond. As they drove away into the forest, he said, "One thing that makes me so keen on you Indians is you truly respect nature."

"Indians exploit nature just like Anglos do."

"No. They live *in* it, not over and outside."

She made a sweeping gesture at the Foxwoods compound. "What do you call that?"

"That doesn't count."

"The only difference is Europeans had better machines than the canoe and the bow and the atlal."

Why am I teasing him like this?

"Sorry, Billy, I'm kidding you. I think Indians had a balance. Nowadays, in order to survive, we human monkeys must make big changes, *immense* changes, and restore the balance. Or else! But why should we survive? Why should I care? It'll hold together till I die. After me, the killer flood."

"But you *do* care."

"Yes. I care."

"I'm not an Indian. I'm a daughter of the Mayflower."

"Me too. I'm pure Anglo, mongrel Anglo, I mean."

"And, like you, I'm a townie. I live in Carmel, a few miles from our casino."

She told him about Carmel and the Ohlone casino, and he told her he roomed close to Foxwoods in Preston, had a B.A. cum-laud from the University of California in Berkeley, was reared by his grandfather in Pacifica, now was in medical school at Johns Hopkins, and, for the summer, was taking all the work here he could get. As they sped along the freeway, conversing, it seemed almost as if Billy were intentionally trying to create a warm intimacy. We're both Berkeley grads---- Old Blues! What a fine fellow! Another Charley. Favored with all the gifts. But *using* them. Consequently, an *anti*-Charley! This lad is making something of himself. Do you jack off? She almost blurted it. Instead, the impulse expressed itself in talking about her son and a request for Billy's phone number so someday she could ask him to call Charley.

He gave his number.

"Phone any time you want, any time at all. You might need my help."

"Help?"

"Is your family name Bruhn?"

"No. It's Braun."

"Braun?"

"Yes."

"That guy you came with, and Laughing Fox, I drove them around yesterday. They kept mentioning someone named Braun. Thought it might be you. I hoped for a chance to tell you Sounded scary. Really *menacing*." He looked back at her. "I just heard bits of it, so I don't have any details or sequences I can describe."

She ruminated on this as she tried to doze and read away the hours in jet-driven capsules of misery hurtling five miles high, first to Chicago, thence to San Jose, California.

Uncomfortable, clothes binding, tasting a bitter flavor in the thought *almost home*, she trudged along in the press of people moving down the aisle and through the passageway into the terminal toward a waiting crowd. As she glanced at it, a sudden warmth surged through her. David! Among the people waiting beyond the barrier, stood David Running Deer. No mistake. Black hair; braided pony tail with a silver clasp; trench coat; radiant energy; otherwise a twin of Braun. *David Running Deer*!

They embraced, hugged. He stood back, smiling.

"Beffle O'Neill, the Morgan awaits."

"Swift Roller of the Deer Clan?"

"Yes, ma'am. Swifty."

"I hate airports. And I was really feeling blue. And now here you are! Turns it all around."

"Weren't you expecting me?"

"No."

"Didn't Two Bears tell you?"

"No. No he didn't."

"He told me on the phone to come meet you. Maybe he forgot."

"Maybe."

They crossed the street to the parking lot, stepped into Swifty, drove to Highway 101, and, listening to a KGO newstalk program, rushed through the heat toward Monterey County. Deer clicked off the radio. "Did Bear tell you?"

"Tell me what?"

"He wants my assistant to supervise the motor pool until the powwow. Me, I'm to stay with you all the time as your bodyguard. From six a.m. till evening. He says you'll have to go places during business hours to put the powwow together and he doesn't want to trust protecting you to dolts like Blood Turtle or George."

"That's thoughtful of him. I enjoy your company."

And what *else* had he told Deer?

"We'll look in on the motor pool when time permits. And you're to keep your eye on the gaming rooms." Silently they sped by sensuous brown hills, turned west and raced toward the Monterey Peninsula. Bear's a fucking slave driver! Got to have time for my sculpture! Fear touched her. What are his real plans? Is Deer a body guard, or prison chaser? The thought both dismayed and comforted. Gay, yes, but still, yet, and nevertheless he'll be continuously with me. Looking at his profile in a half-loving way, once again David Running Deer's striking resemblance to her ex-husband slammed her. If only Arthur had had that *energy*. Then maybe Charley would have inherited it. And be like Billy. Then maybe our marriage would not have been asphyxiated by boredom and today I could think of Charley as Wild Child! High powers, surely not those of the Moron Church, dropped him that eagle feather from the clouds. Maybe I can get Charley to visit! Not . . . likely. He called me a sinner and wants me out of his life. Maybe David Running Deer is bi! AC/DC! DC/AC, that is. I not only love this guy, I *like* him, which is a Hell of a lot more than I ever could say about Braun.

"Long, long ago," Deer said softly, "in Sacred Time, Big Runner was seated on a log by his cooking fire, singing kick-stick songs, wondering what to have for dinner, when along came Rabbit, and challenged him to a race. Big Runner, always fastest on the Spirit Course, and certain sure he could beat Rabbit, offered to stake his favorite arrow, one wrapped in rattlesnake skin to make it sudden, swift, and deadly, an arrow coveted by Rabbit for its power to protect its owner from all hunters. In exchange, Big Runner asked Rabbit to bet his body to serve as dinner. Much to his surprise, Rabbit, the spirit forebear of Bugs Bunny, agreed to do so if Big Runner would allow him to run underground. Big Runner concurred in this and soon the race began, following the one-mile Sacred Course, the Sun Path, to the granite Power Spot. As Big Runner dashed along savoring the thought of roasted rabbit, suddenly from a hole before him appeared the grinning head of Rabbit. Alarmed, Big Runner called on all his guardian spirits for help, and ran at his utmost limit, yet, no matter how hard he tried, every now and then, from a hole ahead, appeared the mocking face of Rabbit. And then, when at last he saw the Power Spot, there upon it stood Rabbit, the winner.

"So after they had caught their breath, they walked back together to Big Runner's camp to get the arrow. But when they got there, instead of fetching the arrow, Big Runner seized Rabbit and laid him on the coals, saying, "I don't know how many of your brothers raised their heads, nor do I know which one you are, but I do know you are going to be my dinner."

"What happened to Rabbit?"

"He got a job in the movies."

Now they were racing up Carmel Hill at a speed not even Bugs Bunny could match, and they turned into the Carmel Valley Road and went through the village by the Running Iron with its tawny stuffed lion and drove up the ridge into the casino compound and stopped inside the motor pool building. "Come on," said Deer, and led back between the two ranks of shining vehicles to his office. "Promised Bear I'd phone when we got here." He sat on his

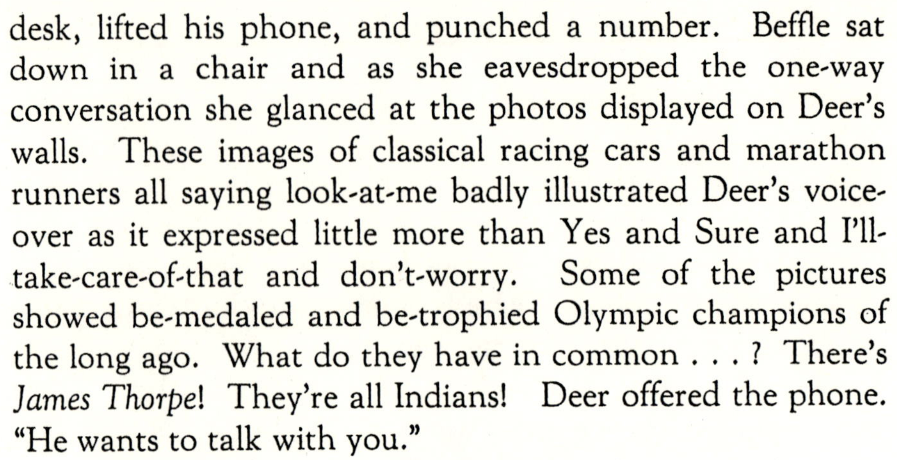

desk, lifted his phone, and punched a number. Beffle sat down in a chair and as she eavesdropped the one-way conversation she glanced at the photos displayed on Deer's walls. These images of classical racing cars and marathon runners all saying look-at-me badly illustrated Deer's voice-over as it expressed little more than Yes and Sure and I'll-take-care-of-that and don't-worry. Some of the pictures showed be-medaled and be-trophied Olympic champions of the long ago. What do they have in common . . . ? There's *James Thorpe*! They're all Indians! Deer offered the phone. "He wants to talk with you."

"Hey, Grease Face. The Pequots scalp you yet."

"No, Owl, they were too busy flaying Anglos."

"So, what you want me to do?"

"Me, I'm going to go around, gathering people and materials for the powwow, and trying to find out who's out to get us, and I want you to stay there at home, and put the powwow together."

"You told me."

"I'll call you once a day on your office phone. Leave messages if I have to. I'll call early, your time, so after we talk you have the whole day ahead of you to get things done. Tomorrow, I'll fax you a plan, a program for the powwow. So, yeah Owl, we have to bear in mind we only have *six weeks* to prepare the Carib Day Festival at Ohlone Valley. Six fucking weeks! First of all, see if you can get some Caribs to come. Doesn't matter how much it costs. Book our guests into the best accommodations. At our place. Or in Pebble Beach. Reserve blocs now! And, oh, yeah. Invite some Spaniards. That way we can serve traditional meat at the traditional Carib barbecue."

"Sure, Bear. I'll take care of it."

"I've thought it over more. You're safe on the compound. But when you want to leave, and your duties mean that'll be often, first go and get Deer from the motor pool. And when you have time, keep an eye on the suckers. Got it?"

"Yes."

"Deer will stay with you all the time you're off the compound. Maybe on occasions he'll bring Hawk. Deer's your security companion. Sure. But he's more than that. He's a resource. He's smart and brave and observant. And he knows one Hell of a lot about Indians. As you do your work, he'll be your reference book, your walking encyclopedia."

"From the look of the art in here, Grease Face, that book'll be a'running, or maybe even a'rolling."

"What?"

"Encyclopedia, dummy. My encyclopedia"

"That's it until tomorrow. I'll have more for you then. But, Beffle, I know you're upset. Between us, Huron or not, nothing has changed. It's just like always. The danger too. The limo I was riding in this afternoon, somebody ran into it. How about that?"

"Anybody hurt?"

"No. We're all okay."

They said good-bye, and Beffle leaned back and looked up at Deer. "I've been admiring your pictures."

"Those pix remind me, when we want to, we can beat the Anglos at their own game."

"A very Anglo thing to say."

He smiled.

"Sure is."

"So, hey, Deer. Can we beat Big Runner at *his* game?"

"After Big Runner put Rabbit's brother in the coals to cook, he sat on a stone by the fire and his mouth watered as he savored the aroma of his dinner as it spread far and wide. Coyote breathed in this fragrant promise and limped over to the fire. 'Big Runner,' said Coyote, let us race to the Power Spot and back while your food cooks. That way you can work up an appetite.' Big Runner had never outrun Coyote, nor had anyone else, even Rabbit, so now that Coyote was lame and limping, Big Runner seized hold of his chance for glory. When their race began, Coyote hobbled and limped, valiantly, and managed to run fast, but not fast enough to keep up with Big Runner, let alone draw ahead. But when Big Runner reached the Power Spot and turned to come back, Coyote came dashing around the spot and by him, no longer limping, fast as the wind. Knowing now Coyote's limp was a trick, when Big Runner got back near the fire he burst out into curses for there sat Coyote, on the rock, licking his lips, devouring the last bite of the dinner."

"That has an Anglo ring as well."

"For sure. Do you run?"

"Going to challenge me to race to the Power Spot?"

"I run every morning. But I never race."

"You jog?"

"I don't think of it that way." He gestured at the photos. "And neither do they, even though they're trapped in the Anglos' maze. Like me, you might say. Or you. You, even more. Half your heart's blood is Anglo. Listen to the other half. Listen to it tell you we don't run for money or glory. Nor do those cars. They extend the man. What do the autos feel? The same thing we---- I feel. Swifty enjoys the run for itself, and runs for those others out there on the floor. Swifty never thinks of who's the fastest. Most are faster than him. No matter. He runs against his own limits, in solidarity with others doing the same. And he never praises oil or tires, nor does he run for the glory of some gasoline. Swifty's beautiful. Swifty's high-strung. Swifty loves the feel of the run, of all his parts moving in harmony, within, with the wind, the road, sunshine, moonlight, rain, snow, ice! He is me; all his wires extend my nerves. Anglos don't understand. Your Hurons? Didn't they explain it to you?"

"No. They didn't."

"I will then. Be ready to run at six in the morning when I knock on your door."

The alarm shocked her awake and shedding covers she sat up in total where?/nowhere? blackness as the light of a dream sank into the sand of the Dream World. Oh . . . ? Yes! My suite in the Ohlone Valley Hotel. Deer! Deer had been at her side in the Dream World. They'd been together in a dreamhouse, a rainhouse, of winds, clouds, and seeds. Shared events in the Dream World. Now beyond memory. Soon he'll be here in the Day World! She washed and drank some water. I'm almost *fifty years old.* What am I doing here? Promising to run! What to wear? She looked at the fat marbled on her fifty-year-old legs. Fifty counting fetus time. Shared events in the fetus world? Dark green shorts. Run off the fat. At fifty, a delusion. Ohlone Valley sweatshirt with the casino's motto: Fun & Fortune. Green again. Hat? Beret. An elementary teacher's voice saying blue and green don't go together, a voice speaking out sharply whenever she used the two in dressing, in art.

And now to await the fulfillment of my absolutely reliable prediction about the meticulous David Running Deer, and here's six of-the-clock, and there's the knock, and my clairvoyance is once again confirmed.

Yes.

Deer carried a big box in and set it on the table. His butt looks good on display in running shorts. In an old-fashioned gesture of courtesy, he doffed his silver & black Oakland Raiders' cap. "I brought your things from Vegas." She dumped the box out onto the bed. Everything I left at Caesar's! All here. Except what the thief took. Even my pirate book! My Oracle. And its last revelation. She recited it in English:

"*With a satisfied air the old person was contemplating the young man's serious attitude and reserve.*"

"Beg pardon?"

She showed Deer the pirate book, and explained the Oracle.

"Relatively, you're a young man. This prediction seems to fit."

"Ask it another question."

"Is it good that we run together?"

She opened the book.

"Do you read French?"

"No."

"So much the better. Choose a line. That will be the answer."

La nouvelle de ce combat, publieé par les gazettes du temps, fit grande sensation en France et en Espagne.

"The news of this battle, published by the journals of the time, made a big sensation in France and in Spain."

David smiled at her. "Our running won't be combat. Running, for us, is ritual, euphoria, mixing into the all, meditation."

They went downstairs, out into the warm morning, and side by side began to trot downhill toward the road to the Village. "Beffle, we should be painted, plastered, and daubed, and carrying some magic medicine as defense against witches and warlocks because they also run."

Deer began singing softly in his Indian language and no longer aware of Beffle's presence, of any presence, drew slowly ahead. Again! Following men! I feel safe. And thrill to Deer's shoulders and legs and butt, a moving harmony, a liquid trot. A my-language mantra:

Running through the Day World,
Running right along,
Mean to keep my toes curled,
Sing a running song.

Well, all right, thinking about what I'm singing about, over and over again, run loosely on my toes, curling up, as each stride begins, with a spring, and ends with a new curl, along and along and along . . . . And David's slowing to a walk.

"Beffle, while you're getting used to running, we'll use the Indian long-distance pace. Run for a while, walk for a while."

Silently they tramped together through the sweet summer morning, and on reaching the highway began to run again, Indian file, against traffic. Maybe *I'm* Big Runner! Big R. can be a *she*. And big in contrast to Rabbit, or even Coyote. Am I following Coyote? Does Coyote have legs and a butt like that? Walk-time again. Talk about doing-it songs. David telling about gambling songs: you sing one to get ready, then make the bets and play the game. The Grass Game Song. The Bone Game song. Time to run again.

Pipe it into the casino. Indian gaming muzak. Civilized. Yet ever so ethnic. Sure . . . :

The Slot Song.
The Baccarat Blues.
The Twenty-One Twist.

The Craps Canticle.
The KENO Chorus.
The Poker Polka!

And now the Village and Deer stopping before the Running Iron.

"Breakfast time."

Deer led along the bar to the table by the tawny stuffed lion.

"You'll be *all* Indian, Ms Owl, before we're finished."

Again a flush of guilt. Must I tell everyone the truth? Deer's not just everyone. "What are you going to have, David? Flavor-free butterfly eyes with milk and sugar?"

"Running's part of the cloth, not a decoration. It's one cheek of life." He stroked the lion. "When he lived up there in the hills, this guy could run. I don't think he ever *jogged* to sweat some fat off his gut and ass. Or worried about thrombosis. That seems most unlikely. So, you know, to run, we eat ritual food, and submit to ritual fasting. Now ain't that one Hell of an answer to: What's for breakfast?"

"What is?"

"You want my recommendation?"

"Yes, please."

"Food."

"Food?"

"That's what I'm having."

"Ritual?"

"All food should be ritual."

"All of one's life is a single ritual and so each part should be lived in awareness of what it is."

"Yes! Now your Huron's talking."

"Motion is life."

"That's the spirit!' He took her hand and pulled her to her feet. "Let's go." On the way out, he bought some blueberry muffins, and, a muffin in each hand, they ate as they ran, he ahead, she behind. If only instead of east they were going all the way west, to Carmel, to her house! I'll make him go there with me! Show him my art! Sculpt an abstract Running Deer trotting through an unseen world of running spirits! His songs drifted back. He slowed to a walk. "What were you singing?"

"Music soothes the Spirit World."

"Soothes?"

"Music's a bridge. But . . . no! Not a bridge. If you sing the right songs, it raises the curtain concealing the Spirit World from our awareness,

"You believe in an unseen world?" she asked, as they turned into their road.

"Yes and no and yes. The unseen world is part of our world. In Sacred Time, we could see it. In Sacred Time, when men and animals all spoke the same language, and were brothers and sisters, man could be animal, and animal, man, and at will. Deer clan? Be a deer or a man, as you like. In those distant times, before we forced the animals to withdraw, in speaking the universal language, some of the best tasting words, said in the right place and time, could have startling, unexpected magical effect." He halted. "Look there!" A deer stood in the road, watching them through its mysterious brown eyes, and then bounded away. "That may be our spirit helper. Some elders say a society is a group of beings held together by mutual dependence. The Spirits, although we can't see them anymore, influence us, and we affect them, so they are part of society. When running sometimes you flow out of yourself, and, as in a dream, the curtain rises. Dreams, you know, are *real.* You race yourself, your own spirit. And that's heroic, but not like Pontiac or Tecumseh, a breed half god and half man.

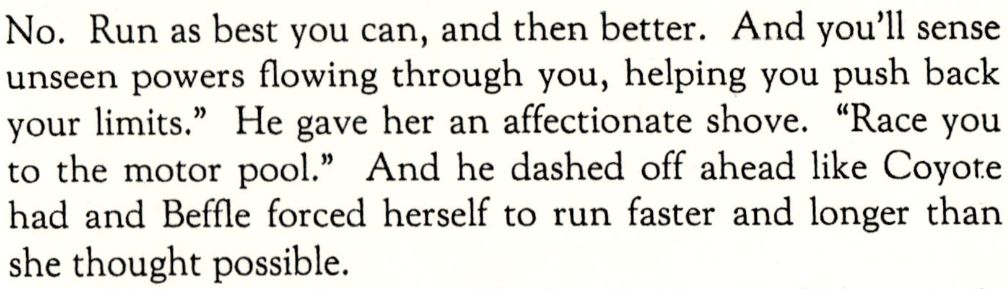

No. Run as best you can, and then better. And you'll sense unseen powers flowing through you, helping you push back your limits." He gave her an affectionate shove. "Race you to the motor pool." And he dashed off ahead like Coyote had and Beffle forced herself to run faster and longer than she thought possible.

Gasping, realizing suddenly she'd not felt a single arthritis tweak, she walked in among the cars. A smiling David held a cold beer out to her. "Here's some seen unseen power."

After drinking the beer, she led Deer to her office to see if Bear had contacted them. She drew the pages of a fresh message out of her fax machine. "It's a preliminary outline of what Two Bears wants at the powwow. He says I can spend all the money I need to and he'll phone this morning at what would be about now."

She passed the papers to Deer, who looked them over, and spread them out on the table. "Look at this!" He wants events, structures, and an Indian market. Set up for three days. "Owl, we'll have to get the biggest tent we can find, and some smaller tents, too." And look at this! He tells us to build examples of North American Indian architecture, on the same principle the Spanish followed in Barcelona to build a town of exemplary Spanish structures. "One thing we'll have, and that's for sure, is fry-bread booths, and one of them will follow my favorite recipe. From Beverly Hungry Wolf's book. Served with jam and hot chocolate, with fresh berries worked into the dough." Okay, we'll have to build some wickiups, and a Hopi stone house, and a Navaho hogan, and an Iroquois longhouse, and an Ohlone-style sweat lodge and tule hut, and tipis and wigwams and a kiva. That Indian architecture book-- the one from Oxford

Bear has in his office . . . we'll call in some contractors, show them what we require, and see who can build it fastest.

"We'll need a lot of room for buses and cars, so we can't put any of this in the parking lot, and the lawn space in front of the buildings won't hold all of it, so where else can we set up?"

"On the golf course."

"Hell yes! I hate golf."

"Me, too, Owl. Let's get old Blind Badger up here and tell him to turn his ground crews loose. We'll sketch out where everything goes and get them started on building some of the market booths."

The phone rang.

"Bear!"

"Did you get my fax?"

"Did you hear about the Cherokee who struck oil and bought a whorehouse?"

"Did you hear about the Boston Brahmin who posed as an Irish Indian?"

"Lay off, Bear."

"Okay. Believe me, I'm busy as a fireman in Hell. Hope you're on top of everything."

"Sure am."

"Spend all the money you want. No need to ask first."

She explained their plans, and then David talked with him. David hung up and said: "That Bear's an Indian O'Neill!"

"*King-Candle* O'Neill, or *Chopped-Hand* O'Neill."

"I don't know. King-Candle, maybe. I've been meaning to tell you. I'm gay."

"Bear told me."

"Good. I've been feeling guilty about not telling you."

"I've been hoping you're bi."

"Sometimes." He smiled. "Yes, sometimes." He sat down on the table. "What Bear doesn't understand is we're not above the rest of life, but are *part* of life and may exploit what our livelihoods require, but no more. Sometimes I wonder if the Cherokee, those called civilized, are Indians at all. Bear . . . ? Sometimes I feel at heart he's no Indian, but pure Anglo." Deer sprang to his feet, and paced around. "What eats me is this casino. I hate it. I can't even go into it without choking. I hide out with my cars. That's okay. But even so, I'm part of it! Bear wants to make it bigger and bigger!" He stopped before her and took her hands. "Beffle, I can't abide it any longer. Anglo gambling is a spiritual disease. At the powwow, in public, I'll warn Indians against it. I'll denounce it to all those chiefs."

"And get fired."

"I can't think about that."

"Why didn't you denounce it before."

"Why? Beffle, one of the most important facts of our times is that thanks to science applied through technology production-per-man-hour is constantly increasing. What took one hour to build yesterday only takes half-an-hour today. So, who gets the benefits. You can keep paying everyone the same, and cut their workweek in half. Or leave the workweek alone, fire half the workers, and cut the price. Or fire them and give the savings to the owners and chiefs. In Europe, some of the benefits go to the workers. To all of them, union and non-union alike. By law. Not so here. Not even through lower prices. Indians are at the bottom of the pile. For us, making a living gets harder every year. And now, suddenly, with our casinos, we're sucking gambling profits which, otherwise, had the money reached Las Vegas or Reno or Atlantic City, would have gone to the super rich and organized crime. We shortstop that money and diffuse it among our tribes. It gives big-buck backing for the principles of AIM. Now Bear is trying to make an AIM confederacy, fed with our immense gambling profits. And, despite what I feel, I'm helping Bear all I can. But more and more I ask myself, is it worth it?"

"Is it?"

"No. Indian casinos, meant to restore our true and ancient life are destroying it! Look at all those Pequots who didn't used to have a pot to piss in, driving around in Mercedes and playing golf! Indian casinos instead of making us more Indian are turning us into Anglos!"

He let go of her hands and slumped into a chair.

"So, Beffle, I've got to speak out no matter what."

Beffle! No more flimflam!

Tell him!

"David. Something I want you to know. All this time I've been faking being half Huron, and half Irish. I'm pure blue-blood rich-kid social-register Anglo."

He looked at her, perplexed.

"Is that why you're so blasted ignorant about everything?"

"Yes."

David Running Deer peered contempt at her, turned his back, and walked out.

TWELVE

BEFFLE LEFT THE PAPERS on the table and crossed over to her desk and sat behind it. *Now what?* I feel as empty as . . . as . . . I feel as empty as dreamless sleep. Bear said *keep it to yourself*, but no, I had to blab it. Deer's honesty had seemed so pure that it exorcised the truth from me. So, now what. Deer despises me for mocking all he holds dear. Holds *deer!* David Holding Dear. Yes. Telling the truth was right. Should have leveled the first week working here instead of putting it off so long. A lot of Anglos work here. She looked at her neatly arranged desk top. A little dusty. She grasped her pen & pencil vessel, a turn-of-the-last-century German regimental beer stein, one showing the officers of the regiment among whom was Charley's great grandfather. Which one? I've forgotten! They all look much alike under their spiked helmets and in their identical high-collared tunics. A forgotten world! All of them dead now, one of them replaced by Arthur, by Charley. All the thoughts they are hiding so well behind their Prussian army masks diffused into the firmament and lost forever. What's for me? Resign? Bear's bound to fire me now. So where can an old broad like me get another good job? Any job? I'll be on the street. Homeless. Someone or some group maybe still out to get me. This desk and the Morgan and Deer and Two Bears and all the others will soon recede like Eddy and Braun into a group cameo on some memory mug. But not the Beer Fairy. Everything the Beer Fairy has ever said in the AOL chatrooms can be called up and printed out on their immense computer. Of all of it, only Beer Fairy dialog and the BF's imaginary bio are immortal. And maybe my employment application with the line in my own hand saying fifty-percent Huron will engage the scrutiny of the historians. So maybe only the Beer Fairy will survive into the next century. The Beer Fairy was half Pilsner and half Huron! I'm getting a little crazy. Have to talk with someone! The Twins? But how to find them? Pearl? Forget it. Braun? Yes. No. Where is he? Charley. No! Billy? That cabby in Vegas? I have their numbers. Well, maybe, but . . . ? Ed! Yes . . . ! *Ed.*

She lifted the phone and touched 1-800-MURDER-1.

It's ringing!

Connection!

A recorded voice.

"You have reached the office of Mr. Edward Jones. He's out of town at the moment. Leave your number and he'll return your call as soon as possible."

"Shit!"

She hung up.

Now what?

Get busy!

She went to the table and fetched Two Bears' fax; then she phoned Blind Badger, and asked him to come up for lunch. If only he were *Badger* and I, Mr. Toad. *That* Badger could talk sense to me. I'll go to Bear's office and get his Indian architecture book. We don't need contractors. With the help of those illustrations and descriptions, and his own wide knowledge of Native American customs, Badger can supervise building everything Bear wants, and maybe think of more. We'll have fry bread. Tortillas. Nothing but Native American foods! Turkey, corn, squash, string beans, sugar. Sure. Strawberries and blackberries and cranberries. And melons and bananas and coffee and chocolate and cocoa and avocados and salmon and bass and trout and of course potatoes and peanuts and peppers and . . . peas. Peas? Have to look that up. And buffalo, and barbecued dog to make it ethnically correct. I'll call the hotels; I'll reserve rooms in blocs-- and I'll make sure our best suites are kept open. And I'll invite drummers and dancers and musicians and poets and singers. The best. But who are the stars in the Indian empyrean? What stars shine brightest in David's sky? I'll ask Badger. Ace'll know. And I'll call a press conference when we've caught some stars and are closer to ready. In about two weeks. And now for the fun part. Designing a poster. She thought over her thoughts. Pure Anglothink! Bear would approve. David? How would pure Indianthink perceive it? She went next door to Bear's office to get the book.

She picked up his lucky stone, the marble fragment, worn smooth by the sea. Bear had found it on Patmos, an island in Greece, on Lambi Beach, where Bishop John wrote *Revelations*, the last book of the Bible, scripture about 666 and seven seals and lakes of fire and the Four Horse*persons* of the Apocalypse. A tidy desktop. Furnished with the minimum. A cardboard box full of mail. Look it over so you can tell him if there's anything important. Junk junk junk. Flimflam cousins. Related by their convergence in requests for money. A new *Native Peoples* magazine. And *Gaming Today*. And *News from Native California*. And the Yale University alumni magazine! *Two Bears at Yale*!

Shelve that one along with *The Rover Boys at Yale.* Next to *Cherokee Scholars in the Ivy League.* Rough and Tough Two Bears Jones. At Yale. Well, these days, anything is possible. Anything we can imagine can happen.

And more.

Still feeling all empty inside, dreading the call from Bear, she kept on trying to fill the vacuum with work. Bear's call came. Formal and businesslike and approving of what she had done. No mention of Deer. Homesick for her own house and studio, but hesitant to go there alone, she went downstairs into the rattle and rush of the casino to patrol. All the stoats and weasels seemed still sufficiently intimidated to eschew temptations to loaf and steal. Bear would approve of that. While she was gone, her spirit had stayed here, as phantom pit boss on the job, or maybe as her animal helper. Whatever form it had taken, it had held the lid on. She met with Badger, who assured her he could supervise the building projects. He pledged authenticity and, barring invasion by the wild boars, assured her he could finish on time. Bearing in mind that for Indians what their entertainers do is much deeper than entertainment, she spent the afternoon making phone calls to artists Badger had recommended. Two groups agreed to come. She sketched a poster and wrote a press release, then ate supper in the casino buffet. Feeling utterly isolated and alone, no longer diverted by work, she went up to her suite, stripped off her clothes, and spent the evening listening to KGO talk radio while playing solitaire on her computer. She slipped into bed and imagined the powwow's Indian market with its variety of structures and the casino buildings looming behind and it all began to seem like fun as she strolled along Indian Street chatting with people until she crossed into Dream Time and found herself in a woods with David wandering among Blackfoot death platforms where bodies of his forebears slowly dried in the sun and decayed and fed the birds in the mournful deathland of lost spirits.

Loud knocking from . . . the Day World . . . intruded . . . and awakening . . . she blinked sunshine . . . and rubbed her eyes and . . . too disoriented to be afraid . . . she squirmed into her robe and opened the door.

There stood David!

He doffed his Raiders' cap and made a sweeping bow.

"Wake up Beffle. Time to run."

She joyfully embraced him and holding his hand pulled him inside.

"You were in my dreams," he said. "You were running after a deer. You caught up to it, and vaulted over its rump onto its back and rode away."

"I dreamed about *you*." The macabre scene returned. Tell him? No. "But I can't remember anything about it." She pecked a kiss onto his cheek. "Make some coffee and grits while I get ready."

Dressed, her pager tucked into her bra, drinking coffee and eating at her table, she gushed all she had accomplished and warmed to his compliments.

Soon they were trotting side-by-side downhill toward the highway.

She looked at him tenderly.

"So you don't care?"

"Of course I care."

"Then why'd you come back?"

"I imagined being you."

She laughed.

"Sometimes I imagine being me. Or I even *act* like me."

"Once you puked in my face."

That slammed into her being.

She stopped.

"That was *you?*"

"I think they mean to kill you because you know too much."

Panicked, she dashed away.

Like Coyote, he caught up.

"You can't get away from me. So *trust* me."

She ran even faster.

"There's a lot you have to know."

Buy a gun!

"They *want* you to run."

Go home and go inside and sculpt and never come out.

"I think they're going to do something *today.*"

She sobbed for breath.

"We'll go to the garden at the Iron and talk."

They were on the highway, running with traffic, squeezed by traffic, running close to parked cars.

Dial 911.

The observer within laughed at her fright.

The pager chafed.

She could hear her heart.

David ran easily alongside.

"Ms Braun," said the pager in Badger's voice, "I want to borrow that building book so I can get started today."

A woman stopped her car close ahead at the side of the road meaning to take her dog for a walk.

A deer darted from a field and trotted toward them making them run single file even closer to the parked cars.

Beffle sprinted away from David.

Crooning at her Dalmatian, meaning to get out, the woman abruptly swung open her door.

Beffle slammed into it.

. . . Beffle came to in bed in the Monterey Peninsula Community Hospital.

A woman's voice was saying, over and over, "You poor deer."

No. *Dear.*

Maybe she'd only said it once.

"You poor dear."

Beffle sat up.

In chairs by her bed sat a stranger . . . and David Running Deer.

"You have a black eye and cracked ribs and a broken pager, but you're going to be all right," said David.

"And the pager?" inquired the observer within.

David smiled. "Kaput."

"That's German."

"That's from when I was stationed in Germany."

"I love Germans," said the dog woman. "They're so . . . *talented.*"

"Dada ist für Ruhe und Orden," said Beffle. "And for Indian running."

"But not for car doors," said David.

"I'm so sorry!" said the dog owner.

In came a nurse. She told them to leave because the doctor was due.

"You poor dear," said the matronly stranger, laying a gentle hand on Beffle's bandaged shoulder. "I'll pay the bill and file an insurance report."

The nurse escorted them out. The doctor said he'd like her to stay a few days for observation, then left her alone. A single room. A gorgeous view of Monterey and Monterey Bay. A TV. A bandaged upper torso. An aching chest. Someone can bring my new laptop. On the nightstand, a check-off lunch and dinner menu with choices of three entrées and drinks, even of beers and wines. I'm in a railroad dining car! The menu says I can order for guests! Stay here forever, Wild Child. For Ever! The situation outside is just too complicated. *Deer* kidnapped me. *Deer* had me push Swifty off the bluff. I puked in *Deer*'s face. What would they have done had I not escaped? Bear runs the place. Like me, they all do what he says. And what might that be? Kill me? Tease me to death? And now the phone's ringing. Can't do anything about the danger, except enjoy it, from here, the safest place there is. It's rather like living in London during the Blitz. Sure. "Hello."

Bear!

Got to keep working on the powwow as if nothing has happened. What a bloody hypocrite! He's talking sympathetically about my accident, and assuring me we can keep everything covered even though I'm in here, and now my voice assures him, no problem, I can handle it. Says keep calling me every morning. A strong feeling flares. David will *not* tell him I know about the kidnapping and my danger. And now his voice expressing a sweet rapscallion wish for a quick recovery and making a friendly good-bye. Maybe now I can get all my ducks in a row. She squirmed seeking a more comfortable position and felt a sharp stab of pain. Mind over matter! Will power! My new mantra: Pain doesn't hurt! Beffle opened a complimentary San Francisco *Chronicle* she found on the bedtstand and began reading it, and at ease for the first time in a long time, she began imagining ways to get the best press coverage.

"Beffle! Beffle!"

That shrieking voice!

"*Beffle!*"

Pearl! Bedecked with more imitation pearls than ever. Some as big as walnuts. *Pearl.*

Pearl rushed to the bed and hugged Beffle, and pain flamed up, and it hurt. Beffle gasped and shoved her away.

"I'm sorry hon," said Pearl, "I forgot."

Can this be my animal helper?

"Oh you poor sweetie."

She has a tiara of pearls worked into her hair!

"How'd you find me?"

"When I went to look for you, out at your casino, they told me where."

"Do you like my place?"

"You betcha!" Pearl drew a pint of rum out of her purse and offered it. "This'll put hair on your chest."

"Thanks, no. It's against doctor's orders."

"Come on, just one dinky little drink."

"No!"

"Well, don't fly off the handle." Pearl gulped some rum, extended the bottle. "Here's looking at you."

"How'd you find me?"

"The Twins told me all about how you comped them to your place. And they had a darned good time there, and met some nice folks who got them jobs in Frisco. And so now they're moving to Frisco, to a cheesy little flat in a really freaky neighborhood, and when they came back to Cleveland to get their stuff and move out here, I helped them load up, and they gave me their address. And just between you and me, I don't think they wanted to. But you know me, live and let live, so I'm going up there now to help them move in."

"That's dog-gone nice of you, Pearl."

"You betcha!" Pearl, smiling widely, settled into a chair and talked of Lakewood, and said she'd not seen Eddy since the reunion, or, for that matter, Melissa, you know, good old Carrot Top. That mystery man with Eddy . . . ? *David.* He'd been David! Pearl had it wrong. She'd seen *David* walking with *Eddy* in Beffle drag. Beffle pressed the call button and a nurse appeared. Beffle winked at her. "Can you find my doctor? I'm getting dizzy."

"Right away, Ms Braun." She turned to Pearl. "I'm afraid you'll have to leave, ma'am."

Pearl stood. "Well I guess! Now I don't have to make up an excuse to go tinkle."

Watching them go out, the fat and the thin, Beffle imagined Pearl seating herself on the throne and preparing to tinkle. Then she found some jazz on the radio, lay back, and closed her eyes. Yes. Stay here forever. Hold my daily powwow court. Watch the powwow on TV. Thoroughly rested, and but slightly distracted by a dull chest ache, she ordered a pasta dinner with red wine, did the crossword puzzles in the *Chronicle*, and the Monterey County *Herald.* After that it was eat, excuse herself for watching TV, enjoy a good night's sleep, and greet the morning, hospital-style. They made grits for her, and brought the papers. Then in came a doctor to whom she exaggerated her chest pains, and after he left, she thought of Running Deer running, and then it was mid-morning, and in came Running Deer himself, and, as he gave her her new laptop and her cellular phone, the hospital phone brought another of Two Bears' hypocritical solicitous colloquies. They both talked with Bear, and when the call was over, Deer sat down by the bed and said: "You can't get away from me, so you'll have to trust me."

"Okay. I'll trust you. But only after you say why you helped Eddy to do that number on me at the reunion."

"When Bear tells me to do something, I do it. Not always because I want to, but because I believe in him."

"For the same reason women follow men and men follow their mothers?" She glared at him. "I want my old laptop and that other stuff *back*."

"Beffle, I wish I could explain everything. But I think I've said too much already. What you don't know won't scare you, and you can't tell others."

"So what's the dark secret."

"For me, Two Bears is The O'Neill. He's the only guy who can make good our claim to the island. AIM's object, build a confederacy of tribes, a well-financed confederacy. Bear's the only guy I know who can put it together. He hopes this powwow will be our constitutional convention. It's what I believe in, what I'd give my life for, and I can't jeopardize it."

She sat up straight and offered her hand. "I lied to you; you lied to me. Now we're beyond that." They clasped hands, firmly, sincerely. "Here's the plan. Come visit me every morning. We'll talk with Bear, and organize our day. We'll make the best goddamned powwow ever seen this side of Sacred Time." And then I'll move to Mendocino County and forget this place forever. "Agreed?"

Deer embraced her gently. They sketched out the day's duties, and he left. In the afternoon the dog lady appeared. She asked about Beffle's condition, and then said, "You're Theodora Braun, aren't you."

"Yes. But please call me Beffle."

"Beffle, my name is Margaret Neumann. I feel terrible about having been the cause of your accident and will do anything, anything within reason, to make amends."

"I want to stay here as long as I can."

"Don't you want to get out and go back to work at the casino?"

"No. Please help me stay." In a rush of emotion, Beffle told her new acquaintance the whole story, avoiding nothing.

Margaret sat back, looking sympathetic, thinking it over.

"Beffle, I don't think you could have picked a better door to run into."

"Should have found a softer one."

"I recognized you, and stopped to talk with you, where it would be private, but I misjudged your speed, and the dog distracted me."

"Recognized me?"

"I'm on the Monterey County Grand Jury. I don't like casinos. They exploit the weak. Your place sucks money out of the county and delivers it to God knows where. We're making an informal investigation of the Ohlone Valley Casino because we sense there's something wrong. But your casino's on a reservation. Virtually an independent nation. Do we have *any* jurisdiction in there, or just over people when they're outside? We don't know. Also, well, I don't mind telling you. I'm rich. I live nearby in the valley. I've hired my own private investigator to informally vet the important people at your place. I know about you. I know about David Running Deer. And, above all, I know about James Two Bears Jones. Perhaps you recognize my detective agency. They're in San Francisco. Edward Jones Associates."

"Edward *Jones*."

Yes, Jones. But Two Bears isn't really a Jones. James Two Bears Jones is a pseudonym. His real name is Henry

Maxwell Adams. And he's no more an Indian than *I* am. Or you, for that matter."

"So who is he?"

"He was born in Oyster Bay, New York in 1948. He went to Yale, and then to the CIA, where he worked in proprietaries, and then he served as station chief in Nairobi, Kenya." She gazed at Beffle and began polishing her glasses. Thin, rimless. A grand jury prop, perhaps. "After twenty years, Adams retired, went to Hastings School of Law in San Francisco, passed the bar, and then eased himself into this casino racket."

"How, I mean---- his act? How could he be so good at it?"

"He spent at least ten years working in bogus CIA businesses, living a cover story, pretending to be someone he's not. He's a trained actor, a thespian, performing on the stage of the real world."

"You mean somewhere he jumped the footlights, and guided by his director and producer, he keeps the play going in our world."

"Yes. He's always on stage."

"In a country which worships actors."

"Yes, Beffle. We're *all* actors, at least in public life. Hypocrisy is the new god. Be your dream without actually *being* it. Live a lie. His sin is he does so more fervently than we do."

"Pathological drama," she replied. "Truthful lies. Purified hypocrisy. And all the same, just maybe, he really *wants* to be an Indian." Memory images of Two Bears rushed through her mind. "I'm thinking, Margaret, sometimes he *believes* he's an Indian!"

"Possibly. But there's something really fishy about all this. It still smells like CIA. As when he used CIA resources and hired detectives to find or fake enough Rumsen Ohlones to qualify in law as a tribe."

"So *that's* how it is?"

"Yes."

They sat in silence studying each other. She's not motherly, but *matronly*, and she *cares*. Elegant. Perfectly groomed. Slightly younger than me. But *matronly*. At the same moment, seemingly having concluded something, they both smiled. I'll trust Margaret and I'll trust Deer. Maybe. "Does David Running Deer know about that?"

"I doubt it." Margaret glanced at the urban/ocean view and back. "What we have to understand, Beffle, is there's an immense amount of money involved in this. Enough to give rise to *any* excess, no matter how costly or how criminal. We may be looking at another Vegas-style money laundry. Imagine! The CIA and some Indian gambling casinos are immensely rich, but do not have to tell anyone where they get their money, or account for what they do with it. Both, at some points, are connected with organized crime. Remember, back in ninety-five or ninety-six, the CIA discovered a *billion dollars* everyone had forgotten about? The CIA sets up and runs bogus businesses-- proprietaries-- as cover for secret operations. Most of them lose money. The taxpayer covers the loss. Some make money. The CIA keeps the profits. Some agents, like Adams, become high executives in these companies-- or in legitimate firms where agents have been placed-- and get large salaries, and perks, all of which they must return to CIA. They can only keep their CIA paychecks. CIA never returns to the government the money it has left over at the end of each fiscal year. It keeps the surplus. For years, as a big-time sideline, the CIA brought hard drugs into the country, and kept part of the proceeds. And it has other sources of income. Much of this capital it invests, in speculations, in bonds, in stocks, in futures, generating private wealth, which it reinvests. All right. On top of that . . . . Information within CIA is distributed only on a need-to-know basis. Records are concealed or destroyed. That's been going on so long that at times these days when the *Director* wants to know something, nobody can find it. A journalist accuses them of a heinous crime? Nobody there can find out whether they did it or not. Their policy on committing crimes is prepare the alibi beforehand. They call that plausible deniability. The other side of the coin? Plausible culpability. The principal agency dedicated to preserving the security of all cannot uncover the truth about itself. So how many billions of dollars have been mislaid in some forgotten drawer, how many billions more stolen by CIA's own agents?" She lit a cigarette, then crushed it in a tray. "So what do you think about all that?"

"I think it's time to dance in the skins of our enemies."

Margaret nodded her head and smiled. "You and I both care. That makes us sisters. We both know too much. That makes us sisters in trouble."

"Members of a new order. The Skin Dancing Sisters of Perpetual Peril and Anxiety."

"Yes, Beffle. We'd best dance in their skins before they dance in ours."

And that adds another dimension to Fun & Fortune!

Beffle speculated and Margaret agreed that maybe quondam CIA men had infiltrated and captured other Indian casinos as well, and that the Ohlone powwow would bring them together and help them establish dominion over the legitimate chiefs who would come, and eventually over the entire movement, meaning *billions* of ill-accounted-for dollars. "A significant portion of this does help Indians," said Beffle. "The Pequots are Mafia free and incorruptible. But, nonetheless, if those CIA people have taken over elsewhere, Two Bears and his associates must be skimming an immense sum off the top, and will skim even more."

"The Pequots," said Margaret, "got there first. They are autonomous, established, world-class players in the power game, and, probably, are safe from infiltration. But the rest of the tribes better watch out!"

"Where does all that rakeoff money go?"

"I don't know, but I suspect they're using it to finance a confederacy of white supremacists which will field political candidates, buy media, and arm patriots. Understand, Beffle, these men are utterly a-moral. People like Adams don't believe in *anything*. These CIA grads were produced by post-Christian society, and mean to combine leagues of the angry and disillusioned into a united force. KKKlanners, Sierra Clubbers, Male Chauvinists Piggers, Christian militias, AIM, Neo Nazis, Professional Patriots, Black Muslims, Populists of all kinds, America Firsters, and more and more. They mean to combine these coordinated groups and sympathizers into a united force to carry out a coup d'état, a putsch, against the federal government. It resembles the Roman Revolution. A republican city government proved unable to govern an empire. Hence, convulsion, transformation. One national government cannot govern the world. Not even that of the American Empire. Economic power is fast integrating into a multi-national pattern. The world political order, the nation-state system, no longer fits the economic order. These CIA graduates, like Augustus Caesar, would direct the coming convulsion into reconstituting into a new government with jurisdiction everywhere, one which uses the old names, but is in fact a new, authoritarian, constellation of powers."

"But you're not sure of that."

"No. All I'm sure of is if they get much farther down that road, the whole thing will self-destruct."

Sensing the futility of standing against this Tiananmen tank, this Juggernaut, and, whether or not it was really there, convinced they both knew too much, they gazed at each other. "Sister Theodora. Neither one of us wants to be here. We've been shanghaied."

"Yes, Sister Margaret, and we're about to jump off the ship, and we'll drown, but we'll drown swimming."

They embraced. Margaret said she'd be back every afternoon, and she'd make sure Beffle would not be discharged. And they laughed about Eddy's part in the affair. And Margaret told her about the hospital's snack bar and garden lounge, arranged about an ornamental pool, home to big multicolored Chinese carp "Put in slots and tables and we'll have a hospital casino!" said Beffle to her friend by way of good-bye.

And now to call Eddy! But, no. Not such a good idea. Bear needs me. Make the powwow happen. I'll be safe till he gets back. Pretend to be the good Girl Friday today I really was yesterday. I'll work under the cover of organizing the powwow and go with the flow.

THIRTEEN

THEY WERE TALKING of Charley and eagles, and, as so often happens, not saying what they were really saying. Deer had come every morning for two weeks, bringing news, and polaroid photos of the rising architectural Native American market. For artistic reasons, for reasons of responsibility, Beffle had been feeling increasingly guilty for not being there in person to oversee the project. Does David think me a prisoner of cowardice? *I* do! "The feather floated down out of the fog and settled right at my boy's feet. As if he'd been *selected* and presented with a *sign*."

"I have an eagle feather," said David.

"Did it fall from the sky?"

"No. There's another way to get a feather."

"Sure. Buy it."

"True."

"So, did you buy it?"

"No."

"So, Angel Face, how'd you get yours?"

"You scale the cliff, up to the eagle's nest."

"And take one out of the nest."

"No, Caged Owl, not even if you find one there." He sat on the bed and took her hands. "You wait."

"You wait?"

"You wait until the eagle comes back."

"And . . . ?"

"You pull one out of the eagle."

"You did that?"

He said yes, and she told him about vacationing in India, sitting with Braun and Charley in a posh garden restaurant, admiring a steak the waiter had just set before her, when a huge roc swooped out of the sky and snatched it off her plate, and as she told the story, and asked if that had been a sign, she thought of Charley and the special Moron underwear he never takes off and his loathing of masturbation and his two years of moron missionary work and his research of his family roots, so all his ancestors could be identified and beamed up to Moron Heaven. Is that officer in his spiked helmet and Prussian uniform ranging Moron Heaven right now? What joys other than gluttony and polygamy do they relish up there? Is Feral Frank at his side? Has he reserved a place for me? David smiled and touched her cheek. "Time to move on." He stood. "The press conference Saturday. It's going to be on local TV. You can watch me run it."

"I'm going to *be* there." Another urge. "I'll watch *me* run it." Did I really say that? "I'll leave here Friday." Emotional sovereignty! "Come get me about this time." Blurt power! "Don't want to miss lunch."

The next day, which as ever did not turn out to be tomorrow, came fueled by grits and maple syrup, and some arthritic twinges, and the sense that living her lie had gained a new dimension. Not only did she have to fake being an Irish Indian, but now she had to feign loyalty as well. What *will* I say at that press conference? Bear missed his morning call. She pictured a VIP love nest arranged for him by the

Oneida Nation's Turning Stone Casino in upstate New York or that big Indian operation in Wisconsin. What kind of love nest would suit me? David would be in it. Waiting to snatch a feather. But what else in this paradise? Would one of those Vegas casinos set one up for me? What would *they* deem appropriate? Badger called. "To build everything in this book we'll need the whole golf course and at least a year." A *year*. Where will I be in a year? "Take all the room you want. Hire all the people you need. Build what you like that you can finish by Carib Day. And see if you can heap up an Ohlone mound of decayed abalone shells." Bear's relying on me, so I'll be safe till he returns. And then lunch came and then Margaret. Once again, Margaret's arrival made Beff's day. As usual, they talked over details of what they knew about Bear and the casino and casinos generally, none of which had given them new insight into the situation, but, this time, Beffle told Margaret about her own life, about Feral Frank, and her mother, and Charley, and her brother, who'd been drafted, then killed in Vietnam.

"I think Frank was as disappointed in his son as I am in mine." Beffle said she'd never liked her brother. "He picked on me all the time. Once I got so pissed at him I burned his car!" She took Margaret's hand in hers. "He told me about interrogating prisoners. You take some up in an airplane. If the first doesn't answer questions, you push him out the door, and ask the second. No answer? Out he goes. Now ask number three. My brother said that was *policy*, not just spontaneity. And he loved it, too. And then he burned alive in a helicopter, and it makes me feel terrible to think about any of it. He took after my mother. Frank felt he'd failed. Parenting. Try try, and fail. Feral Frank could not bear to think of any of this any more than I can."

Margaret was as sympathetic as ever. She promised to bring Ed's agency report about Two Bears. "It's absolutely *miraculous* what those investigators can find." After she left, it struck Beffle that Margaret's personal life remained a mystery. Back to work! She ordered coffee, then made some phone calls and sent some e-mail and posted an announcement of the press conference on the internet. What in bloody Hell am I going to say? Promote Bear? And the confederacy? Expose Bear as its enemy? David had postponed his morning visit. When he came later that afternoon, they exchanged news of what they'd been doing. She noted Bear had forgot to check in. They ran through more details. "Hey, pal, looks like we're still on top of it!"

David smiled in agreement.

"I set up my tipi today," said he, "right on Number-One Green. It's a Deer Clan Tipi, made and painted by my great-grands."

"You can show it to me on Friday."

"It's a real beauty. You probably won't understand it, though."

"I understand everything."

"In that case you'll know the dark stripe circling the base represents earth, the tall white central stripe is the deer vision that inspired my forebears to make the tipi, and the black top is night sky. And in each space you'll find inhabitants depicted: holy places, a deer, stars, spirit trails, all united by the poles. Inside, it's a separate, somewhere-else world. Believe me, you'll *feel* it when you're sitting in there. The poles convey prayers from inside, up through dream space, into the sky, and on, through the sky, out of the universe, into sacred time."

"It's our turn. Let's us build our own tipi to set on Number-Two Green. The earth will show holy places:

banks and sports arenas. Swifty the Morgan, the Flying Green Horse, will stretch rushing across the white dream band; and space trash will stir among the stars."

David whooped and grasped her shoulder and they talked about details and whats and whens until they heard an intense screechy voice outside and in came Pearl. "Those broads out there tried to keep me from coming in to visit. They actually called security! And I thought *I* had balls!"

"Pearl. We're talking business. I have to do my work from here. In my room. We're in *conference.* I told them not to let *anyone else* in. Nothing personal, you understand."

"I should be sore at you, but I ain't."

She barged out.

"I told them not to let *her* in. Everyone else is all right. But not *her.*"

"Our tipi has a repertoire of songs and dances coming from deep in the years, but always changing, alive."

"We'll have to do the same for the motor pool and Swifty."

"And the medicine bundle. What will we do for that?"

"Wait for dreams to tell us." What if they told you Two Bears is no more an Indian than I am? "Some things are stranger than dreams." I hope Margaret keeps her promise to bring me Eddy's agency report about Two Bears. "Do some of your colleagues still call me One Bear?"

"Could be, but I haven't heard it for a while."

I'll show him the report.

Does he know already?

"We Blackfeet used to build the biggest tipis of all. Imagine. Forty buffalo hides for the cover. Four fire pits inside." He stood to go. "See you in my dreams."

In came Two Bears.

Two Bears flashed his friendly threatening snile.

Two Bears said hello.

Two Bears sat on the bed.

Two Bears peered at Beffle and asked about her health.

Beffle said she felt fine. "I'll be out tomorrow."

Two Bears rubbed some snuff onto his gums.

Two Bears, still peering at her, said: "Sometimes I think you're accident prone."

Beffle glared back.

"Sometimes, Grease Face, I look forward to dancing in your skin."

He laughed. "My skin would be one Hell of a loose fit." He walked over to the dresser, and sat on it. "I've just been at the compound. You people are doing a good job."

"Did you see my tipi?" asked David, hungry for approval.

"Deer Clan. A real beauty."

"We're going to design a tipi for the cars."

"If anybody could make one, I'd bet on the Blackfeet to do it."

"We'll build it for the second annual Ohlone Carib Day Fair."

"Sure, David, sure we will," said Bear, in a patronizing way.

They asked him what he'd accomplished.

"It turned out even better than I thought it would. We'll have about fifty chiefs here, some from tribes with casinos, some from wannabees and others from the not-until-the-sun-stops-rising kind." He took some snuff. "What I told them is what I believe. It all rests on what's called the yin-yang, from ancient China, but I think Indians all believe it too, and we may have passed it on to the chinks when we still lived in Siberia. Now me. You both know me. I don't have to fake anything with you, which is one Hell of a lot more than you can say, Beffle. Me. I'm a pagan. I believe all the gods exist, or none of them exist, because the proof of the existence of any of them is always the same, but either way, it doesn't matter."

He stood and began pacing.

"I know that because they haven't shot me down yet."

He snorted some snuff and leaned against the wall.

"Yin-yang. Life is a progression of changing opposites. Seeming opposites. Beneath is a union we can sense but cannot express. Our duty, as a society, and as individuals, is to keep these changing opposites in balance. Preserve the harmony. That was central to the philosophy of the Ohlone tribelets. For millennia. Right here! Before the either/or Catholics came and enslaved them in the Missions. It curbed the tribelets' hatred and mistrust of one another. In recent times Clio has immensely distorted the balance. Modern history is the biography of white supremacy. You don't believe that? Read it! These days, the human family is moving back toward an Ohlone sort of equity. Consider China. Korea. Japan. Southeast Asia. We Native Americans are in a position to help push life back toward harmonious balance. If we unite. And have enough money. And now goddamn it to Hell, we've got the form and the bucks. And we're putting it together right fucking here!"

"So far, so good," said a smiling Deer. "We've done our part. Everything will be ready and on time. You can count on us."

"I do. That's why I put Beffle in charge."

"Bear. I told Deer I've been pretending to be part Indian. He knows. But *you* didn't know that. I resent your bringing it up! It's no big deal. When the phone company in Monterey laid me off, here I was, a menopause woman

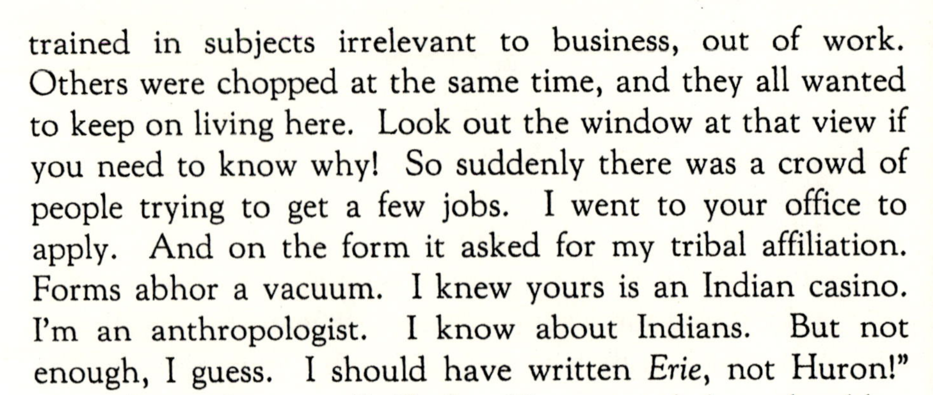

trained in subjects irrelevant to business, out of work. Others were chopped at the same time, and they all wanted to keep on living here. Look out the window at that view if you need to know why! So suddenly there was a crowd of people trying to get a few jobs. I went to your office to apply. And on the form it asked for my tribal affiliation. Forms abhor a vacuum. I knew yours is an Indian casino. I'm an anthropologist. I know about Indians. But not enough, I guess. I should have written *Erie*, not Huron!"

"Easy does it, Beffle." He grasped her shoulder. "You're really good at what you do. I've no complaints. You two have done a fucking good job of getting things ready."

"I do my best. Why? I may not be an Indian, but I share your yin-yang view and will do anything within reason to help realize your dream about creating a tribal confederacy." That's true enough. And Two Bears Adams is the man who'll destroy it! Anger, rage against this arrant hypocrite churning inside, she listened to her voice saying girl-Friday things to the boss. "So what's the plan from now till the press conference?"

They talked over details of getting ready. Bear called their decision to charge twenty dollars for general admission and make everything else free a stroke of genius. Bear looked at Beffle. "You're smart and brave. And spirited. I like that."

"And I look forward to dancing on the brink of the world." Don't say it! "In your skin."

Bear replied with his trademark snile.

No fucking wonder revealing my Indian act didn't phase him.

"So, Bear, why'd you come back so early?"

"To do the press conference."

"*I'm* going to conduct the conference."

"From the hospital? A bedside levée like Louis the Fourteenth?"

"No. From the casino like Theodora the First."

"You told me all that on the phone, but I couldn't be sure."

"When they brought me here, and *I* wasn't sure, I was going to have David Running Deer do it."

He glared contempt at Deer.

"You're fucking jerking me off."

"I'm telling you I was going to have David do it."

"That fucking engine doctor?"

"That fucking *honest* engine doctor would do one Hell of a lot better then *you* will."

Bear's voice snarled at her.

"Woman, no fucking wonder you're accident prone."

"Deer would do a good job."

"That weak passive bastard would fuck up!"

"At least, you big fat fraudulent phony, he's a real Indian!"

Flushing with rage, Two Bears sprang to his feet.

"Woman, you better watch your step."

"Sure. The only good Indian is a dead Indian."

He stomped out and slammed the door.

"Well, David, how about *them* bananas?"

"Long ago he told me *you* were faking it."

"He told you I'm not really an Indian?"

"Yes."

Beffle told David Running Deer all that Margaret had told her. "So I guess from now on we'll have to be bärenjägers," he said.

"Bear Hunters. Yes sir! And we'll need all our animal helpers and then some."

"Animal spirit helpers are amoral, tricky, greedy, irritable, deceitful, and full of magic. Coyote is the worst."

"Just like Bear's CIA." She smiled at him. "Tomorrow, when you come to get me, come for lunch. I want you to meet my friend Margaret."

David sat on the bed and grasped her hands. "Two Bears and AIM. They both seemed congruent. I still love his dream of an Indian confederacy sustained by Anglo gambling losses. But now I see he's faking it." David squeezed her hands. "*Bärenjäger.*"

PART FIVE

Thanks to genetic control, Nature-driven evolution is becoming commerce-driven *evil*ution. Is that why to most people future generations are of no concern?

--Beffle a.k.a. Ms Braun
Carmel, CA, 2003

FOURTEEN

DR. DEER ARRIVED FIRST. He found Beffle sitting at the table by the window, scanning the *Chronicle*, enjoying the view. She poured him some coffee. "Two Bears didn't have it quite right," he said. "A sense of oneness with all, *that's* the central Ohlone concept. If he were a real Indian, he would have known. Sure they balanced opposites, but . . . when I was sixteen, I scaled a giant butte, and built a stone and grass platform on top, fasted, and, for days and days, I waited for revelations and visits from spirit beings. And eventually I crossed into the pure world of dream time, and, well, I went up a child, and came down a man."

"Believing the earth is the back of a great turtle."

He smiled and shook his head, and asked about the press conference. Beffle said they had to keep the AIM dream going, so they should produce the conference as planned and expose Two Bears later. "I brought my magic helper," said David Running Deer, turning his back to the door. He drew a 9mm automatic from his coat and laid it on the table. "Here's Glock."

"I remember. I met him before."

He slid the pistol back into its holster.

"They gave me a permit for Glock because sometimes I take our money to the bank."

The door opened, admitting Margaret.

. . . and Ed!

Beffle rose and embraced him.

She stood back, holding his hands.

"Well, Eddy, I guess we can call this our second reonion." She introduced David to Margaret, and Margaret said they'd met already, and they all sat at the table. "Eddy Jones!" She shook her head in wonder. "I guess you know David."

"We left Westlake together."

"And didn't tell me."

"I was you and you were Melissa. So by definition *you* knew. And I wasn't morally obliged to tell Carrot Top. Or, to look at it another way, David was watching you for Bear and I was investigating you for Margaret. We couldn't tell you that. But we wanted to scare you so you'd get a sense of the depth of your danger."

"It worked. You scared the shit out of me."

"Here's something else to tweak your nerves." He gave her a spiral-bound folder. "Here's my report on Henry Maxwell Adams. Two Bears. Margaret wants you to keep it."

She thumbed through the booklet.

"It's amazing! How did you manage to find out so much!"

"These days, Beffle, there are no secrets."

"As in you're retired CIA."

"Where'd you hear that?"

"I guessed it." And blurted it. "After all, you told me you're in law enforcement."

"You told me you raise rats." As for him, he said, in a way, he does indeed work in law enforcement, at least, like now, this unusual case of finding facts for a grand jury. His agency's main office is in Cleveland, and he maintains others on the coasts, one in San Francisco, one in Key West, one in Philadelphia. "And would you believe it, I started this business as a CIA proprietary, and built it into a profitable enterprise. What? True. "Our main job is gathering information for defendants. And we specialize in federal cases." As he talked along, exuding benevolent confidence, Eddy seemed a rock-solid boss type without a care in the world, not the dream-terrified man who'd cuddled and wept and then submitted to being Beffle in a yellow dress. "My favorite office is Frisco, because when I'm out here I can come down to the Monterey Peninsula and play on these gorgeous golf courses." Ask him why the best golfers need more than one club. Remind him I know every inch of his body. And he, of mine! And Margaret chatters politely, and he asks for a dinner date. "I can't promise anything till after Carib Day." I'll be watching out for you. "Good old Eddy. My favorite golf Nazi. Going to keep me alive so we can dine together after our powwow fair."

When they got up to go, Beffle invited Margaret to visit her any time at her house in Carmel Meadows. "Hell with the casino. I'm staying at home in my studio from now on." They embraced, and Beffle followed them out the door. "Eddy, if you want to have some fun, jine the cavalry."

"Looks like we both already did."

He beamed good-bye.

"And, Eddy, maybe you'll get some dreams from me."

I still like the bastard, she thought, as she went back in.

"And now, David, you can take me home."

He made a joke about her being homesick as they carried her stuff out to the parking lot.

"All right! You brought Swifty!" She stroked Swifty's waxy polished hood. "Remember, when Bear and me---- when we flew away in this flying green horse! That was absolutely awesome! Talk about floating disembodied in Dream Time! I wish you'd been there. It was dazzling! A high point in my life! You'd have loved it!"

"You went up with the eagles."

They swung into the Morgan and drove out to the Holman Highway and downhill by pines and around curves toward Pacific Grove. "Ms Owl," said David. "There's something wrong with that Margaret. I don't think you should trust her."

"I don't trust anybody."

"And you raise rats."

"Because I don't trust anybody, with a few exceptions, I trust everybody."

In Pacific Grove, they went to the business center and xeroxed Deer a copy of Ed's report, and then they drove by Victorian houses to the ocean and along it toward Pebble Beach. "For ten thousand years," said David Running Deer, pointing at a dune, "the Ohlone lived here, and except for those mounds of abalone shells, did not leave a single scar on the face of nature. Not one! And now, look!" Ahead loomed the Spanish Bay hotel complex and golf course, where some deer were grazing. "Europeans have been here for less than three hundred years and have ripped Nature's face right off!" Swifty rushed up Sunset Drive, by houses and the high school, and ascended Holman Highway and turned south on Route One. "In Indian Time, multi-life was a much much thicker presence around here than today. Elk. Bear. Huge crowds of water fowl. An ocean alive with abalone and fish! And now! You don't even hear birdsong!"

"Yes. And back in Ohlone Time only about ten thousand people lived between Big Sur and the Golden Gate. Now, there are millions!"

"And they hold dominion over the birds of the air, the beasts of the land, and the fish of the sea."

"Worse! That's not all they master. Thanks to genetic control, Nature-driven evolution is becoming commerce-driven *evil*ution. Is that why to most people future generations are of no concern?"

Deer switched on classical music and they left Highway One and went down into Carmel. "We Indians are homesick for Never-Was Used-to-Be-Land, and so are you, Mayflower daughter." He parked, and led toward the Jack London. "And, Beffle, the Ohlones couldn't step into a saloon for a beer." They sat at the oval bar. "Two Bears is right when he says there are no Indians any more, just like there are millions of Norwegians but no Vikings, and there never *will* be any Indians again. What we have to do is plan ahead, and make a world suited to the children of the future age." Talking it over, they found themselves in full agreement. "So," said Beffle, "that's why we have to produce the Columbus/Carib Day powwow as planned."

"No matter what?"

"No matter what!"

They grasped hands, went back to Swifty, and rushed over to the Mission and went behind it toward the lagoon, and on to Beffle's house.

"Here's what I'm homesick for," said she as they walked by the dusty old car in the drive and into her studio. Everything was exactly as she'd left it: sculptures taking shape, unmade bed, an open book, a sink full of dishes; over it a fake oak cabinet, doors ajar, with peeling veneer and particleboard shelves. In all the place looked like a rich and promising life had been chopped off by Death himself. "David. That cabinet looks like oak, so it *is* oak, okay?"

"Sure. I'll believe its skin is it."

She opened the fridge and confronted a dried head of lettuce and an ice covered freezer and some beer. She took out two cans and they sat down at her worktable. "Now, watch." She stood and fetched a mask and a red wig and disguised herself as Melissa. "This'll be my cover until the conference. I've a phony press credential for the *Plain Dealer* which I noted in our main computer and put on the comp list, so Melissa Green, ace reporter, can wander around with you, looking at everything. And after the conference, we'll come back here, and I'll start working on a sculpture of you. Eventually, we'll cast it ten feet high, in bronze, and it will be our King Candle, standing at the entrance to the Indian Architecture Park, which we'll keep building and adjusting and refining and perfecting as a gift to coming generations."

David smiled and raised his glass.

"To Melissa!"

"To fun and fortune."

Beffle stood.

"Here's the plan. They know my car at the casino, and of course they'll recognize the parking medallion, so I'll drive my car to the Village, and you take Swifty, and I'll meet you at the Running Iron, and you can drive me to the compound, and we'll walk around, and look at everything, and make sure we're ready for the press conference."

Beffle parked beside the road just beyond the Village where she could leave her car for a few days if necessary, and walked to the Running Iron. She could hike or even run to her car if need be. David was sitting inside at the table by the stuffed cougar and had a beer waiting for her. "They should call this place the Tawny Lion."

"Or the Cornered Cougar."

"Or the Woozy Wildcat."

They sipped their beer and listened to music.

Then, in from the garden came Two Bears.

He strode over to their table, drew up a chair, and sat.

"This," said David, "is Melissa Green." He turned to Beffle. "This, Melissa, is Two Bears Jones."

Two Bears stared at Beffle.

"You've got that wrong, David. Try Theodora Braun."

"David, you've got *both* parts wrong," she blurted quite without thinking. "Try Henry Maxwell Adams."

Bear made an evil snile. "Theodora, you know too fucking much."

"Nevertheless, tomorrow, as the mistress of ceremonies, when I introduce you, I won't tell all."

Bear rose part way from his seat and leaned toward Beffle raging into her face. "You rotten bitch you fucking better not."

"You think you know what I see? You got that wrong, too. I see you, yes. I see a fat infant, squalling, drooling, sniveling, puking, shitting all over itself, yelling *me me me.*"

"Listen, cuntface. You're both deep in it and can't get out."

Two Bears stood and stalked out the door.

"David, we'll do our best to make the conference run smoothly."

"We're sworn to it."

David drove them to the casino compound. They left Swifty in the motor pool and walked by the hotel and past the casino to the Number One Fairway, which was being transformed into an architectural park. At the entrance stood some Ohlone tule huts and a sweathouse. Just beyond, they came to the flat-topped vestibule of an arched-roof five-fire Iroquois longhouse, covered with canvas rectangles instead of birch bark, an edifice which was to be the site of the press conference. About twenty-five feet by one-hundred, it had plenty of room for the podium, chairs, buffet, and bar, at which a few early journalists were already drinking. Beffle and Deer ordered orange juice, and a man next to her, whose credential accredited him to some local magazine, asked her what could have possibly attracted a representative of the Cleveland *Plain Dealer*. "The Ohlone case parallels ours. All the land titles between Big Sur and the Golden Gate are phony, rest on deceptions and lies. The Ohlone, you see, never signed a treaty or any other kind of land-transfer document with the Spanish, who, in the name of their king, arbitrarily made the land grants to which all current titles refer. As with Oh-lone, so it is with O-hio. We have to think of the Erie Indians. After all, they're the ones we named our lake after. Show me a treaty transferring their rights to us. To anyone. You can't. It doesn't exist. They never signed anything. The Erie Indians still own Greater Cleveland." David, acting as casino docent, created a blizzard of imaginary details and anecdotes, and, once back outside, he burst into peals of laughter.

He led the way to Number-One Green.

There, right in the middle, over the sacred hole itself, stood his heirloom tipi, a **KEEP OUT** sign staked in front.

They went inside, where David took beers out of an ice chest.

With the door flap closed, and no windows to preserve connections, they sat on an island, out of the outside world, in a cone, in Dream Time, immersed in a foreign fragrance. Matte filtered sunlight made the walls radiant, limned the uniting poles into a superimposed line drawing. You could see through the ancient hides behind it just well enough to discern the low ochre band of Earth; the white middle band of Spirit World, the star-studded black top band of sky. "Look there, Owl, that butterfly on the white, it brings dreams." A very different private ur-world, this---- one utterly detached from the moveable sets of the outside theater, golf-to-architecture, and tomorrow's staged press conference.

Back in her car, driving home, Beffle felt the presence of this new reality, and knew it would last long enough to help her render David in clay. With rebar and wood, she built an armature, about three-feet high, and began packing and kneading clay onto it, seeking for the outer and inner likeness of David Running Deer. Occasionally, she stood back, and walked around her emerging piece, to view it from all angles, and adjust it, and at times she even stood on a stool to study its top.

And then she thrust a pencil into it.

And the shaft of a brush.

Why in the fuck am I making this voodoo doll?

She drew out the pencil, and the brush, and smoothed over the wounds, healing them.

She walked around her David again.

Sure beats Barbie's Traveling Ken.

And suddenly the sculpture seemed remote, an entity, another self, play-acting for the great world.

And she sat down at her desk and began reading Eddy's report.

Two Bears had been arrested in an anti-war demonstration at Columbia University.

And then he'd joined the CIA.

And now he'll burst into my house and kill me.

She hurled the report at the wall.

I'll hire Eddy to investigate Eddy.

What will *that* report say?

I'll hire Eddy to investigate me!

That report doubtless already exists.

And now Eddy will kick in my door and kill me.

For mocking golf.

A ghastly feeling of emptiness, of vulnerability, enveloped her. Tomorrow. What will I do? What should I do? What's the right thing? Will I live till then. Alone. Defenseless. *I* don't have a Glock. Got to talk with somebody. Get a ouija board and talk with Feral Frank. The Twins? My Charley? He belongs to the god of the Morons. Charles, the Vegas cabby? Sure. Find cab 667, and then speak in my rough Beer Fairy voice, all the time remembering I'm a half-breed auto sales-*man* from Saint Louis. Wet dark loneliness overwhelmed her. That boy, yes . . . Billy, that limousine kid from Foxwoods. She dug through her papers and found his number. He sensed the truth before I did. Tell him the story. Learn what he'd do in my place. She touched the numbers and listened to the phone ring in far off Connecticut.

"Hello," said a young woman's voice.

"Is Billy there?"

"That no-good dirty rotten son-of-a-bitch ain't here and he'd goddamned well better not come back no more if he knows what's good for him."

The woman hung up.

It had become so windy there were no waves at all.

It had become so awful it was funny.

So what am I going to say tomorrow?

Ask me on Sunday.

FIFTEEN

IN THE MORNING, ill-refreshed after a fitful sleep and poisonous dreams, Beffle fried some leftover grits, slopped them with corn syrup, ate, dressed in gray-streaked redhead scar-faced green-dress dead-Melissa drag, pinned on her credential, slung a shoulder bag containing her Beffle costume, and drove out to the Village to where Swifty and David waited at roadside. A rush in Swifty up the grade through sweet air to the motor pool restored her spirits. At the longhouse door, Ace and High Hawk checked credentials; inside, tables offered the guests a variety of free T-shirts emblazoned with the Ohlone Valley Casino's emblem and slogan: ***Fun and Fortune***, and at the bar stood early-bird journalists. Melissa/Beffle, conversing, learned one major succulent in the bait that had been swallowed by so many media types and caused them to be reeled into Carmel Valley for the conference was the fact that the casino would ask Indians everywhere to celebrate Carib Day-- October 12th-- as Anti-Columbus Day, in all an offer of dramatic copy and photo ops to balance the coverage of Columbus Day parades in Frisco and elsewhere.

Outside once more, Beffle paused to admire the faux-- or was it mock?-- birchbark covering the longhouse. Each rectangle had been painted to resemble the real thing. Whence the *blind* in Blind Badger, considering what an excellent artist and builder he is? Just down the street, declaiming before a round house framed by saplings and covered with reed mats, at the center of a group of journalists, stood Badger himself, the official guide. He described the hut as a Kickapoo wickiup and then, in response to a question, said, "What you see here are only *examples* of native American structures, removed from their social, religious, and even *meteorological* context." He gestured at all the construction. "To do this right would take the whole golf course. A Creek Square Ground alone, with the sacred fire and the ball field and appropriate buildings, would occupy two fairways. What? My sources?" He produced the book. "Look! I recommend this to you as background. Yes? *Native American Architecture* by Peter Nabokov and Robert Easton. Oxford University Press. And, of course, what I learned from the old people on the Klamath Reservation where I grew up, and the fruits of curiosity generally." He guided the party to the next building, a large plank Kwakiutl house you enter through a painted mouth, because, as he put it, houses swallow their visitors. Next came a Cherokee notched-log cabin; a Seminole star fire in an open, thatched hut; a Pueblo adobe house with an outside beehive oven; a dome-shaped Chippewa bark-covered wigwam; and after that a six-sided wooden Chippewa Drum Dance Lodge, its shingled roof sloping downward from a turret. Then they came to a Pawnee earthlodge, one appearing from ground level as a flat, verdant cone thanks to the sod covering Badger's workers had stripped from Number Two Green.

Badger led them down inside.

A TV reporter remarked to Beffle: "These houses are all so . . . so *raw* and *ugly*."

Beffle stared angrily at her. "Raw and ugly! What you're seeing is *classical*. This architecture is severely restricted by materials and tools, and perfected by slow change deriving from millennia of living."

"Look at this primitive basement they call home! And then tell me we don't have to keep trying to civilize the savages."

"Yeah! Sure! Look around at it! It's better than the dugouts Europeans built on the Western Front."

"The Western what?"

"Verdun! World War One! Ypres!"

"I don't know much about that, but all this, everything we've seen here, is nasty and crude, and so is that old man."

"Listen Fart Face! Show some fucking respect!"

Beffle, the coals of anger blown red-hot by this puffing moron, stalked out of the earthlodge, resolved to make AIM's dream come true, Bear or no Bear. She paced by structures and a Thunderbird perched on a pole to the tipis, and up onto Number One Green into David Running Deer's heirloom tipi world. She tied the flap shut and waited in Spirit Space between earth and sky to calm down. Why should Indians, why should *anyone*, have to struggle for the respect and equity that should be birthright? She unslung her bag and began transforming herself into Beffle; then, finished, seated herself on the lush sod carpet, looking at the sunbright lines and shapes on the tipi wall, remembering the similar design painted beneath that Vegas overpass Bear had shown her, imagining ghosts of golfers who had once congregated on this spot.

Time to leave!

Have to walk around a little, to make sure everything's running smoothly, then go confront Bear and open the conference.

And say what?

She packed Melissa Green, Fearless Reporter, into her shoulder bag, placed it on Number One Hole to thwart ghostly golfers and golf-course gophers, untied the flap, and strode out, leaving it there.

She strolled around, looking at everything, and then, on the way back to the longhouse, came across Blind Badger standing before a Hopi stone dwelling, speaking passionately to the journalists. He was talking about the rising of 1680, the only successful revolt of Indians against the Europeans in all of North America's history. "Pueblo runners carried messages to elders of all the towns, Pueblo, Navajo, Hopi, to attack the Spaniards at the rising of the moon." Beffle began humming "The Rising of the Moon," an Irish song about the revolt of 1799 against the English, which began with the same signal, and Badger told of the virtual slavery Spaniards had imposed and of the triumphant Indians killing priests and livestock and burning churches and routing armed forces and driving off all the settlers.

He'd sunk so deeply into it he'd forgotten about time, and, consequently, might make his audience late to the conference, so Beffle told him to conclude. He nodded, and she walked back to the longhouse. Did he still worry about wild boar rooting up the turf? As before, Ace, a.k.a. Blood Turtle, and High Hawk stood by the door, checking credentials. They greeted her and chatted about Las Vegas. Some media types were networking at the bar or lounging in the chairs. The stage was now decorated with multi-colored ears of Indian corn, tomatoes, squash, pumpkins, chocolates, peanuts, avocados, and potatoes to symbolize the Native

American origin of sixty-percent of the world's food crops. George stood nearby. Even without his Roman armor, dressed in a white suit, he presented a massive and formidable presence, even more so than did Two Bears.

"Hey, broad ass, where you been hiding?"

"George, something you need to consider."

"And what the fuck is that?"

"Imperious Caesar, dead and turned to clay, might stop a hole and keep the wind away."

"What?"

"Might not the guts of Alexander plug up a beer barrel?"

Shakespeare to the rescue, thought she, as she went backstage.

There, at a table, sat Two Bears, dressed in a gray suit, rubbing snuff onto his gums.

"Good morning, Theodora."

"Good morning, Henry."

Bear stood, awkwardly.

"That George out there, Henry. We should call him Big-ot for short."

That produced a smile, and then a look of pain.

"My back's been acting up."

"I'm sorry. Sciatica's even worse than arthritis."

He replied with his usual snile.

She offered a hand. "Truce?"

"Truce." He sat on the table. "You've done one Hell of a job, Beff. There's reporters from everywhere out there, and more keep coming."

"They like the contrast, the irony, the dramatic promise of our organizing a continental Anti-Columbus Day. They're hoping for a cultural Super Bowl. Our handouts and press kits stress that the first Carib Day

Powwow will also be the Native American Fourth of July, our own Independence Day and Constitutional Convention combined. And all that rests on the romantic---- you know, a foundation of casino glamour and big bucks."

"I have the same impression."

She embraced him, and stood back. "We can make this the story-du-jour! Today *and* on the twelfth!"

"It's about time to start." Abruptly, his face turned hard and he peered into her eyes. "Don't double-cross me."

"Bear. I intensely want this dream to come *true*!"

"Don't forget you're accident prone."

"Don't forget, I can puke at will."

He held up a hand and said, "Wish me luck."

"What will Clio tell future generations about today?"

"Clio's going to say we kicked ass!"

They walked out on stage and sat.

There were fifty or sixty people, including Margaret and Eddy, to whom she'd given chimerical credentials. Some guests wore ***Fun and Fortune*** T-shirts. "Bear. See that guy at the left end of the third row? In the blazer? Yes. That's Eddy Jones, the bloke I told you about when I came back from Ohio. You know, from my high school reunion. Remember? The guy who vanished."

She rose, walked upstage to the mike, scratched it for attention, and as they hushed, glanced from face to face. Running Deer. Smiling. At Bear? At me? Blind Badger seemed a grave elder abstracted from some ancient movie. Eddy: winking! No gravitas there. Margaret radiating dignified Carmel elegance. The white bulk of Big Ot-- of George-- standing behind. And the Pequots' Laughing Fox! And there sits that despicable TV-reporter. Whom we'll manipulate like all the rest of them to trumpet our arrogant ambitions to the world. Yes and no. The Indian confederacy will be more than that. Thoughts of everything being yes-and-no more-and-less hubris-and-humility reeled through her head whilst she listened to her voice making a short but sweet introduction "of the man behind it all, Two Bears Jones."

In a breeze of polite applause Two Bears came forward to the mike, and Beffle, giving herself no applause for collaborating in this deception, sat down.

In his beautiful baritone singing voice, Two Bears thanked them for coming, said he'd make a short introduction, and then open the floor to questions. "This," said he, pushing the mike aside, and coming up to the edge of the stage, "this is a time of transition, of immense change, accelerating, accelerating. For the first time in all history the young people live in an everyday world where anything they imagine can come true. Anything, and *more*. In the real world, to a great degree, previous generations had but to copy their elders. Previous generations could and did speculate, imagine, dream, live in myth and fantasy. Now, the dreams and reality are converging. Today's youth is building a new way, a way that will serve as a model for future generations. Present times, their accelerating transition to who knows what, are extremely dangerous for all of us. We now are building a bridge to the other side. But is it well engineered? Is it being built by honest contractors?"

Two Bears paused and swiftly glanced into the eyes of each auditor.

"The original peoples of this continent must play a primary part in shaping the future. To that end we here call upon all the tribes to send representatives to the first annual Carib Day Powwow, the details of which are described at length in the updated press kits we will now distribute."

George and some others quickly passed out big envelopes fat with text, charts, photographs, graphics.

"Right here, in two weeks time, we will form a confederacy of North American tribes. All Indians will be admitted to the grounds free; others will be charged twenty dollars. City Indians, who have no tribe, I urge to seek tribal adoption. Adoption of strangers as full members is totally consistent with our ancient traditions."

His hands clasped behind him, Two Bears paced along the front of the stage, came back to the center.

"We have pre-registered forty-nine tribal chiefs. We will not be satisfied until all premier chiefs agree to come. Carib Day will be *our* Fourth of July, *our* Independence Day, *our* Constitutional Convention. Tribes will elect delegates to the Continental Congress which will convene here, next year, on Columbus Day---- Carib Powwow Day. Our motto henceforth will be: All for each; each for all."

Arms crossed on the lectern, leaning across it toward the auditors, his voice radiating at once great energy and beauty, Two Bears called for questions, and responded, as one after another reporters stood and made their inquiries. He converted *how* questions into whats and whys, and his replies seemed truth driven, *passion* driven. This guy understands! This guy *believes*. He's so eloquent I almost accept what he says without any reservations, and *would*, were it not that I know what a flimflam artist and cunning hypocrite he really is. Beffle shifted on her hard plastic chair, and felt arthritis stab her knee. And his hubris beard has grown back in defiance of us shaving it in Vegas. Navajo men need only shave once a week, and it's much the same with other tribes. That beard should have clued me long ago to the truth. Two Bears cannot *possibly* be a full-blooded Indian. What arrogance! What contempt for the rest of us that beard represents. Why am I acting as an accessory when I should be denouncing him?

And now *he's* talking about deceptions.

"When hunting, Ohlone men, who lived right here for thousands of years, would trot alongside deer, wearing deer horns and skins, so their prey would trust them well enough to let them approach within killing distance. Deception is central to humanity. At heart we're all alike. Human history is the biography of Coyote reacting to changing circumstances, climates and technologies."

A reporter stood up.

"Can you give us an example?"

"Once upon a time, Coyote, Cougar, and Fox went hunting together. Luck smiled on them. They were quite successful. That evening, when it came time to divide up the game, Cougar told Fox to do the honors. Fox divided the proceeds into three equal piles, then asked Cougar to take his choice. Cougar paced around the piles, sprang upon Fox, and devoured him. Cougar then asked Coyote to divide their wealth again into two piles. Coyote put everything good into one pile, a few scraps into another, and asked Cougar to choose between them. After doing so, Cougar asked Coyote how he'd managed to make such an equitable division. Coyote smiled and said: 'I remembered you did most of the hunting.'"

Responding to the next question, Two Bears said the US Constitution was modeled in part on that of the Iroquois Confederacy.

To an inquiry about architectural context, he replied: "That can be elusive, even to me. For example, as traditional Navajo see it, or *feel* it, the house is home to spirits as well as people. They burn cedar there to convey their prayers up to the powers. Spirituality saturates everything. The house is too holy, too ceremonial, to admit of indoor plumbing."

Some seemed to be following what he was saying, some not. The TV reporter who yesterday had been badgering Badger rose. "What," she asked, "do coyotes and plumbing have to do with Columbus Day?"

Bear leaned forward on the podium and glared at her. "Coyote is one of the old people from Dream Time who made us and all this you see around us."

Silent, peering at her, fists closed, sniling his nasty snile, Bear seemed ready to spring out and eat her.

She stood her ground. "Carib Day? Are you telling us you want to replace Columbus Day with some sort of trumped-up coyote dream?"

"Dream Time is still with us. You go there every night. And it scares the Hell out of you."

A reporter stood.

"Answer the lady's questions."

Bear smiled. "Not long ago, last week I think, Coyote was strolling along a hiking trail. That one down in Pacific Grove. He came across Raccoon, which surprised him, because Raccoon never comes out in the sun if he can help it. Raccoon caught sight of him too late to run away. Coyote's much too swift. If you don't believe me, read Mark Twain's account of how fast Coyote really is. So Raccoon bent over and mooned Coyote. 'Isn't that just special,' said Coyote, 'being mooned by my dinner.'

"'Maybe that's how it looks to you, but you've got it wrong. See! My ear's to the ground. I'm listening to what they're saying beneath the earth.'

"'What are they saying?'

"'They're talking about you.'

"'Me?'

"'Yes. Quiet.'

"Coyote stood there in silence till he could bear it no longer. 'Tell me.'

"'They're saying so many joggers and bike riders and little children use this trail it should be kept clean. Always. They just caught two dogs who pooped on the trail and burned them alive. Now they're looking for another animal who left a big stinking pile of shit back there by Asilomar.'

"'Wait here,' said Coyote, and he rushed back along the trail, found his excrement steaming in the sun, and using a cypress branch, pushed it off. Then he brushed away his footprints and found a puddle on someone's lawn and washed his feet. When he came back, Raccoon was gone. Well, he must have got tired of waiting for me. So, okay, no dinner, but at least I know what they're talking about underground.'"

The room hushed for a moment.

Then *Eddy* stood, and held up his kit.

"Mr. Jones. In this handout, here, have you addressed every important aspect of the story?"

"Well, yes, mainly. I forgot to say, if the Pueblo have it right, human life emerged from underground."

"You also forgot to say your name is really Henry Maxwell Adams and you're no more an Indian than I am." Eddy turned to the others, handed a pile of folders to Margaret. "She'll pass these around. They document the details, including Adams' career in the CIA."

George came up behind Eddy, grasped his wrist, twisted his arm, and began to run him out. Bear spoke into the mike. "George! No! Let him go! Truth is truth." He stepped forward, leaving the mike, and gestured for silence.

"Truth is truth. Carib Day will proceed, unchanged, but without me."

SIXTEEN

BEFFLE BOLTED BACKSTAGE and out the door. That makes Eddy the champion bear hunter. She walked swiftly to Deer's tipi, snatched her bag off Hole Number One, and trotted to the casino, paced through the rattle and honk of the gaming floor to the private elevator, and rode it up to her suite. Once inside, she locked and chained the door, shut the blinds, stripped naked, took a hot shower, and flopped on her bed to nap, to plan the next move. Have to quit. Gather my stuff. Take it home. Find another job. Never ever come back! But who can replace me! I cannot cripple our Carib Day event! Adrift in a cold dark sea of doubt she slid into a nervous sleep whose current carried her into caverns of imageless nightmare. A persistent Day World ringing shocked her awake. *Telephone*! The clock showed 6:22. "Hello." Badger! Saying an emergency meeting of the Ohlone Council had deposed Two Bears as of now and replaced him with David Running Deer. "I called to assure you your job is secure. They confirmed you in it."

Beffle thanked him and arose.

She went to the bathroom.

Would the spirits let the traditional Navajo plumb their hotel/casino? She sniffed the air, looked at hardware and ceramics. What manner of holy spirits would call this house home? Somewhat refreshed, she put on her Melissa Green skin. I'll go home and hide out. She went down in the elevator, and crossed the gaming floor, where scores of suckers sat feeding the matronly machines as if nothing at all had ever happened. Who will wean them? Outside, Beffle hiked downhill toward the Village where she'd parked her car, trudging along the same road where David daily ran and sang to the Ohlone spirits. In chorus with them? A convertible stopped beside her. The local magazine writer with whom Melissa'd shared drinks. "Want a ride"

"Sure. Thanks. Just going to the Village."

He expressed wonder at the day's events, and she told him about the Ohlone Council. "The tribal polity resembles a council-manager city government. Think of the big chief as mayor; the council, of which he is a part, as the policy-making body; and the CEO-- Two Bears, now D.R. Deer-- as city manager. Deer's assistant, a gal named Braun, is the chief of staff."

She had him drop her by the Running Iron.

In the garden, wild turkeys fluttered and paced and fanned their tails.

Beffle went inside.

There, at the lion table, before a liter of wine, sat Two Bears, his hand ruffling and smoothing the dead cougar's fur.

He glanced her way, and saw her.

Sniling his nasty snile, he motioned her to a seat.

"You fucking set me up, Theodora."

"You won't believe me, but I didn't set you up. Eddy surprised the Hell out of me, too."

"We could really have done it. We *were doing* it. And now, thanks to you, they've fired me."

"I heard."

"And you?"

"Not yet."

"That's bad for my reputation."

"How so, Grease Face?"

"A really good man leaves a trail of broken women."

"And boys."

"I don't look at boys."

"But you do smell bike seats."

"Meaning?"

"When I was a child, bike seats, they shaped them differently. So you'd know which ones to smell. And, remember? The boy's bike had a bar, from seat to handles, but not the girls' bike. Why? Dresses. Nobody but a moron would wear a frock on a bike. So, why? Why those needless distinctions? Is that the way it's supposed to be?"

"Beffle, Melissa, or whoever in fucking Hell you are today, you tell *me* how it's supposed to be. Go ahead!"

"I ought to know, but I don't."

"Ain't that a fact."

"You can say Beffle is baffled."

"Something nobody around here knows . . . . Mix this into your confusion! Me, I came out here as part of CIA Emeritus, an underground group of retired case officers and station chiefs with immense financial resources. By means of professional application of tradecraft and money, Emeritus is slowly gaining control of Indian casinos. Living my cover story, both bears of it, kept me in contact with AIM and its plans. The longer I worked with Indians, the better I came to understand AIM's objective, and the more sympathetic I became. I was an a-moral romantic. This is the first time since adolescence I truly believed in something. And you fucked it up! You tore me up by the roots."

"I know you don't believe me, but I didn't double-cross you."

"Well, anyway, I guess you'll have to admit I made one Hell of an Indian."

"You sure had me fooled."

"My plan was build the confederacy and chop the Emeritus cancer. Dig out the deep-cover types like me. Give the casinos back to the Indians. And zap whoever it is that keeps hitting us. And it was happening." He made a nasty snile. "Woman, you're enough to make me homesick for CIA."

"I'm going up to the casino tomorrow, Bear, and quit my job."

"What will you do then?"

"Art. Frolic and romp where the eternal and the temporal meet. Be a marginal. Smear art around on the border between the cultural and the universal."

"You can't eat art."

"Food sculpture?"

"Where can you get another job, an old broad like you?"

"I don't know. But I can't work up there any more. I'll resign."

"Don't."

"What are *you* going to do, Bear?"

"When you came in, I was dreaming my way into it."

"Into what?"

"I'm writing an operetta called 'Abalone.' Like Gilbert & Sullivan. Not John L. I-can-lick-anybody-in-the-house Sullivan. No! Think Pinafore-Mikado-Penzance Sullivan. I'm building it around the 'Abalone Song.'" He softly sang: "Rich folks boast/ Of quail on toast/ Because they think it tony/ But I'm content/ To owe my rent/ And live on abalone." He rubbed snuff onto his gum. "It's set in Monterey and Carmel, mainly near where you live. In the old days, while singing the song, and inventing new verses, writers and artists sat on the beach around a driftwood fire, drinking wine and pounding abalone to tenderize it. So, hey-- here's a classic." He began singing again. "Some say that/ God is fat/ Others say he's bo-ny/ But as for me/ I disagree/ He resembles abalone." Bear drank some wine. "When I finish writing it, I'll get some people together, and do it."

"Just get them together, and they do it."

"When I tell people to do something Owl Face, you for example, they always do it. Oh, sure, I may have to push a little, but I always get my way, and they do it."

"Like try to kill me."

"I don't know any more about that than you do. Are they still after us? I don't know. But we have to stay one step ahead."

"D.R. Deer?"

"Looks like he won big."

"He could be deep-cover Emeritus."

Bear sat silently considering this. "Could be. He kidnapped you, and may be part of our other troubles. And, Beff, think about it, if he *is*, we know too much, so he needs us dead." He stroked the lion. "Personally, I'd have given my job to Badger."

"David still needs me to finish producing the powwow. . . . or does he?"

They discussed this dilemma, until a sudden roar of motorcycles intruded.

In came the Twins, and *Pearl*, dressed all in leathers.

On her breast she wore the legend *PEARL*, spelled out in big white beads.

Bear began introducing Melissa to them.

"We know her, from high school," said a twin.

"And we both sucked her *pussy*," said the other.

Pearl gave Bear a big hug, then stroked the lion. "I like *your* pussy."

"So, hey, Mel," said a twin, "we're going out to see Beffle. Surprise her. Have a big party."

"And me," said Pearl, "I'm going to kick some Beffle ass!"

"Why?" asked Melissa/Beffle.

"She so stuck up! So dog-gone *highbrow*. Look at how she always treated *you*."

"We're staying in Monterey," said a twin, offering a card. "At this hotel. Give us a call."

"May love and luck ride with you," said Melissa/Beffle. "May you catch up with Rabbit, and give Beffle Hell."

The women went to the bar, asked for beer, chugged it, and trekked out. Beffle tore up the card and dropped it in the ashtray. "Remember, back in Vegas, when you pushed them all out of our room?"

Two Bears nodded yes, and burst into quiet song:

"In Carmel Bay/ Some folks say/ They feed the lazaroni/ On Harley Twins/ Fried Pearl skins/ And chunks of abalone." Two Bears beamed at her, an openness she'd not seen before. "Maybe I should write a book," he said. "About my life. Because then I could change the parts I don't like. Looking back from here I see that CIA, not by accident but by policy, as in Operation Phoenix and MKULTRA, has continuously committed heinous crimes, and keeps on doing so, not in the name of some revealed religion, but in that of a high god called National Security. Any felony is acceptable, or even praiseworthy, if done in the name of that deity." He scratched the lion's brow.

Hoping for a purr? "Right now, everything's loose, waiting to take a new form. Since Spirit Time, the tribes have not managed to come together. It's now or never. I want to make a *together* for them all, based on our assets merged with other casino profits. Almost five hundred tribes sponsor gambling of some kind. More come in every day! CIA Emeritus and who knows what other crime syndicates and speculators are infiltrating and trying to take over. We have to stop it, dig out the deep cover, build the confederacy. I think the Pequots will help us. So, Beffle, you keep your job, and I can work through you, just as before."

"So you want me to keep on being your mirror."

"I want you to help me. Together we can do it."

Is this win/win?

If not, it's lose/lose.

Yes or no? Which is right?

One thing for sure! Reason won't give me the answer.

"If we keep on trying, Lying Lion, we better start practicing our death songs."

"Nobody's going to kill me, Owl Face. Me, I'm immortal."

"At death, Ohlone become birds, and carry family messages to the powers."

"At death, casino clients go to their sky home, losers. But, if they've had fun, they go home happy." He stood. "We'll meet here tomorrow noon and start putting a plan together."

"All right." They shook on it. "Now, Bear, I'm going home to think it over."

He walked her to the door.

She took him by the shoulders and smiled up at him.

"How many Cherokee does it take to screw in a light bulb?"

He made a sour face.

"All of them. The big chief holds the bulb, and the rest turn the building around."

They hugged good-bye and he went back inside.

Turkeys still paced in the garden.

Beffle started her car and drove toward the sea.

A sudden thought from nowhere:

Coyotes mark their boundaries with urine.

On the dashboard, mocking her, stood the wind-up Jesus she'd found at a junk sale.

When I get home, I'll phone somebody.

But whom?

Or I'll reach out with my computer.

How about Feralfrank.org/heaven?

She imagined David Running Deer jogging alongside the road.

Face it. I've nobody at all to talk to!

She wound Jesus.

"Sweetie, you look like what people want to think they truly are. But if you're part human, you're really like the rest of us, Coyote in drag."

She released the winding key.

"You should mark your boundaries with urine."

Jesus began twitching on his cross.

"Is Two Bears still deceiving me? Play acting? Believe it! Flimflamming this audience of one-- me-- is easy. I know too much; I'm too naive, and, yes, despite all my disguises, too honest."

She sped past the mid-valley shopping center where she liked to go to movies.

Is Emeritus Rabbit winning the race?

Traffic thickened, clotted, as she came close to Highway One.

Should I help Bear organize a new tribe?

Called the Casino Indians?

A car rushed around her, forcing an approaching pickup onto the shoulder.

Or will it really be the Deep Cover Indians?

"Hey old pal, stop twitching on your cross, and tell Wild Child what to do!"

A red light told Wild Child to stop.

"The Hell with deceptions!"

She stripped off her carrot top, and hurled it to the floor.

"No more pretending!"

Off with the mask! Leap the footlights! End the play!

She peeled Dead Melissa's features, flung them down onto the Dead Red wig.

She turned into the Barnyard Shopping Center.

She drove through it, went west on Rio Road toward Carmel, and headed for the Mission, and the Lagoon, and home sweet home.

Will there be Harleys in the drive?

The drive, empty.

The apricot tree beside it hung heavy with neglected fruit; windfall rotted in the shade beneath.

She limped to the tree, plucked and ate.

From far off, the whuc! *coooo coooo coooo* of the rain dove.

Parakeets chattered and chirped somewhere nearby.

The latest and most flamboyant class of illegal immigrants.

Maybe I can talk with them?

She limped to her door, gathered an accumulation of junk newspapers and circulars, then went in.

There, at the worktable, by his three-foot clay image, his silver-and-black Oakland Raiders hat placed before him, sat David Running Deer.

Silently, they peered at each other.

Then he spoke.

"Understand, Beffle, I'm immensely pissed off. At you and Two Bears, both pure Anglo, using CIA money, and deceptions and lies trying to take over the Native American future."

She let the ad-trash drop to the floor.

"Two Bears is gone, Beffle. It's your turn now."

She did not reply.

"Pearl's gone too."

Either he's with them or with us.

"They've been using Pearl to watch you."

That piece helped fill in the puzzle.

"Take your last look at the sea and the sky."

My next move?

It flashed into consciousness, the answer.

"David. Together. The three of us. You, and me, and Two Bears. We'll do it. We'll make it happen. Carib Day. The Native American Confederacy, freed from infiltrators, composed of rich Indians and poor Indians alike, nourished by big money from the casinos, consecrated to liberty and justice for all---- together, you and Bear and me, we can do it. We *are doing* it! It's *our* turn now!"

David Running Deer lifted his hat, and set it aside, exposing his Glock automatic pistol.

A smile touched his lips.

Meaning . . . ?

Glock or love?

She couldn't read it.

What now?

Crack my knuckles?

What now?

A kiss, a sigh, indifference?

A pledge to help?

Or stabbing pain sliding into eternal black void where nothing hurts.

Eternal night?

Happily ever after?

He laid a hand on the pistol.

Beffle glared rage at him.

Silent, motionless, he seated and she, erect, they stared at one another.

He hefted the pistol in his left hand, and as she serenely made ready to die, his right hand closed over it, and he began working the slide, ejecting the bullets one at a time.

"I can't do it," he said.

The crazy thought hit he could not kill her because his fastidious nature revolted at the prospect of the bloody mess.

She peered scorn at him.

He stood, expressionless, confronting her stare.

Time lost its velocity.

Time seemed frozen in this ancient photograph.

David Running Deer turned, and leaving the pistol and his Raiders' cap, he strode out the back door.

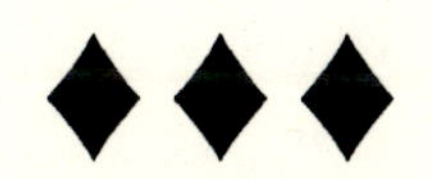

Books by Richard Miller

Amerloque (a factual fiction about responsibility and injustice, set in French Morocco): Crown Publishers, Inc., New York, 1966.

Bohemia (a history of the Bohemian tradition): Nelson-Hall, Inc., Chicago, 1977, 1978.

Snail (a satirical fantasy about love and war): Henry Holt, Inc., New York, 1984; Owl, Holt, NY, 1985; Abacus: Sphere Books, Ltd., London, 1986.

Squed (a lively tale about death and the dead set mainly on the Other Side): Bloomsbury Publishing, Ltd., London, 1989.

Sowboy (a fictional fiction about life on a hog farm and beyond): Bloomsbury, London, 1991.

Mosca (the story of an artificial fly secretly sworn to killing off humankind so life may live): Dada Foundation Imprints, LLC: DFI Books, Monterey, CA, 1997; Synergy International of the Americas, Ltd., Miami, (with Lightning Source/Ingram, LaVergne, TN), 2000.

Coyote (a fiction about deceptions set in Native American and Las Vegan casinos): Synergy, Miami, with Lightning Source/ Ingram, 2001.

As yet unpublished

OTIS AND HIS *TIMES* (a biography of the early publisher of the *Los Angeles Times*): revised Ph.D. dissertation, University of California, Berkeley, 1961, 1963.

ROMANCE RUN (a working-class sea story), 1956, 1996.

COMES NOW PETITIONER (a fiction about youth in the mid- sixties), 1968.

CANAM (a Canadian-American adventure and family history), 1997.

TANGLEFOOT (a factual fiction about Chicago's Streeterville), 2000.

Comments

Amerloque: "Perhaps the elements that place this novel of the postwar generation above the usual are its setting, Casablanca in 1952, and its international roster of characters." ***Library Journal***

Bohemia: Miller "has performed an important service by introducing the survivors of the counterculture to their illustrious forebears."

The Journal of American History

- a "masterpiece of scholarship and interpretation . . . ." ***New Age***
- "a major intellectual synthesis." ***Human Behavior***
- "wherever and whenever youth dropped out to paint, write poetry, find themselves, defy the established order . . . Miller has sought out their story, researched it exhaustively, and told it well." Kevin Starr in ***The San Francisco Examiner***

Snail: "This action-packed picaresque novel . . . moves on the high grounds of the fantasy genre." ***The New York Times***

- "this novel will make the readers' flesh crawl, trigger daytime nightmares, and, finally, leave them laughing." ***Publishers Weekly***
- "Funky . . . Flaky . . . Insightful . . . . It's a dandy." ***The Tampa Tribune***
- "a hugely enjoyable cosmic crusade." ***The*** (London) ***Times Literary Supplement.***
- "adolescent, shallow, devoid of craft, tasteless, scatological . . . self-indulgent . . . silly, self-serving, pretentious, a blot on . . . an otherwise honorable and distinguished publisher . . . ." ***The Washington Post***

Squed: "Miller's imagination is astonishingly fertile, his manipulations of language and situations impressive, his tortuous perspectives both entertaining and thought provoking." ***Venue***

- "interesting and entertaining . . . a bizarre black comedy." ***Oxford Times***
- "Blackly comic and quite delirious." ***Time Out***

Sowboy: "COWBOYS are the stuff films are made of . . . . But who are the sowboys?" ***Evening Gazette***

- a "fast-moving piece of inspired lunacy, dedicated 'to joy and genius,' . . . a distinctly strange but exhilarating ride." ***Scotland on Sunday***
- "I thought Sowboy must be the work of a young man just into his 20's, . . . but then I learned Richard Miller is an old buffer . . . who simply writes young." ***The Guardian***

Mosca: "a strong sense of irony coupled with an unconventional cast of characters could make this utterly offbeat tale an underground or cult classic."

The Monterey County Herald

OTIS: "among the best of the lot . . . . (in a bibliography). ***The Californians, The Magazine of California History.***

9 780965 842334